TITLES BY DAWN ADDONIZIO

Novels Of The Faerie Realm:

A RISKY PROPOSITION, Book 1 of
The Third Wish Duology

SOUL SEDUCTION, Book 2 of
The Third Wish Duology

PASSIONATE MAGIC

GREY'S MAGIC

Published by Nouveau Ventures Unlimited
3606 Woods Walk Blvd
Lake Worth, FL 33467

Edited by DM Eburn
Cover Image courtesy of Can Stock Photo Inc / neotakezo

PASSIONATE MAGIC

First paperback printing February 2014

For information contact:
Dawn Addonizio
Dawn@DawnsBoutique.Org

This is a work of fiction. All of the characters, organizations, locales and events portrayed in this novel are either products of the author's imagination, or are used purely for fictitious purposes.

Passionate Magic is dedicated to:

Every reader who holds onto the belief that magic really does exist, no matter what life throws at them.

And to every writer who has struggled through NaNoWriMo (National Novel Writers' Month), and come out the other side, better for it.

Much Love & Faerie Blessings Upon You All!   -Dawn

Table of Contents

Chapter One

The summer sun blazed down onto Violet's upturned face, soaking into her body to melt away the tension that had been building since she'd arrived in Key Largo two days ago. Dazzling points of sunlight glinted across countless rippling waves as the boat sped toward a nearby coral reef, the rush of wind softening the heat and sending her long, dark hair fluttering out behind her. The sweet scent of orange and coconut tanning oil teased her senses.

She was on summer vacation from her job teaching fourth grade, although it didn't feel like much of a vacation. She'd been putting off this trip, but with the end of the school year she'd run out of excuses. She couldn't believe it had already been two whole months since the day she'd stood beside the ugly upturned earth that marked her parents' graves.

Vicki and George Hendrickson had always loved the ocean, reveled in its mystery and magic, and they had instilled that love in their only daughter. Even now, being on the ocean soothed and calmed Violet—despite the fact that, in the end, it had been this very expanse of water that had stolen her parents' lives.

Violet sighed. She'd thought she was almost at peace with the unfair way in which they'd been taken from her. But two days spent alone in their cozy garden villa, going through closets scattered with Hawaiian shirts that carried traces of her dad's aftershave, and her mom's eclectic collection of hats, had stirred her grief back up to the surface.

She needed a break, intending to go for a walk down by the docks and maybe a swim on the beach. But she'd happened past this snorkeling tour just as it was leaving and joined it on a whim.

Maybe it was the boat's name that called to her—*Ocean Magic*—painted in bright, glowing blue against the vessel's crisp, white-washed stern. Or perhaps she was drawn by the challenge of embracing the ocean again after what had happened; proving that she held neither fear nor blame for it.

Violet couldn't help a small smirk as she admitted to herself that it also might have had something to do with the sexy boat captain rounding up customers from the dock as she passed. The husky timbre of his voice had lured her over, Irish if she wasn't mistaken. She was a sucker for that particular accent. Of course, it didn't hurt that he was built like a Celtic god.

She stole a peek at him through the dark lenses of her sunglasses. He stood at the polished mahogany captain's wheel, the wind ruffling his short honey-brown hair, all easy self-assurance as he chatted with a pair of women who sat nearby.

Just her luck, they both looked like supermodels. She inhaled the brisk salt-air and turned away to stare out at the fathomless aquamarine water, determined to enjoy her adventure with or without the attention of the handsome boat captain.

As the boat coasted to a halt, she peeled off her shorts and top, bending to retrieve her fluorescent orange snorkel vest and mask. She sucked in a breath as she rose in time to see the mouth-watering captain casually pull off his shirt, revealing a wide, well-defined chest and abs with just a hint of a six-pack. The pair of women beside him appeared to appreciate the view as well.

Violet refused to join them in their ogling, doubting he needed his ego inflated further. When he began instructing them on water safety, however, he drew her attention once more. He had the loveliest voice, with that rich Irish brogue of his, and his sea-green eyes sparkled with warmth when he smiled.

He caught her gaze for a moment, holding it as he finished his speech, almost as if he was speaking to her alone. He seemed to start toward her, and heat rose to her already flushed cheeks. Flustered, she looked away and hurried to the back of the line to await her turn to descend the ladder into the water.

∞∞∞∞∞∞∞∞∞∞

Doyle forced a smile at the scantily clad young woman sitting in front of him. She was tracing a manicured fingertip over her glossed pink lips in what was obviously meant to be an enticing manner. She and her giggling, gum chewing friend had rushed to sit by him as soon as they'd boarded the boat.

"Brittany and I were giving each other belly button shots at the bar last night. It was a blast." She gave him a coy look from beneath lashes thick with mascara. "You should come hang out with us tonight. If you buy the shots, we'll feed them to you."

Brittany giggled and Doyle laughed politely. "That's quite an offer, ladies."

They were certainly pretty enough, but he met the same type of girl day in and day out. He'd enjoyed his share of them, taking advantage of what they were only too willing to give, but he wasn't in the mood for another meaningless romp with a tourist.

It was his last snorkel trip of the day and he was eager to be done with it. He loved his business, but he was wiped out from the brutal heat and his four earlier groups. It wasn't so bad when he had a turn in the water and his partner, Manny, stayed on the boat to supervise the scene from above. But it was Manny's turn to swim.

He'd never thought anything could make him miss Ireland's wet, aching cold until he experienced mid-summer in the subtropics.

The flirtier of the two girls leaned into him. "That's not all I have to offer, handsome," she whispered on a drawn out breath. The cloying aroma of smoke and cloves nearly made him choke. "Come swimming with me and I'll show you."

Doyle gave a noncommittal chuckle and hid a grimace. Maybe sweating on the boat was the better alternative after all. He reminded himself that he couldn't complain. He'd said he wanted sun and sand, and he had it in spades here in the Florida Keys.

He'd never regretted his decision to leave Ireland. Although he wasn't sure his poor parents would ever get over the shock of it. That he'd chosen to venture so far from home was only a part of their dismay; it was more that he'd bucked convention and decided to live in the *human* world. Because, despite appearances, Doyle wasn't human.

I wonder if knowing that would be enough to make these two leave me alone, he thought dryly. But he would never reveal his secret, the satisfaction of chasing away overbearing tourists notwithstanding. He hadn't even told Manny, and they'd been friends and business partners for ten years.

Doyle steered the boat alongside the reef, giving his first-mate a nod to indicate they were stopping. Manny winked in salute as he dropped anchor, the wiry muscles of his arms and bare chest shifting beneath summer-darkened skin that had started out a deep, Costa Rican brown. Doyle stripped off his t-shirt with the *Ocean Magic*'s logo, ignoring the increased giggling from the college girls, and began to give his rote safety spiel before he sent the group into the water.

He almost stumbled over his words as his eyes fell upon the beautiful young woman watching him solemnly from the aft railing. He'd been busy piloting the boat and fending off advances from the 'girls gone wild', but he couldn't believe he hadn't noticed *her*.

She had a solitary air, standing apart from the couples who were helping each other with their lifevests, and not joining in the laughter of the other clustered groups of passengers. But she didn't look like she minded being alone. Her posture was selfpossessed and confident, though a veiled sorrow seemed to linger beneath the tranquility of her expression.

She was several inches shorter than he, with a firm but curvaceous body. Her breasts and hips were full and ripe, her pale golden skin clear and sunblushed. Her long, dark hair fell in waves to frame a soft face with extraordinarily blue, almost purple, eyes. She locked gazes with him as he finished speaking, and he began to move toward her, as if in a dream. But at the last moment she turned away and joined the queue to get in the water.

Disappointed, he faltered to a stop, oblivious to the giggling blonde who threaded her arm through his and asked if he would be her snorkel partner. He mumbled something about having to stay on the boat as he disentangled himself, earning a pretty pout.

Absorbed with thoughts of the mysterious brunette, and determined to introduce himself on the return ride, he picked up the clipboard with the passenger roster and tried to guess her name. As he scanned the page, he smiled in triumph. Hendrickson, Violet. The name reflected the color of her eyes. And she was the only passenger traveling alone.

∞∞∞∞∞∞∞∞∞

Violet admonished herself for being foolish as she waited, her mask looped around her wrist and fins dangling from her fingers. The captain was far too good-looking for his own, or her, good. Out of the corner of her eye she saw one of the blondes hanging on his arm, and she turned away, shoving him resolutely from her mind. What had she been thinking? There was no way he'd been about pass up that free lunch to come talk to *her*.

She reached the ladder and was soon lowering herself into the warm, soothing water; all other thoughts forgotten as the buoyant swells welcomed her into their embrace. She had forgotten how good it felt to be out here in the middle of the ocean. It was far different from swimming near the shore with the rolling whitecaps crashing onto the beach. Here it was like another world, with only an unbroken expanse of blue-green serenity as far as the eye could see.

She quickly donned her snorkel mask and fins, and worked her way out over the jumble of pitted and maze-like corals that made up the reef. Lacy sea fans waved lazily in the currents and multitudes of colorful fish flitted every which way. She lost herself in exploring the teeming marine life, following a couple of parrot fish that were chasing each other for a while, and then stopping to admire a large anemone with purple-pink tentacles.

She floated past a school of butterfly fish, flashing silver and yellow in the water-muted sunlight, and held her breath to dive down for a closer look at a huge grouper that she'd nearly missed. Its mouth gaped open and its fins barely moved as it hovered in a dark crevice, waiting for prey. Trigger fish darted by as she returned to the surface to clear out her breathing tube.

Violet's gasp of delight sounded hollow inside her snorkel as she caught sight of a sea turtle in the distance. She hurried toward it, trying to minimize her movements so as not to startle the creature. A large shadow moved past, and she blinked, jerking her face around to see what it was.

Something smacked hard against the side of her head and her vision went grey. She was stunned for a moment, and then pain crashed over her. She realized suddenly that she could no longer breathe. Her mask was filling with water, blinding her, and something was dragging her down, down, away from the air and the light. She panicked, struggling and flailing against its merciless pull.

Her lungs burned and tightened until they felt as if they would implode. No longer able to stop herself, Violet inhaled seawater.

∞∞∞∞∞∞∞∞∞

Doyle paced from stern to bow in frustration. The group had dispersed out over the reef, and from this distance he couldn't tell who was who. They were just a collection of bright orange blobs. They would be floating around out there for another half hour before he would get the chance to talk to the lovely Violet Hendrickson.

Who was she? And why would someone like her be vacationing alone? With his luck, she had a fiancée waiting for her back at her hotel room.

He continued his pacing, staring moodily out over the water, and then he went stock still. *That was odd.* He could have sworn he'd just seen a merrow's tail break the surface out beyond the reef, its large, silvery green scales sparkling in the sunlight.

The merrow were mer-folk, and notorious for keeping to themselves. There had been tales of sailors spotting them throughout history, but he'd never seen a hint of their existence in all his years in the Keys. It was strange that one would be anywhere near a place that was so populated by humans. His eyes scanned the water, searching for another glimpse.

Instead, he saw something that made his blood run cold despite the blazing afternoon heat. There was a single orange jersey floating about a hundred yards off the starboard bow, like so much abandoned flotsam.

Without a second thought he dove over the side of the boat and began a furious swim toward the empty snorkeling vest. He realized too late that he should have donned a mask, as he squinted through blurry, salt-stung eyes to gauge his surroundings. As soon as he reached the solitary jersey, he plunged deeper.

This was where the reef started to become the territory of divers. The seafloor dropped and the coral became a rocky landscape of peaks and valleys, jutting out to create hundreds of miniature caves. Many were large enough to conceal a human body. Had some fool decided to go exploring on their own and gotten stuck? Inadvisable though it was, he began feeling around inside the dark dens with his ungloved hands.

A perturbed moray eel shot out at him, its jagged teeth nearly clamping onto his fingers. He jerked his hand back and moved onto the next opening, growing frantic. The human brain could only go without oxygen for about five minutes. It must have been at least two since he'd jumped in the water. And though Doyle wasn't human, whoever had been wearing that orange snorkeling vest was. And they were running out of time.

A large, sleek shape rushed past him, creating its own wake beneath the surface. Doyle squinted at it, thinking it was a shark. But then he glimpsed something that seemed out of place on the seafloor below and he dismissed the creature as he lunged toward it.

A clump of dark wisps floated at the edge of a recess of rock, disappearing into a hidden cavity beneath. His fingers tangled in the mass, identifying the clinging strands as human hair. He reached deeper, past the curve of an unmoving head, to grasp a lifeless body beneath the shoulders. He tugged, and found himself holding an unconscious Violet in his arms.

He felt as if he was looking at her in slow motion. Her beautiful face was pale and eerily still, her long hair hovering in a weightless raven cloud. Then time caught up with him and he pushed off the rock, his leg muscles stroking for the surface.

"There they are!" someone shouted.

Doyle barely registered the sound as he rolled onto his back, pulling Violet's limp form with him, desperate to get her to the boat where he could perform CPR. His arms tightened beneath her ribcage as he struggled to position her, and suddenly she was choking and sputtering as she coughed up water and gasped for breath.

Doyle didn't think he'd ever felt such stark relief in his almost two hundred years of existence.

His first mate reached his side and began trying to pull Violet from him. Doyle's grip on her tightened reflexively, some primal instinct roaring to life, unwilling to relinquish her to another.

"Easy now," Manny soothed.

Doyle wasn't sure whether the calming words were meant for him or for Violet, but he relaxed his hold and allowed Manny to slide her down so that she was supported between them.

"We'll have you out of the water soon," Doyle assured her gently as they began working their way back to the boat. She murmured a sound of gratitude between coughing sputters.

The rest of the group bobbed in loose knots around them, treading water and staring. Doyle knew they were only concerned, but it was all he could do not to shout at them to get out of the way. He heard a faint, agitated buzz and looked up to find a distraught faerie hovering overhead, her wings sifting sparkling purple dust that scattered behind her on the wind.

She was a sprite, approximately three inches tall with dark shining hair that fell past her knees. Her skin glowed with silvery light and her pastel dress shimmered in shades of pink, blue and yellow. From the anxious stare she was directing at Violet, Doyle guessed that she must be the young woman's faerie guardian.

Faerie guardians bonded with certain mortals at birth, following them throughout their lives to bring them aid and protection. Most mortals had no idea of the existence of the faerie realm or any of its denizens. If they had a faerie guardian helping them they simply attributed it to luck, when they noticed it at all.

Doyle had a bone to pick with this particular faerie. Where the hell had she been when her charge was drowning, and why hadn't she steered Violet away from the danger?

"How the devil could you let this happen, little sister?" he muttered up at her, his jaw set in a grim line.

Her tilted eyes widened a fraction. "You're sidhe," she gasped in surprise.

He was just about to let loose a scathing reply, when he realized that Violet was trying to speak, her voice coming out stilted and hoarse from a throat raw with saltwater.

"Excuse me?" she managed finally. "I didn't *let* anything happen," she croaked. "Something knocked into me and dragged me under!"

She sent him a *how-dare-you* scowl and looked to the other group members for support.

"Of course it's not your fault, sweetie," a plump, motherly woman cooed. Her flowered rubber bathing cap was askew, leaving her kindly expression lopsided, but Violet smiled back at her in gratitude.

Some of the others nodded their agreement, staunchly remaining nearby, but several people were rapidly working their way back toward the boat. No doubt it had something to do with Violet's announcement that something had tried to drag her beneath the waves.

"I didn't mean you," Doyle assured her quickly. He directed an aggravated glance at the faerie as he realized his mistake. Of course Violet had assumed he was talking to her.

Violet shot him a disbelieving look. "Who did you mean, then?" she demanded, her voice still husky. "I'm fairly sure you weren't calling your friend here 'little sister'. He looks manly enough to me."

Doyle was forced to tamp down an unreasonable surge of jealousy toward Manny. "I didn't...I'm sorry, okay? Let's just get you back on board," he said with an irritable sigh.

"Captain Doyle's just a little hot with me for no keeping a closer eye on things," Manny said in a smooth tone. "He only wants to keep you safe, *lindita.*" He gave Violet a reassuring smile, but a question flickered in his dark eyes as they traveled to Doyle's.

Doyle shook his head in silent apology and concentrated on guiding Violet to the ladder. He ignored the faerie now flitting back and forth in front of them. Apparently she found the situation humorous, her attempts to stifle her laughter with her small hands failing miserably. The dust from her wings changed from purple to green, and it drifted into his face as the wind changed direction, tickling his nose.

He sent her an irate glare. Most types of faerie dust made humans sneeze, and right on cue, Violet and Manny erupted in unison.

"Bless you," Doyle said, unable to keep the sourness from his tone.

The faerie shot upward with a muffled chortle.

"Just a little salt water in the nose, eh, *lindita*?" Manny chuckled.

Violet tilted a smile in Manny's direction and Doyle fumed.

They reached the ladder and Manny managed to ascend it first, helping Violet up and leading her to a bench. Doyle scrambled after them and hurried to Violet's other side.

"Thank you, Manny. Can you get everyone back aboard while I tend to Miss Hendrickson?"

Manny gave him another questioning look, but rose and did as he asked.

Doyle placed a hand on Violet's shoulder. Though he felt her stiffen, he couldn't seem to make himself stop touching her. Her skin was warm and satiny beneath his palm. His gaze dropped to the rounded tops of her breasts where they peeked from the scooped neckline of her bathing suit. They rose and fell gently with her breath, the sight making his throat go dry.

He jerked his eyes back to her face and found her studying him with a puzzled frown. He swallowed. "I'm sorry." His voice sounded rough and he swallowed again. "I was just checking to make sure you had no visible signs of injury."

One delicate sable brow lifted. "Whatever it was hit me in the head." Violet reached up to gingerly explore her scalp.

"Of course." Doyle nodded quickly, his fingers brushing hers as he began his own examination.

Violet winced and sucked in a breath as he found a tender spot.

"Sorry," he said again, lightening his touch. "The skin doesn't seem to be broken, but you do have quite a bump. Does it hurt anywhere else?"

He gave the faerie, still hovering above them, a meaningful glance. She pulled a small cloth pouch from inside her dress and darted down to sprinkle silvery healing dust over the area he was probing with his fingers.

Violet shook her head. "No. I think I'm alright. It's already starting to feel better."

Doyle smiled and Violet's rosy lips quivered upward in response. She smelled of the ocean and sun-ripened fruit. Her hair was drying into shining ripples of silk beneath his hand, and he longed to run his fingers through its length. She was so close, her eyes like wide pools of liquid amethyst. A man could lose himself in their crystalline depths. If he just leaned in a few inches, he would be able to taste her…

An annoying chorus of giggles broke the spell. Doyle shook his head to clear it and reluctantly pulled his hand back from Violet.

∞∞∞∞∞∞∞∞∞

Violet wasn't quite sure what had just happened. First the handsome captain had blamed her for almost drowning. Then he'd insisted on taking care of her himself and sent the other, friendlier man away. She could have sworn she'd caught him ogling her cleavage, but he'd insisted he was only looking for injuries. Her head *had* been throbbing. But when he'd touched her, his fingers had literally soothed away the pain, as if by magic.

To make things even more confusing, just now there had been a moment when she was sure he was about to kiss her. A shiver went through her, her lips still tingling at the enticing thought. His sea-green eyes had held such heat as they stared into hers. But he'd pulled away when his two girlfriends showed up.

"Are you okay?" gasped the woman in the red bikini. Her voice dripped with concern, but her eyes roamed the captain's muscular chest as she spoke. It was the clingy blonde he'd had on his arm earlier.

"What happened?" her friend asked in an anxious tone, steadily grinding a piece of chewing gum between her teeth.

Captain Doyle straightened and crossed his arms over the width of his chest, as if to distance himself from Violet. She felt a bright flash of annoyance at him, mingled with a touch of disgust for herself. She reached down to pull a towel from her backpack, using it as an excuse to scoot away from the fickle captain.

"Something big knocked into me from behind. It was probably a shark," she replied briskly, enjoying the discomfort that flitted across both women's faces as their eyes traveled from her to the water in which they'd just been swimming. "I felt it dragging me down before I passed out."

"Did it bite you?" asked the one with the gum, grinding it harder as she stared at Violet in horrified fascination.

"I..." Violet looked down to make sure she wasn't bleeding. It suddenly occurred to her that the only way a shark could have pulled her down was with its teeth. But all she found were a few light abrasions where her skin had rubbed against rock. Although relieved not to find any more serious injury, she discovered, with a surge of disappointment, that her favorite silver anklet had fallen off.

She looked up to find the woman still looking at her expectantly. "No, I wasn't bitten," she said, feeling foolish. She must have imagined being dragged down.

"Thank Gawd!" the woman exclaimed, appearing not to spot the inconsistency in Violet's shark story.

Violet glanced at Captain Doyle, sure he'd catch it right away. But he was staring off into space, not even listening to her. Apparently she no longer merited his attention. Miffed and a little hurt, she stood up and wrapped her towel tighter around her midsection. "Excuse me. I need to use the restroom."

∞∞∞∞∞∞∞∞∞

"It wasn't a shark," the faerie piped up as soon as the word left Violet's mouth. "It was a merrow. That's why I wasn't able to warn her away in time. Sometimes my signals get crossed when other magical beings are involved."

Doyle stared at her, frustrated with his inability to reply.

"I don't think this was an isolated incident. A couple of months ago... oh, Titania's wand!" she cursed.

"I have to go. My son found his way out of his playpen. Little tyke's getting much too clever. I'll find you later, when you can talk." She gave him an apologetic grimace and was gone.

Doyle blinked and realized that Violet was no longer at his side. He rose, skirting around the college girls, and began walking toward the bow in search of her. He thought he'd seen a merrow. But why would one of the mer-folk want to harm Violet?

Violet exited the head, pointedly avoiding his gaze as she returned to her seat, and Doyle sighed. Apparently he'd upset her again. He'd have to figure out how to make it up to her later. Right now, he needed to get his passengers back to shore.

"Ready to pull anchor, *amigo*?" Manny clapped him on the shoulder.

"Let's take her in," he grumbled.

Chapter Two

Violet couldn't believe the nerve of the man. He'd followed her off the boat asking if they could get together later. When she declined, he asked for her address and phone number, claiming it was for insurance purposes. All the while, those two little blondes had been lurking behind, waiting for him.

Well, they could have him!

She felt a pang of regret, remembering his gentle touch and the way her entire body had tingled to life at the prospect of kissing him. But no. It didn't matter how sexy his accent was, or how amazing his eyes were, or how much she wanted to run her fingers through that soft honey-brown hair and feel what it was like to have his thick arms band around her as their lips joined.

He was obviously some kind of playboy, and she wasn't going to allow herself to become one of his toys.

She opened the white picketed gate and made her way up the cobblestone path that led to her parents' glass-paned front door. Bougainvilleas bloomed in a riot of fuchsia, purple and orange, towering over the trellised fence to either side, intermingled with red and yellow trumpet vines. She really should get someone in here to cut them back, she thought, as she fitted the key in the lock. Maybe she'd ask that nice neighbor who had offered to help her box up her parents' things if she knew of a good yard service.

Violet sighed as the door opened and a blast of cool air washed over her. She moved into the living room and dropped her backpack on the hardwood floor, sagging onto one of the couches. It was upholstered in a thick weave fabric that had been dyed royal blue. The other couch was dark red, and a forest green recliner completed the set, a tribute to her mother's eclectic taste. Mom had loved to mix and match colors and styles, and somehow she had always seemed to make it work.

Which reminded Violet, she'd intended to finish packing up her mom's hat collection today. She allowed herself to rest for a few minutes more, then she rose and trudged toward her parents' bedroom, her feet dragging as she made her way to the walk-in closet. There were already a couple of boxes waiting on the floor, and she began carefully transferring the hats from the shelves down into them.

Her mom had owned hats in every color and style imaginable. Some had feathers or veils. Others were decorated with buckles, flowers, bands or pins. She found two almost identical berets made out of shiny red vinyl. Violet smiled and shook her head, wondering how a person could possibly find the occasions to wear them all. But her mom had probably worn every single one without worrying whether or not they matched the occasion. Both Vicky and George Hendrickson had been the types of people to live for the moment and experience all the joy that life had to offer.

The magnitude of their loss slammed into Violet, combining with the vestiges of her earlier fright in the water, leaving her too overwhelmed to fight her grief. She sank to the floor of the closet, between the boxes of hats. Her fingers clutched at one of her dad's favorite Hawaiian shirts, pulling it off its hanger as she went.

She cried until the shirt was wet with her tears and her nose was too stuffy to smell the lingering scent of his aftershave.

∞∞∞∞∞∞∞∞∞

"I'm sorry I didn't see the *lindita* go under, *hermano*."

Doyle looked up from hosing off *Ocean Magic*'s deck. He'd been staring at the bench where Violet was sitting earlier, lost in thoughts of her. "It wasn't your fault, man."

Manny eyed him doubtfully. "I was supposed to be watching the group, no? And you been cranky as a wet *gato* ever since. If you no mad at me, then what's eating you, *hermano*?"

Doyle exhaled heavily as he debated how much to tell Manny. The Costa Rican was a stand-up guy and a good friend. They'd been partners for ten years now, and Doyle trusted him almost as much as he trusted his best friend, Pat. But he'd never entrusted any human with the knowledge that he was *sidhe*, descended from a noble line of immortal warriors that made their homes in the faerie realm.

He settled, as always, for giving his friend a partial truth.

"I like her, man," he said simply. "I liked her from the moment I saw her. I wanted to ask her out, but those two blondes kept after me and I think she got the wrong idea."

Manny's face broke into a huge grin that pushed his cheeks up into rounded pouches. "You had me worried there for a minute, *hermano*. I was wondering how come you did no want to sample what those two were offering."

Doyle smirked as he bent to pick up a discarded soda can left behind by one of the passengers. "I've got my mind set on sampling something a bit more exotic than those two, and I'm afraid Miss Violet Hendrickson is the only thing that will do."

"I know what you mean, *hermano*. I have been dating this new *chica* for several weeks now, and no other can turn my eye from her. I think I am in love."

Manny crossed his hands over his chest and raised his face heavenward.

"I hope she feel the same. Her name is Melody. Beautiful, no? I will bring her to meet you some time soon."

Doyle smiled. "I'd love to meet the woman who's finally stolen your heart, brother."

They finished cleaning the boat in companionable silence and agreed to meet back at the docks in a couple of days for their next round of tours.

Doyle walked the few blocks to the secluded, residential street where his old-Florida-style house was situated on a two acre lot. It was a white rectangle of a building, with a low, flat roof and green-trimmed windows with jalousie shutters.

Coconut palms dotted the property and a veritable forest of waxy-leaved sea-grapes fenced it in. Grass grew sparsely at best in the sandy soil, but it was less for him to mow and it gave the place a distinctly tropical feel. As soon as he opened the slat-paned front door, his Irish wolfhound, Bruno, nearly knocked him over in a frenzied, slobbery rush to get outside.

"Sorry buddy. Couldn't make it back for your afternoon walk. Tourists kept me busy all day. I met a bonnie one, though." He rubbed the pony-sized dog's soft ears and Bruno looked at him reproachfully before trotting out into the yard.

Doyle grinned and went inside, knowing the dog would return to the door when he was ready to come in. He dropped his keys next to a pile of mail on the shelf in the entryway, kicked his shoes off, and made his way barefoot across the cool tile toward his bedroom to take a shower. Manny had helped him lay the flooring a month ago, and it was still shiny and new, adding to his home's growing contrast of modern updates and vintage fixtures.

He was scrubbing the salt out of his hair, his eyes screwed tight against the soapy water, when a faint high-pitched whistle sounded in his ears. "What the devil?" he mumbled.

Laughter tinkled over him. His eyes shot open and he cursed as shampoo ran into them.

"Yer a fine specimen of man, ye are, Doyle Thresher," Violet's faerie guardian mimicked in an exaggerated Irish accent, casting an appreciative eye over Doyle's naked form.

"I don't sound anything like that." Doyle scowled and continued rinsing his hair, not bothering to give the sprite the satisfaction of trying to shield the parts of him she'd obviously already seen. "And you wouldn't know what to do with me, ye bloomin' faerie, so get yourself out of here before I mistake you for the soap and wash my *specimens* with you."

The faerie chuckled. "You can call me Eleanor, sweetie."

"Nice to be on a first name basis after all we've shared," Doyle replied in a sarcastic burr. "Get out then, *Eleanor*. Why don't you go wait in the living room like a normal guest?"

"Alright, don't get huffy. I just wanted to let you know that there's a monstrous creature currently attempting to break down your front door. It looks a bit flimsy and I'm not sure how much longer it will hold up against the beast. I've got some dust that simulates extra-strength catnip, but I'm not sure what it will do to this brute. I could put it to sleep for a while if you want..."

Doyle tucked a towel around his waist and sprinted from the bathroom before she could finish her offer. Eleanor trailed after him and found him sitting on the edge of a worn brown leather recliner, bending down to rub the creature's belly as it rolled on the floor. Its tongue lolled from its mouth like pulled taffy, its huge paws flailing in the air at the tips of ridiculously long, lanky legs.

"You're a good puppy, yes you are Bruno," Doyle growled in a doltish, sing-song voice.

Eleanor's eyebrows climbed up her silvery forehead. "You call that thing a *puppy*?" she asked in horrified amusement.

Doyle raised his eyes and just missed being whacked in the face by a stray paw. "Well, he probably won't grow any more. But you'll always be my puppy, won't you, boy?" he asked the dog fondly as he rose and straightened his towel.

"Now just wait here while I throw on some clothes. And no peeking this time, ye pint-sized pervert," he warned as he closed his bedroom door with slightly more force than necessary.

Faeries, Doyle thought with disgust as he yanked on a pair of cargo shorts and the first t-shirt he pulled from his drawer. They were always sticking their noses in other people's business, especially if they thought they could gain the slightest favor for their charges. And they could usually talk the teeth out of a saw when they had a mind to. If Violet wasn't this one's charge, he'd flick the little blighter right out the window. The audacity of her spying on him in the shower...

He ran his fingers through his damp hair and fixed a polite smile to his face as he returned to the living room. He stumbled to a halt at the sight of what appeared to be Bruno's attempt to ingest the annoying little menace.

"Bruno, NO!" he shouted, hurrying forward to grip the dog's massive jaws in his hands before he could clamp them around Eleanor's tiny frame. Despite the satisfaction it would give him, he couldn't allow his dog to eat Violet's faerie guardian.

Eleanor whizzed out of Bruno's mouth, giving Doyle a bemused look. "Relax, big boy. The pup had a bit of a toothache and I thought I'd save you a trip to the vet. Bruno would never try to eat me. Would you, pumpkin?" she asked the enormous dog.

The faerie landed on the dog's sloping snout and began scratching him between the eyes. He stared at her with a blissful expression, one of his rear legs kicking reflexively against the tile floor.

Speechless, Doyle released Bruno's jaws. "Traitor," he mumbled, stalking toward the kitchen. "Can I get you anything to drink?" he called, forcing a pleasant tone. *A thimble full of cyanide perhaps*, he added to himself. He opened the stainless steel refrigerator door, pasted with photos of Bruno and landscape scenes shot from the *Ocean Magic*.

Eleanor darted over the long breakfast bar to hover above his shoulder. "I don't suppose you have any decent champagne?" she asked in a hopeful voice.

He looked at her askance. "Let me just check the wine cellar," he answered dryly.

Eleanor sighed. "I figured. But it never hurts to aim high. What are you having, then?"

"Beer." He punctuated the word with the thump of the bottle on the ancient olive-green countertop. "It's beer, o.j., whiskey or water. Take your pick," he added, grabbing a frosty mug from the freezer.

Eleanor sniffed. "I'll just have a nip of yours, then." She pulled a tiny earthenware mug from somewhere within her color shifting dress and held it beneath the foamy, amber stream as he poured.

Doyle led the way back into the living room and dropped onto his leather recliner, murmuring in contentment as he took a long, cold swallow of carbonated heaven. He waited for Eleanor to seat herself on the edge of the gently scuffed wooden coffee table in front of him.

"So, now that I can talk to you without your charge thinking I'm a complete jackass," Doyle gave the faerie an accusing look, "why is it that you think a merrow would be trying to drown Violet?"

"I have no idea," Eleanor said glumly. "Like I said before, I didn't sense she was in danger until it was too late to help her avoid it. But I did get there in time to see one of them pulling her down. Doesn't make much sense, does it?"

Doyle frowned and shook his head. "From the little I know of merrows, they tend to stay as far from humans as possible. And they're not known to be violent. You said something happened to Violet a couple of months ago as well?"

"Not to Violet, to her parents." The faerie grimaced. "They were killed at sea. The human authorities said a freak wave must have sunk their boat and they drowned before they could be rescued. She's here to pack up their house."

"Poor lass," Doyle murmured softly. What courage it must have taken for her to go in the water today. And to nearly suffer the same fate as her parents, then have to return to their house and all the memories awaiting her there.

"But what makes you think her parents' deaths had anything to do with what happened today? It sounds like it was just a tragic accident."

Eleanor shrugged. "It's a feeling I have."

Doyle stared at her. "A feeling? Anything more solid than that?"

"Just that it's my job to sense anything that might be a danger to Violet," she retorted, her wings giving off a mutinous buzz, "and my feelings are rarely mistaken."

"Alright. I meant no offense." Doyle held his hands up. "It's just a bit hard to believe that we have a rogue merrow on our hands, out there murdering humans for no apparent reason."

"Three humans from the same family? There must be a reason, Doyle," Eleanor insisted. "And I don't want her going back in the water until I know she's safe."

"So warn her away from it." He shrugged as if that resolved the matter.

Eleanor huffed in annoyance. "It's not that simple. Violet loves the ocean. I can't warn her away from it forever!"

"So how do you intend to keep her safe?" Doyle demanded.

"I'm glad you asked," the faerie replied, pursing her tiny lips as if trying to hide a smile. "Since I can only do so much to keep her out of the water, and there's even less I can do to keep her safe once she's in it, what Violet needs is someone to protect her. Someone who's an even match for a determined merrow. Someone like an immortal warrior, for instance."

Doyle gaped at her. "You mean me. You want me to protect your charge for you."

"I know you like her," Eleanor pronounced with a look of sly satisfaction.

"Be that as it may," Doyle sputtered, "I fear her opinion of *me* leaves much to be desired. Thanks in large part to *you*, I might add."

Eleanor waved her hand dismissively. "A misunderstanding that's easy enough to fix. I have every confidence that, once you turn on that Irish charm of yours, she'll warm right up. You're a fine looking man. And believe me when I tell you that Violet noticed, whether she wanted to or not."

Doyle rubbed his thumb across his stubbly chin as he considered her words. Had Violet really found him attractive, despite the piss poor way he'd handled the situation with her today? "Fine," he agreed after a moment. "I'd be more than happy to improve upon Violet's first impression of me."

He narrowed his eyes and pointed at the faerie. "But don't think I don't know when I'm being maneuvered by flattery."

Eleanor gave him an innocent smile.

"How shall I meet up with her? Where is she now?" he asked, attempting to sound more casual than he felt. In truth, he was as eager as a schoolboy to see her again.

Eleanor's wings drooped and she stared down into her mug. "She's sitting alone in her parents' closet, surrounded by their things, crying."

Doyle shot to his feet, startling a yelp from Bruno. "What are you doing here with me, then?" he demanded. "Go...do whatever it is you do. Comfort her!"

When the faerie raised her face to look at him again, there were tears sparkling in her eyes. "She's grieving, Doyle. There's only so much I can do. I can share her sorrow, but I can't take it from her. It's something she needs to feel."

Doyle lowered himself back into his chair, cursing helplessly. "What she needs is to get out of that house. Can't you persuade her to go out for a bite to eat somewhere? Then I can meet her and try to take her mind off it for a bit."

Eleanor wiped at her eyes and nodded, tucking her mug back into her dress and rising from the coffee table. "I think I can manage that. I'll nudge her toward that crab shack, next to the docks. The rest will be up to you."

Doyle's lips quirked up in a mirthless smile. "I'll do my best to win the lady over. Just keep in mind that I'll probably be more successful this time if it doesn't appear that I'm conversing with my imaginary friend."

"Agreed. Oh and one more thing," Eleanor added, crossing her arms and rising to look him directly in the eye. "If you hurt her, I'll make sure you regret it for the rest of your immortal life."

She blinked out of sight wearing a threatening glower. It was far more formidable than it should have been, considering her diminutive stature.

Doyle stared after her with the confused expression of someone who'd just been put in his place by a cotton ball.

Chapter Three

Violet decided that there wasn't anything much better than enjoying the evening breeze, and sipping a mojito, while you gazed out over the ocean at a spectacular sunset.

She inhaled deeply, thinking that her parents had probably spent many evenings in this very spot doing precisely the same thing. The idea filled her with a strange serenity, as if they were with her now, lending her their strength despite their physical absence.

"How you doin' honey? You need a refill?"

Violet transferred her tranquil smile to the amiable waitress and glanced down at a glass that was mostly ice and mint leaves. She was on vacation. And she was walking home. She ordered mojito number two and a blackened grouper sandwich with fries and extra tartar sauce.

The waitress clomped away across the rustic wooden deck planks, hips swaying beneath her cutoff t-shirt. She was waylaid by a pair of cute guys who appeared to be more interested in flirting than ordering. Violet grinned and swiveled in her plastic seat to take in the rest of the scene.

The place was lively, without being too loud and crowded. Jimmy Buffet was singing about a cheeseburger in paradise over the speakers. And as the sun sank below the horizon, hundreds of tiny multicolored lights sprang to life, like a miniature fireworks display. They were everywhere, wrapped across the wooden railings and woven around the poles and spokes of the table umbrellas, casting the restaurant in an enchanted glow.

To top it all off, the bartender made a damn good mojito. Violet didn't usually venture beyond beer and wine, but she was glad she had tried something new. She was thinking that things were definitely looking brighter, when her eyes rose to find Captain Doyle standing beside her chair.

Violet nearly groaned at the appetizing package he presented: more than six feet of gorgeous, muscled man, freshly showered and shaven, and wearing just a hint of crisp, clean cologne. She couldn't deny the jolt of attraction, but the last thing she needed was to get involved with some local skirt chaser.

"Miss Hendrickson," he greeted affably. "Nice to see you again. I hope you're not feeling any ill effects from your earlier mishap?"

His rich brogue teased her ears and his warm demeanor relaxed her defenses, but she hadn't forgotten about his hot and cold treatment of her on the boat. "I'm fine, thank you," she answered warily.

"I'm glad I ran into you," he said, softening his tone. "I've been wanting to apologize to you for the way I acted earlier. I believe we got off on the wrong foot, so to speak. If I seemed a bit gruff, it was just that I was truly concerned for you—not only because you were my responsibility as a passenger, but because you seem like a genuinely nice person."

He gave her a wry smile. "I'm afraid I was also a bit preoccupied with a couple of the other passengers. I don't know if you noticed, but there were two in particular who were making a nuisance of themselves the entire trip. Though I would have liked to tell them to clear off, I was obliged to humor them somewhat. I've built my business from scratch, and I've learned it doesn't pay to be rude to the customers."

Violet blinked up at him, touching her tongue to lips that had suddenly gone dry. Though dressed casually in canvas shorts and a plain red t-shirt, he radiated a quiet confidence and sexuality that quickened her heartbeat and stole her breath. Maybe she had misread him before. He sounded so sincere. His eyes shone that mesmerizing sea-green in the glint of the colored lights, seeming to convey a heartfelt appeal.

Doyle stuck his hands into his pockets and cleared his throat. "Miss Hendrickson?"

"Please call me Violet," she exhaled on a quick breath.

He smiled uncertainly. "Violet. I was wondering if you'd allow me to buy you a drink."

Her pulse skipped at the way he said her name, the syllables lingering on his tongue as if he was savoring them. Should she? It was only a drink, but the force of her response to him made her skittish. She'd had a couple of serious boyfriends, but none of them had made her entire body hum with sensual current the way this man did. If she wasn't careful, the handsome Captain Doyle might end up breaking her heart.

But if her parents' deaths had taught her anything, it was that life was short. She made her decision and spoke before she could change her mind. "I'd like that. Please, have a seat." She pointed to the vacant chair across from her.

Doyle hid his sigh of relief as he joined Violet at the table. For a moment he'd been sure she was going to refuse him. She seemed nervous, and he decided he needed to make more of an effort to put her at ease.

"Thank heaven you're kind enough to give me the chance to redeem myself," he said with mock solemnity, purposely thickening his accent. "I promise to be on my best behavior from now on. Doyle Thresher, at your service." He held his hand out in a formal gesture.

He ruined it by winking at her and Violet laughed. She took his proffered hand, the brief contact sending a tingle of electricity zinging across her skin.

"Well, you already know I make my living giving tours on the *Ocean Magic*," he continued in a light tone. "So what do you do, Miss Violet Hendrickson? It is Miss, isn't it?" he added with a cheeky grin.

Her lips twitched with humor. "I teach fourth grade at an elementary school in Boynton Beach, a couple of hours north of here. And yes, my students call me Miss Hendrickson."

"A prim and proper school teacher," Doyle teased, "now I'll really have to watch my P's and Q's. Ah, here comes your drink."

The smiling waitress carefully placed a fresh mojito in front of Violet and whisked away her empty glass. "The food's coming right up," she promised before turning to Doyle. "Can I get you anything?"

Doyle eyed Violet's strange concoction. There seemed to be a bunch of leaves mixed in with the ice and someone had stuck a twig in it. "Just your special on draft tonight, please. And a large order of hot wings with fries."

"They have the best wings here," he confided to Violet. "So what exactly is that you're drinking? It appears to be sprouting some manner of foliage."

Violet chuckled. "It's a mojito—rum, sugar syrup, lime, mint leaves and club soda."

"And why is there a twig in it?" he asked dubiously.

She snorted in mirth. "It's sugar cane, but it doubles nicely as a garnish and a stir. Here, try it. It's actually quite refreshing." She pushed the glass across the table.

He wrinkled his nose in a charmingly boyish gesture. "I suppose you're one of those people who insists you have to try something before you can say you don't like it."

"I am," Violet agreed with a grin. Then she added, "Unless it's made from the internal organs of animals. I draw the line there."

He considered her with silent amusement. "What about liver and onions? Now there's a tasty dish. It was one of my mum's specialties when I was growing up. Have you ever tried it?"

"No." Her face scrunched up in disgust and she shook her head.

"Haggis?" he inquired innocently. "Ever tried that?"

"Blech." Violet made an involuntary sound of revulsion.

"Then how do you know you don't like it? You realize you're breaking your own rules, here, Violet." He feigned a disappointed sigh. "That's not very prim and proper of you. Doesn't set a good example for the impressionable youth with which you've been entrusted."

Violet smirked. "You're stalling, Doyle." She picked up the glass and held it out to him. "And there's nothing disgusting in a mojito. Try it. You'll like it."

"What about the sticks and leaves!" he exclaimed. "I prefer my beverages a little less...nature-y."

She tilted her head at him, an irresistible challenge in her gaze. He met her eyes and held them as he reached for the icy glass. His warm fingers brushed her cool ones. She made to pull away, but he slid his forefinger over hers, gently imprisoning it, as he leaned forward to take the straw between his lips. His teasing look melted into something deeper, and far more enticing.

He pulled a slow draw of the liquid, brushing his finger over hers in an unhurried caress that hinted at a heady world of possibilities and sent molten desire cascading through her belly. He released the straw, his finger continuing to draw lazy circles over hers, his eyes smoldering with heat and promise.

"You're right." The husky timbre of his voice was languid with seduction. "That was nice. Sweet. I wouldn't mind a bit more."

Violet could scarcely breathe as they stared at each other, the air between them crackling with intensity. She jerked back to reality as the waitress brought Doyle's beer, forcing herself to pull away as another server stepped up with their food. By the time they were alone again, she was flushed with embarrassed uncertainty. Had she made more out of his attentions than was really there?

∞∞∞∞∞∞∞∞∞

Doyle had only intended a bit of light teasing to make Violet feel more comfortable, but as soon as he looked into her eyes and his hand brushed against hers, he was ensnared. It was as if her touch held the power to bewitch him, stripping away all else and reducing him into a torrent of need.

Her skin had taken on a sun-kissed glow from her afternoon on the water, and he could just see a tantalizing edge of delicate lace peeking out from beneath the strap of her top. His fingers itched for the excuse to smooth across her shoulder and tuck it back into place. The thought of touching her bare, satiny flesh drove him wild.

But the bedeviled waitress had come back at the worst possible moment, and Violet had pulled away again. He could have shouted with the frustration of it. He took a bracing breath and reminded himself that he needed to go slow with her. She was still grieving for her parents. And he was supposed to be protecting her, not seducing her. She was an innocent young woman, a schoolteacher, for heaven's sake!

She looked uncomfortable, and it was his fault. He racked his brain for a way to put her back at ease. He couldn't pretend there hadn't been a moment between them. That would only make things worse. He decided it would be best to try to pick up where they had left off in conversation, neither drawing attention to, nor denying, the episode.

He caught her eyes as she took a nervous sip from her straw, and he gave her a somewhat sheepish smile. "I'll know better than to question your taste in beverages next time," he told her softly.

He was rewarded with a shy grin.

"Now you have to try my wings, unless you don't think you can handle the heat," he goaded.

"Bring it on," she taunted, dipping a french-fry in ketchup and popping it into her mouth.

Doyle studied her surreptitiously as he chose a drumette and rolled it in hot sauce before placing it on the edge of her plate. She was smiling again, and the tense set of her shoulders had relaxed. She was an intriguing blend of contrasts, seeming reserved one moment and turning playful the next. He found himself wanting to know more about her.

"So, do you like teaching? How long have you been at it?" he asked, just as she was taking a bite of her sandwich.

She gave him a derisive look as she chewed and he chuckled. "Sorry. Take your time." He started on a wing so she wouldn't feel like he was watching her eat.

She swallowed and sipped at the last of her mojito. "Three years. And I love it. I love working with the kids. My administration and my co-workers are great too…for the most part," she added, shaking her head in amused acceptance. "There're always a few aggravations to contend with. But overall I get along with everyone. And my school's only about five minutes from my apartment."

"How did you know that was what you wanted to do?" he prodded, enjoying the way her eyes sparkled when she talked about her job.

"I grew up around it," she answered with a wistful smile, "both my parents were teachers."

Doyle froze, and then covered the reaction by downing the rest of his beer. He wasn't supposed to know about her parents' deaths, and he didn't want to influence her decision to talk about it.

"So it was in your blood from the start," he commented.

"I suppose so," she agreed, her expression turning remote. "I always admired the way they were able to inspire their students to learn. They had this knack for making knowledge seem exciting, and the most amazing way of turning the process of figuring things out into a game.

"When I was younger and I was stuck on a subject, usually math," she said with a self-deprecating smirk, "they were always able to explain it in a way that made the light-bulb click on in my head. I wanted to be able to do that for kids."

"They sound like really great people," Doyle said gently.

Violet hesitated. She didn't want to bring down the evening, but it seemed strange not to tell him about her parents' deaths now that she'd gushed on about them.

"They *were* great people. They retired down here and bought a sweet little villa just up the street. But they were killed in a boating accident a couple of months ago. That's why I'm here. I'm packing up their house." She gave him a reassuring smile, hoping she hadn't made him uncomfortable.

"I'm so sorry, Violet." Relieved not to have to pretend he didn't know, he reached out and briefly squeezed her hand where it rested on the table. His warm palm engulfed her fingers in a gesture of strength and comfort. He was reluctant to stop touching her, but quashed the unseemly urge.

"I'm around the docks most days, and I only live a couple of blocks from here. I'd be happy to help with anything you need."

To his surprise, she reached for his hand as he started to pull away, clasping it tightly in her own. "Thanks, Doyle. That means a lot to me."

She smiled into his eyes for a moment before releasing him, sparking a curiously warm sensation deep within his chest.

"So what about your family?" she asked, nibbling on the chicken wing he'd given her and nodding her acceptance to the waitress for another drink.

"Well, originally I hail from Ireland."

"I guessed," Violet admitted with a grin.

"From a small town in County Kerry, to be precise," Doyle continued. "My family still lives there—my mum and pop, and my sister."

He bit into a sauce-drenched wing and nodded gratefully when the waitress dropped off his beer.

"Why did you leave?" Violet studied his handsome face with curiosity as she sampled her new mojito. She was beginning to feel pleasantly giddy.

Doyle shrugged as he chewed. "Ever since I was a lad, I've felt the call to explore. I was always getting into trouble, wandering off across the countryside, trespassing where I shouldn't, or getting myself lost. I think it was my small way of getting my parents used to the idea of me leaving.

"They were quite distressed when I told them I was going to university in Dublin." He grinned and took another swig of cold beer. "You can imagine their reaction when I decided to leave the country. I had to move out in steps across Europe—England, then France, then Spain—before I dared drop the bomb that I was going across the ocean to America."

Violet laughed. "It sounds like a well-thought-out escape plan. Do you go back to visit them often?"

"Honestly?" Doyle made a guilty face. "As little as I can. They're always coming up with a new scheme to get me to move back home, usually involving some single village girl in whom I inevitably have no interest."

"Ah, the age-old parental interference tactic: trying to tell you whom you should date." Violet chuckled. Her cheeks felt flushed and she gulped down more of the icy mojito.

"More like trying to set up an arranged marriage," Doyle grumbled. "Which is why having an ocean between us suits me just fine. Scarlett, my sister, comes to visit now and then. I love her, but she's not much fun to take out. She doesn't like hum... uh, people very much."

Doyle stuffed a couple of fries in his mouth, appalled that he'd almost slipped up in front of Violet like that. He'd been about to say that his sister didn't like humans, which was entirely true, but sounded rather odd considering *he* was supposed to be human. He'd never had a problem keeping his secret before. Apparently he needed to watch himself more carefully around Violet.

He glanced at her to see if she caught his stumble, but she didn't appear to notice. Her eyes were bright and happy, and she was wearing a rather large smile. Relieved, he decided to change the subject.

"Well, enough about me. Tell me something about yourself."

"Like what?" she demanded with a giggle.

"I don't know," his grin broadened at her playful mood. "Do you have any pets?"

"Yes," she answered with an emphatic nod. "Lots of fish. They're on a holiday feeder right now, and some of them are probably starving to death as we speak. They're not very bright, you see," she said with a rueful expression. "They're used to eating the flakes from the top. But the feeder sinks to the bottom."

Her eyes drifted away from his and she pointed across the deck. "Hey, isn't that your friend from the boat? And I think he's with my neighbor, Melody."

He followed her gaze to find Manny waiting for a table with a slim, attractive red-head. Doyle waved them over.

Manny clasped Doyle's hand and cast an interested look toward Violet. "*Lindita,* nice to see you feeling better. You too, *hermano.* Doyle was very cranky after you left today," he added in a confidential tone to Violet, ignoring Doyle's warning look. He put his arm around his female companion. "This is my lady friend, Melody. She is a beauty, no?"

Manny's eyes glowed with adoration as he introduced the red-head, who was indeed beautiful. She was tall and slender, with clouds of curly red hair and blue-green eyes that appeared huge above her high cheekbones. The hem of her filmy blouse floated over the low waistband of her jeans, and a matching blue beret was perched at a slant atop her curls.

She wore the hat with aplomb, and Violet grinned, thinking her mom would have approved.

"Nice to finally meet you," Doyle greeted. "Manny speaks of you highly. And often."

Manny narrowed his eyes and shook his finger at Doyle, who smirked back at him.

"Nice to see you, Melody," Violet added cheerfully. "And thanks again for offering to help me pack the other day. Why don't you guys sit with us?"

They pulled up two more chairs, and the waitress came by for their drink orders.

"It is nice that you two ladies know each other already," Manny com-

mented with a pleased nod at Melody and Violet.

"Yes, Violet is staying in one of the villas up the street from mine," Melody explained, looking sympathetic.

Violet smiled. All traces of sadness seemed to have fled from her blissfully fuzzy head. "Melody was nice enough to offer to help me pack up my parents' house."

"And the offer still stands," Melody insisted. "I'm not working at the moment, and would be more than happy to come by and help. Maybe you'll take me up on it now that I'm not such a stranger." Her expression turned melancholy as she added, "Violet's parents were very nice people."

"Oh, *lindita*," Manny tutted in sudden understanding, "I am very sorry for your loss."

"Thank you, Manny. And I appreciate the offer, Melody. But let's talk about something else," Violet suggested brightly.

She was more than content to sit back and drink her fresh mojito as Doyle and Manny launched into an amusing story involving a woman who had paid extra to bring her cat snorkeling with her. She insisted that the unimaginatively named 'Kitty' would love snorkeling because he spent hours on top of the aquarium at home, dipping his face and paws into the water as he watched the fish.

The tale, not surprisingly, ended with a wet, terrified cat and its severely scratched owner demanding her money back.

Laughing, Violet finished her drink and excused herself to the ladies room, only to discover that her ability to walk in a straight line had been somewhat compromised. Fortunately, Melody went with her and prevented her from taking a rather nasty spill on a warped deck-board.

"*Hermano*," Manny whispered, his eyes trailing worriedly after the girls, "how many of those has she had?"

Doyle followed his friend's gaze to Violet's empty mojito glass and he frowned. "I don't know. A few. But I tasted one and they're mostly mint soda."

Manny chortled. "No, *hermano*, there's a good shot of rum in there. That's what happens with those fancy drinks—you don't feel the liquor 'til it bites you in the *culo*."

Violet stumbled back to the table, Melody's hand steady at her elbow, and dropped heavily into her chair. "I'm sorry you guys. I think I drank too much," she announced.

"No need to apologize," Melody assured her in a kindly tone.

Manny chuckled. "Not at all, *lindita*."

"I didn't realize how potent twigs and leaves could be," Doyle joked.

Violet blinked at him, bemused. "Me either."

Doyle gave her a guilty smile, hoping she didn't think he was trying to get her drunk. And heaven help him if her faerie guardian thought so. "I think I should walk you home, though. When you're ready," he suggested, hesitantly.

"I think you're right." Violet realized she was having trouble focusing. "And I'm ready if you are."

Doyle flagged the waitress and handed her some bills, keeping one eye on Violet as he did so. "Please allow me to buy you dinner," he offered.

Violet nodded her thanks. She would normally have protested, but at the moment she couldn't find it within herself to care.

They said goodbye to Melody and Manny, and Doyle helped Violet down the wooden ramp leading to the dusty parking lot. The sky had clouded over to obscure the moon and stars, leaving the night humid and dark. Doyle steered her toward a level stretch of sidewalk, bright with pooling light from the streetlamps. He draped his arm over her shoulders to help steady her, and sucked in a sharp breath when she snuggled into his side.

Her nearness drove him to distraction. She smelled so lovely, like an orchard in the sunlight. And her skin felt like satin where his hand rested on her arm. He longed to run his fingers over its softness. He told himself to think virtuous thoughts, but the friction of her body rubbing against his as they walked was a delicate torture.

"Have I thanked you properly for saving my life today?" she asked, her voice a melodic sigh.

He stiffened at the question. He could think of several ways he'd like to be properly thanked by the angelic temptress beside him.

"Well, in case I haven't," she said sweetly, "thank you, Doyle." She hugged him tighter to her side for a moment.

He clenched his jaw, disgusted with his train of thought. He was obviously not fit to be walking her home. He should have asked Manny to do it.

He leaned down to place a chaste kiss on the top of her head. "Any time, Violet."

She let out a contented murmur, and an unexpected tenderness moved through him. It didn't quench the fire he felt for her, but it helped it to burn a little slower. They continued walking in silence and Doyle smiled to himself as he thought about the intriguing young woman at his side. He'd only known her for a few hours, but he already feared that he was becoming addicted to her company.

They were turning onto her street when a clap of thunder rumbled through the night, rattling the windowpanes of a garage door as they passed. Jagged bolts of lighting followed it across the sky, casting the neat row of villas in eerie brightness, just as the clouds burst open in a flash downpour. Doyle cursed, trying to shield Violet, but to his surprise she erupted in delighted laughter.

"I love storms!" She broke away from him and did a twirling spin with her face held up in supplication to the deluge.

Doyle snorted and shook his head. "You're going to fall right on your can, Violet."

She giggled. "Dance with me." She took Doyle's hands in hers, pulling him along with her contagious joy.

"You're mad, you realize that," Doyle laughed as he whirled her around.

She merely smiled up at him, her damp hair spilling down her back in a silken waterfall. Her eyes shone like jewels in the darkness, reminding him of nothing so much as a beautiful nymph that had stepped from the faerie realm to take on human form.

Doyle grinned down at her and decided that, if she was indeed mad, sanity was highly overrated.

Chapter Four

Violet awoke with a groan, wondering why the sun had crawled down from the sky to beam directly into her bedroom window. She must have forgotten to close the blinds before going to sleep last night. That was odd. Usually the possibility of someone skulking outside the window, watching her sleep, would keep her awake until she got up to shut them.

She made a vexed sound and rolled off the mattress, shading her eyes with one hand as she staggered across the rug to the window. She twisted the blinds closed and drew the layered muslin curtains, sighing with relief at the resulting darkness. A dull ache was beginning to form behind her temples, and all she wanted was to dissolve back into sleep. She turned and stumbled forward to collapse on her pillow, and froze.

Doyle's sleeping form was partially tucked beneath the covers on the opposite side of her parents' king-sized bed. The thick comforter was pushed down around his waist to reveal the tanned, muscular contours of his chest. One arm was thrown carelessly over his head and his lips were slightly parted to take in deep, even breaths. She stared at him as the night's events came crashing back.

She was such an idiot. She'd been sucking down those mojitos like they were water. And she couldn't remember a thing after her vague recollection of saying goodnight to Melody and Manny. She glanced down and her head started to pound in earnest. She wasn't wearing anything except for her lacy white bra and panties.

She blinked at Doyle in trepidation, wondering what she would find if she pulled the covers just a little lower. She couldn't have…he wouldn't have…oh, crap. She needed an aspirin. She lurched toward the bathroom to pull on her robe, cinching the soft, over-washed fabric tightly around her waist. Then she dug some pills out of the medicine cabinet, and shuffled off to the kitchen for a glass of water.

She was sitting at the mosaic-tiled table in the nook by the west-facing box window, pressing a cool waterglass to her forehead and waiting for the painkillers to do their work, when Doyle wandered out of the bedroom. He stretched and yawned, his arms and bare chest shifting tantalizingly with the movement. A pair of plaid cotton boxers rode low on his trim hips.

He gave her a warm, slumberous smile. "Good morning, Sunshine. How are you feeling?" His voice held a sexy, sleep-roughened quality that sent a shiver across her nerve-endings.

"Okay," she answered, more shrilly than she intended.

He frowned. "Are you sure? You look a bit peaky. Does your head hurt?" He started forward. "I know an amazing massage technique…" He faltered.

Her eyes had gone wide, almost panicked, at his approach.

"Violet?" he asked in concern.

"Uh huh," she squeaked, her muscles tightening as if in preparation to flee.

"Have I done something to upset you?"

"I..." her hand trembled slightly as she lowered her waterglass to the table, her eyes following it down. "I can't remember what happened last night," she mumbled, refusing to look at him.

Doyle made a sound suspiciously akin to a laugh. He closed the distance between them, his bare feet slapping against the wood floor, and lowered himself onto the empty wrought iron chair next to Violet. His knee brushed hers where her robe had fallen open, and she squeezed her eyes shut in mortification. But she didn't pull away; she didn't want to. And that was part of the problem.

Doyle took one of her hands and gently lifted her chin with the fingers of his other hand. "Violet, look at me."

He was right. She was acting like a child. She forced herself to face him, feeling embarrassingly unsophisticated.

"Nothing happened." His sea-green eyes were solemn, but mirth sparkled within their depths.

She bit her lip. "But, the bed, and I was kind of undressed..."

"Sweetheart, we were caught in a downpour on the way home, and you insisted on dancing in the rain," he told her with an amused snort. "You were soaked. It was all I could do to get the wet clothes off you before you passed out."

She pulled back from him, a comical expression of horror flitting across her face. "You undressed me?"

"I couldn't let you sleep in a puddle of water! And it's not as if it's anything I haven't seen before," he pointed out, exasperated.

Violet's eyebrows drew together dangerously and he knew he'd said the wrong thing. "You've never seen *me* before."

"Violet, come on. It's just like seeing you in a bikini," he implored in a cautious attempt to backtrack.

"You've never seen me in a bikini," she said stubbornly. "And that still doesn't explain why we were in bed together."

Doyle gaped at the way she'd turned the tables on him so quickly. An uncomfortable lump of guilt formed in his chest, leaving him unable to come up with a clever explanation for why he'd spent the night with her. In the same bed.

"I'm going to take a shower." Her tone was flat as she rose and went back to the bedroom, shutting the door quietly behind her.

Doyle groaned and dropped his head into his hands. He'd been the perfect gentleman. How had he ended up with her mad at him? Well, maybe he'd enjoyed undressing her a bit more than he should have. The thought of those lacy wisps of white surrounded by all that bare, creamy skin was enough to make his cock twitch even now. But he hadn't touched her any more than necessary to get her out of her wet clothes and into bed.

And the fact that he'd crawled into bed with her...well, he hadn't wanted to walk home in that storm. He'd thought about sleeping on the couch, but he didn't know where the extra linens were kept. Okay, so the truth was that he'd wanted to be near Violet. But the bed was huge, and he'd kept to his side.

∞∞∞∞∞∞∞∞∞

Violet closed her eyes and leaned against the inside of her parents' bedroom door. What was wrong with her? She'd gotten drunk and Doyle had taken care of her. And she had turned it around and picked a fight with him. She should be relieved that he cared enough to make sure she got home safe, and was enough of a gentleman not to take advantage of her impaired judgment.

But the truth was, she was sober now and her judgment was still impaired. She'd only met him yesterday, and a part of her knew that she probably *would* have slept with him last night if he'd asked, liquor or no.

She headed into the bathroom to find both their clothes still wet, but draped neatly over the racks in the bathtub. She transferred them to the sink with a sigh, feeling a guilty comfort in the fact that he couldn't leave without her apology. Not unless he wanted to walk home half naked anyway.

∞∞∞∞∞∞∞∞∞

Doyle wondered what he should do. He didn't want to leave, but he didn't know if Violet wanted him to stay. Not to mention the fact that poor Bruno was probably crossing his hind legs by now. It was a beach community and no one would look at him twice for walking the streets in his boxers. And although he wasn't supposed to, he could always use magic.

But he wanted to make things up with Violet. He stood and wandered listlessly over to the refrigerator. It was barren except for a couple of yogurt cups, an old jar of mustard, some bottled water, and a rather dodgy looking Tupperware container. The pantry was similarly vacant, revealing a patchwork of colorfully lined shelves. A coffee pot sat next to a toaster on the speckled corian countertop, but sadly, there were no beans to be found.

He headed past the bright, mismatched living room furniture and opened a door that he correctly guessed led into the garage, an idea taking shape. The space was dim and tidy, with an old Ford woody wagon parked in the midst of several stacks of boxes. Doyle slipped into the red vinyl driver's seat, encouraged when the interior light flicked on, and he found the keys tucked above the visor.

He grinned at the pewter depiction of a sprite hanging from the rear-view mirror as he turned the key in the ignition. The motor rumbled to life on the first try. He clicked the remote for the garage door, counting a silent two for two when it worked as well, and carefully backed the car out into the street. He should be back before Violet even noticed he was gone...

Violet finished brushing the tangles from her hair and stood over her suitcases, debating what to wear. She was feeling ridiculously nervous at the prospect of opening the door and facing Doyle again. She chose a snug black t-shirt, with a feminine ruffle at the sleeves, which molded nicely to her breasts and flattered her waist. Then she pulled on a pair of soft khaki lounging shorts and added some dangly earrings to liven up the outfit.

Her stomach fluttering, she opened the door. Her senses were immediately assailed by an amazing smell, and she quizzically made her way to the kitchen. There stood Doyle, in a fresh t-shirt and shorts, flipping what appeared to be a giant omelet in one pan, while bacon sizzled enthusiastically in another. As if that wasn't wonderful enough, he was making coffee. And he'd brought sugar and cream.

She jumped as the toast popped up, and Doyle saw her as he turned to check it. He gave her a hangdog grin, and her face slowly stretched into an incredulous smile.

"I'm sorry," they both said at the same time, and then laughed.

"No, listen, Doyle," Violet said anxiously. "I really appreciate you getting me home safe and taking care of me last night. I shouldn't have snapped at you. I was just a little unnerved," she felt her face grow warm and finished in a determined rush, "to find you in my bed and not remember how you got there."

She looked so pretty standing there, a blush staining her freshly scrubbed cheeks, her raven hair gleaming beneath the soft kitchen lights. "It was my fault," Doyle said automatically. "I should have slept on the couch."

"No," Violet denied, shaking her head. "You were fine. That bed is huge. I was just being priggish."

Doyle grinned at her pronouncing herself a prude. "You *are* a prim and proper school teacher," he joked. Her face started to fall into a scowl and he backtracked quickly, "I'm kidding. Your reaction was perfectly understandable. I shouldn't have assumed it was okay to share the bed. And I promise you, I would never have taken advantage of you in such a state."

The lines that had begun to form in her forehead smoothed away and he smiled in relief. But he couldn't help teasing her just a bit more. "Other than that, though, was it really so terrible to wake up beside me," he asked in a husky brogue.

Violet's blush deepened and she didn't answer. "Do you need any help with breakfast?" she asked, looking flustered.

Doyle jerked in surprise and hurried back to what was now sure to be extra crispy bacon and a browned omelet. That would teach him to discomfit his shy school teacher. "No, I've got it under control," he replied with a grimace. "But I hope you like your breakfast well done."

"It's got to be better than the yogurt cups I've been eating for the past two days," she said, grinning. "What's in the omelet?"

"Tomato, mushroom, onion, and lots of cheddar," he answered, taking it off the burner and splitting it in half with the spatula. He scooped one of the pieces onto a waiting plate, melted cheese bubbling and stretching out in long strings before separating.

"A man after my own heart," Violet sighed. "I'll set the table."

Violet pulled out a couple of silky, tasseled placemats and matching cloth napkins, and lit the taper candle sitting at the center of the table's mosaic swirl. In moments they were tucking into coffee and large plates of food.

"Mmf is really good!" she exclaimed around a mouthful of omelet.

Doyle smirked at her over his bacon. "You sound surprised."

Her eyes crinkled with humor as she swallowed and took a scalding sip of coffee. "Not at all," she denied. "I'm just not used to having guys cook for me."

"No?" he teased. "Well, you've been hanging around the wrong sort, then. I always cook a woman breakfast after spending the night in bed with her."

Violet snorted, refusing to touch that one. She did wonder, though, just how many other women had been treated to Doyle's culinary talents. They ate in silence for a while, accompanied only by the clink of forks on ceramic plates and the faint twitter of birds from the garden.

Violet took a final bite and sat back with a sigh. "That was delicious. Thank you, Doyle. I must have been in the shower longer than I thought, for you to be able to go shopping and cook all that."

"Actually, I borrowed your car," Doyle admitted with a guilty twist of his lips. "I had to run home to walk my dog and get some dry clothes, so I just grabbed some stuff from my pantry while I was there. I only live a few blocks away. And I put the car right back where I found it. I hope that was okay."

Violet looked surprised. "It's fine. It was my parents' car. But I love driving around in that old thing. I had a friend drop me off here because I'm planning on bringing it home with me."

"I can see why." Doyle grinned. "It's a bit like riding in a time capsule. Not to mention that it's probably built like a tank compared to most of the newer models."

"Yeah." Violet sighed. "My parents were old hippies at heart. It'll be kind of like taking a piece of them with me. I'm getting rid of most everything else. Which reminds me, I should probably get back to packing," she said regretfully.

"I'd like to help you, if you'll let me," Doyle offered. "I can clean, pack boxes, move stuff, whatever you need me to do."

"Oh, Doyle. That's very sweet of you, but you don't have to do that. I've already kidnapped you for a night and finagled breakfast out of you. I'm sure you have other things to do today."

"Nope," Doyle disagreed bluntly. "It's my day off, and I'd like nothing better than to spend it with you, whatever you're doing."

Violet's heart fluttered at the statement. How could she say no to that? "Okay," she conceded softly.

"Good."

The air between them practically vibrated with electricity. With a word and a smile, he quickened her pulse and made her ache for his touch. Did he feel it too? Violet took a shuddering breath and attempted to keep her expression casual.

"Thank you."

"You're welcome." He leaned forward to brush a kiss across her forehead, and then briskly began clearing away their plates.

Violet's heart skipped a beat, maybe two, and it was a moment before she remembered to inhale again. She had almost believed he would kiss her. Not that chaste peck he'd given her, but a *real* kiss, full on the lips, preferably with the use of his clever tongue.

She really needed to get a handle on herself. She debated the wisdom of taking another, much colder, shower before they spent the day cooped up in the villa together.

She sighed and rose to take over the cleanup. She felt bad leaving it to Doyle after he had cooked and then kindly offered to help her pack.

∞∞∞∞∞∞∞∞∞

Doyle scrubbed furiously at a plate, silently applauding his self control. He ought to win a medal for restraining himself from tasting Violet's delectable lips just now. He subjected a coffee mug to equally rough treatment, as he tortured himself with thoughts of where that kiss might have led, with that lovely king-sized bed beckoning from the other room.

No, he was here to help her pack up her parents' things. And to make sure she didn't go back in the ocean until the sprite found out why the merrow had attacked her. Nothing more. But he swore that with one more spark, the atmosphere between them would burst into flames. Could she not feel it? He was going to have to concentrate on baseball and his sister's upcoming visit just to get through the day in such close quarters with Violet.

"Did that mug do something to piss you off?" Violet asked in startled amusement. Doyle was scouring the thing as if it had been dipped in toxic waste.

Doyle's hands stilled beneath the stream of hot water and he gave Violet an abashed look. "Sorry, I guess I was daydreaming."

"About what, dismembering someone?" Violet laughed as she pulled the immaculate mug from his grip and nudged him out of the way. "You cooked; I'll clean."

She took over, brooking no argument. He grinned at her back as she swayed between the sink and the dish rack, her movements graceful and efficient. His eye was drawn lower to the lush curve of her bottom, enticingly molded by the thin, soft material of her shorts.

He turned abruptly and made himself go check on his drying clothes.

∞∞∞∞∞∞∞∞∞∞∞

Violet found she didn't have to worry about cold showers after all. She put Doyle to work moving boxes out to the garage. Then she gave him the job of packing up the kitchen, the dishes and cookware and such, while she performed the more personal task of wrapping and boxing the various knickknacks and photos on display throughout the villa.

Doyle continued to transfer packed items into the garage and spent some time making new boxes out of flattened stacks of folded cardboard. When he had finished everything he could think to do on his own, he went in search of Violet again and found her in a small office, tucked away in the rear corner of the villa.

It was a neat jumble of bookshelves and filing cabinets. A computer desk faced a window that looked out onto the vibrant splashes of color tumbling across the backyard garden. Violet was sitting cross-legged on the floor, her mauve-painted toes peeking from beneath her knees, amidst scattered stacks of what appeared to be old mail.

"What next, boss?" he asked softly.

Her eyes lifted from the paper she was reading, blank and startled for a moment, before her face melted into a smile. She sat up and raised her arms in a back-popping stretch, groaning the stiffness away.

Doyle stifled his own groan at the way her shirt clung to the ripe fullness of her breasts.

"Sorry. I was just going through these credit card statements. Can you believe my parents were spending over $3000.00 a month on gas? I thought it was a mistake at first. After all, the woody can't be *that* bad on gas mileage. But then I realized it must have been for their boat. I know that boats use a lot of fuel, and gas prices have almost doubled, but isn't that a bit excessive?"

Doyle shrugged and picked his way past the litter of papers to drop into a creaking office chair. "It depends. Manny and I take the *Ocean Magic* out five days a week, to the reefs and back, up to five times a day. And you don't even want to know how much we average per month on gas. Just suffice it to say that we go well over $3000.00 on a slow month. What kind of boat did your parents have?"

Violet's lips curled in a little moue. "I don't really know. It couldn't have been very big though, maybe thirty feet? I think my dad said it had an 'outboard motor'."

Doyle snorted. "Either it had a fuel leak, or they must have been taking it out every day," he replied, lifting one golden-brown eyebrow.

Violet shook her head as if trying to wrap it around the idea. "Well, they *were* retired. And they loved being out on the ocean. So I guess it's not all that strange."

She shrugged and added the statement to a pile she'd already been through. "You're ready for your next assignment?" she asked with an impish grin.

Doyle gave her a sideways smile. "I don't know. What's my reward?"

Her rosy lips formed an 'O' of feigned shock. "I thought you were helping me out of the kindness of your heart."

"I am." His eyes sparkled with laughter. "But I thought kind deeds were meant to be rewarded."

"Hmm," she sounded, biting her lip thoughtfully. "What sort of reward were you expecting?"

Stark heat flared in his expression. "I hadn't quite decided yet," he said huskily.

She let out a soft chuckle and pointed to a bookshelf. "Well start packing up those books, would you, and let me know when you decide what you want." She dropped her head and began reviewing her paperwork once more.

Doyle stared at the top of her head, a slow smile spreading across his face. His little school teacher was starting to flirt back. He went to retrieve some empty boxes for the books, trailing his fingertips lightly over her hair as he passed.

Violet hid her smile, a surge of exhilaration coursing through her. He'd made another of his flustering, charged comments, and she'd given it right back this time. Now there was just one enthralling problem...what would he expect for his reward?

∞∞∞∞∞∞∞∞∞∞

There were four floor-to-ceiling bookshelves in the office. Doyle started on the one farthest from Violet so as not to disturb her paper piles. He glanced over its contents—all reference books, mostly consisting of a bulky old set of encyclopedias, which made for the heaviest work so far as he carried them back to the garage.

The next bookshelf contained a massive collection of dog-eared paperbacks, which were lighter once packed, but took longer to box up because there were more of them. They ranged from classic fiction, to romance, to mysteries, to true crime. He even noticed a few fantasy and horror titles mixed in.

Violet began transferring the papers on the floor into a corner filing cabinet, and Doyle moved to the opposite wall and the third bookshelf. These were all teaching tomes, ranging from books on education, to student textbooks and workbooks for assorted subjects and grades.

At last he reached the final, and most interesting, bookcase. His eyes traveled over multi-colored volumes of varying height and thickness. Some of the jackets were fashioned from cloth or hide as opposed to paper. A few of the titles had faded into illegibility, their spines so brittle they looked as if they might disintegrate on contact.

Here he noted an impressive range of mythology from different cultures throughout the world, alongside folktales, faerie tales, books on mysticism and witchcraft, and even spell grimoires. He opened a rather dusty volume on Celtic legends, with a green cloth cover stenciled in gold lettering, and grinned to find a surprisingly accurate chapter dedicated to his own people, the sidhe.

It was always a bit bizarre when he came across a true account of the faerie realm that the humans had relegated to the category of fiction. It hadn't always been that way. Many years ago, before he was born, contact between the realms had been far more common. The humans had been more in tune with the earth and the ways of magic. They had *believed.*

But as the generations went on they had been taught to ignore his kind, and a veil had fallen over their eyes. As a result, many of the denizens of the faerie realm who could not pass for mortal creatures, such as the sprites, had become invisible to humans.

The Seelie Court, who worked to maintain the eternal balance between good and evil, had been forced to put measures in place to uphold the separation between the realms. They feared mass chaos would erupt if the humans were suddenly confronted with the fact that a realm of immortal beings coexisted alongside their own. Doyle understood, but he thought it was a shame.

The two realms had so much they could learn from each other.

"How do you expect to earn your reward if you keep slacking off?"

Violet's teasing voice interrupted Doyle's musings, and he realized he was staring into space, still holding the book on Celtic legends. He smiled to find her looking up at him from amidst a new stack of papers she had created on the floor.

"This is quite a collection your parents had," he commented, indicating the shelf beside him. "They must have been real mythology buffs. And all these spell and witchcraft books. Were they Wiccan, by any chance?"

Violet snorted softly. "They were…eccentric. They had a lot of romantic notions about magic and alternate realities, and how cross-cultural similarities between myths and legends proved that they contained a core of truth. I swear they probably believed most of the stuff on that shelf was true."

Doyle frowned at her, nettled by the dismissal in her tone. "It doesn't seem all that farfetched to me," he said, trying to sound casual.

Violet's eyes widened and she smiled at him in disbelief. "You're kidding, right?"

His frown deepened. "No, I'm not."

"Oh, come on," she insisted incredulously. "It's a nice fantasy, but mystical creatures and magical worlds, existing right alongside our own, even though no one can see them. How does that work, exactly?"

She laughed as if expecting him to share in the joke.

But Doyle couldn't seem to work up any humor. He told himself he should just concede her point and drop it. Something inside him, though, compelled him to argue with her.

"Do you honestly believe, then, that there is no mystery or magic left to be discovered in this world? That there is nothing out there beyond what you have the ability to see and comprehend?" he demanded in mounting agitation.

She gave him a bewildered look. "I'm sure there's plenty left to be discovered—in the depths of the oceans and in remote jungles and definitely in outerspace. I just think that if there was really some invisible magical world all around us, someone would have caught onto it by now."

Doyle was so exasperated he couldn't speak. The urge to prove Violet wrong was like a live wire burning through his mind. He had to get away from her before he said something rash. He tossed the Celtic book back toward the bookcase and walked out of the office without another word.

Violet stared after him. What in the world was he so worked up about? Then it occurred to her that he had asked if her parents were Wiccan. Maybe *he* was Wiccan and she had just offended his religion. People could be really touchy about that sort of thing. She pushed herself to her feet, thinking she should probably go apologize.

∞∞∞∞∞∞∞∞∞∞

Doyle retreated into the solitude of the bathroom and stood in front of the sink, palms pressed into the cool marble countertop, his reflection looking back at him from the mirror. He made an effort to loosen the frustrated tension tightening his shoulders.

It wasn't Violet he was upset with so much as himself.

What had possessed him to needle her like that? He'd never had a problem keeping the existence of the faerie realm a secret from any of his other human friends, male *or* female. Why was he suddenly so eager to reveal himself to Violet? Whatever the reason, he needed to get over it.

He splashed some water on his face and, feeling more composed, exited back into the bedroom. Violet sat on the edge of the bed waiting for him, her feet crossed at the ankles and her hands clasped as if she was forcing them to remain still.

"Doyle?" she said apprehensively. "I'm really sorry if I offended you. I like you very much and I would never intentionally say anything to ridicule your beliefs. I don't know what I would have done without all your help yesterday and today."

The words were almost as sweet as the lips they had fallen from, and Doyle realized that once again he'd been a jackass. He strode forward to stand before her, trailing the backs of his fingers down her soft cheek.

"You did nothing wrong, Violet. I'm just tired and cranky and I was being argumentative. My blood sugar probably dropped too low and it addled my brain."

"I forgot all about stopping for lunch," she said apologetically. He had been thoughtful enough to make her breakfast, and she'd worked him all afternoon without feeding him. She grimaced as she thought about the empty fridge. "Do you want a yogurt cup to tide you over? I could get us some takeout."

Doyle laughed, but the relief he expected to feel at her acceptance of his excuse was annoyingly absent. "No, thanks. I actually need to get home and take out my poor neglected dog."

"Oh, right." She tried not to sound as disappointed as she felt. But the slow caress of his fingers was addling *her* brain. "Um, do you want a ride?" she asked breathlessly.

"No. The walk'll do me good. I'll catch up with you tomorrow, okay?"

Was there regret in his voice, or was it her imagination looking for reasons to ask him to stay? "Okay, then. Thanks again for all your help," she managed.

Doyle told himself it was for the best. Her very presence wreaked havoc on his control. He needed to put some distance between them, and maybe tomorrow he'd be able to approach her with a fresh perspective.

But it took every ounce of willpower Doyle possessed to turn and walk out her door.

Chapter Five

Violet spent the night tossing and turning, the bed suddenly seeming too big for just one person. She woke up late, grateful for the coffee Doyle had left, and spent a restless afternoon prowling about the empty villa without accomplishing much of anything.

She figured Doyle must be out on the boat. Her traitorous imagination kept spinning out scenes involving him, sexy and shirtless, surrounded by groups of adoring, bikini-clad women who were only too happy to invite him home and have him cook breakfast for them.

Her heart leapt when the doorbell rang a little before 5 p.m. But it wasn't Doyle. It was Melody, standing there in jeans and a t-shirt, looking cute with her blue beret perched atop her fiery curls.

"Hi, Violet," she greeted with an uncertain smile. "I hope you don't mind me stopping by like this. I just wanted to say hello and see if you needed any help."

Violet sighed. "You know, I'm having a hard time getting anything done today. But would you like to come in for a cup of coffee?"

Melody beamed. "That would be great."

Violet led her guest to the little mosaic table in the nook by the window and set about making fresh coffee.

"I'm a little embarrassed about the other night," Violet admitted, crossing her arms over her chest as she leaned against the counter. The rich aroma of percolating java began to waft from the pot behind her.

She shot Melody a self-conscious grin. "I don't usually drink hard liquor. I guess I kind of lost track of how many refills I was ordering."

"You have no reason to feel embarrassed," Melody insisted, her wrought iron chair scraping lightly against the floor as she turned it toward Violet. "You were just letting off a little steam. I know going through your parents' things must be very difficult for you."

"It's not the most fun way to spend my summer vacation," Violet agreed. "But I'm getting through it. Doyle was here yesterday and he helped out a lot. He packed up some stuff for me and did all of the heavy lifting, transferring boxes out to the garage and so forth." She shrugged and turned to check the coffee, which had slowed to an intermittent drip. "A lot of what I have left to do is just going through paperwork."

"Doyle seems like a very nice man," Melody said to Violet's back. "I hadn't met him before the other night, but Manny considers him a good friend. Have the two of you been dating long?"

A teaspoon slipped from Violet's fingers to clatter against the counter. "Uh, no, we're not dating," she corrected. "I only met him day before yesterday, when I went on one of their snorkeling tours. I had an accident in the water and he came to my rescue." She gathered the mugs and spoons and brought them to the table, then went back for the cream and sugar.

"Sorry," Melody said with a chagrinned chuckle. "You two just kind of seemed…well, anyway. So are you married or dating anyone special at home?" she asked.

Violet smiled as she diluted her coffee to the color of pale caramel. "Not really. I teach elementary school and I guess I tend to do my socializing with my co-workers, most of whom are women. There are a few guys, but they're either married or gay," she added on a laugh.

"Really?" Melody asked with a mischievous grin. "Well, perhaps I wasn't so far off after all. Manny says that Doyle is single, in case you were wondering. And I have a hunch that he isn't gay."

"I'll keep that in mind." Violet took a sip from her mug, her eyes dancing with humor over the rim. "So what about you? How long have you and Manny been a couple?"

"Only a few weeks," Melody answered, a dreamy fondness taking over her features, "but I like him very much."

"He seems like a super-sweet guy," Violet replied sincerely, "very warm and friendly."

Melody nodded. "He is. Not at all like my last boyfriend. He was so jealous. He couldn't stand for me to spend time with anyone but him. I tried to break things off, but he wouldn't leave me alone. I had to move to get away from him."

Violet's forehead wrinkled in a frown. "He sounds like some kind of stalker."

"He was a bad choice," Melody agreed softly, regret clouding her blue-green eyes. "But I was feeling lonely, and at first he seemed very charming." She shook her head, her red curls bouncing gently beneath the light cotton fabric of her beret. "Anyway, Manny is much different."

Sensing Melody's discomfort with the topic, Violet gave her a sympathetic look and changed the subject. "So what do you do for work?"

"Well, I'm actually trying to figure that out," Melody answered in a hesitant tone. "I have a little bit of money, but it's running out, and I'm going to need to find a job soon. I don't really have any professional skills, so I was thinking I might try waiting tables at one of the local restaurants."

Melody nibbled her lip anxiously and Violet silently applauded herself for choosing another stellar topic of conversation.

"I'll bet you can make a lot of money waiting tables down here, especially during season," Violet said with confidence. "And I'm sure you'll pick it up quickly. Plus, summer is probably the best time to learn, since it's slower."

"You think?" Melody asked, her angular face seeming to brighten.

"I'm sure you'll be fine," Violet encouraged. "By the way, I've been meaning to tell you that I like your hat. It reminds me of my mom. She used to wear hats all the time. I've been packing up her collection, and it's the hugest I've ever seen."

"Really?" Melody asked with interest. "I've always had something of an addiction for hats too. I'd love to see her collection, if you wouldn't mind."

Violet's lips twisted ruefully. "If you'd asked yesterday, I would have said no problem. But now they're boxed up somewhere in the garage, probably behind a couple hundred pounds worth of encyclopedias and cast iron pots. I promise though, when I'm ready to have everything carted out of here, I'll let you have a look at them before they go anywhere."

"Okay thanks, I'd really appreciate it," Melody said hopefully. "And maybe I can help with some of the other stuff too. You know, if you need a hand taking it anywhere or whatever."

Violet smiled. "Thanks. I didn't expect to have so many offers of assistance when I came down here. You and Doyle have both been so nice. Although, I think the only reason he felt obligated to look after me was because I almost drowned on his tour."

"How did that happen?" Melody exclaimed, her thin form straightening in alarm.

"It was no big deal, really," Violet assured her with a laugh. "I was trying to get a closer look at a sea turtle, and I guess I got away from the rest of the group. Something knocked into me and I was unconscious for a few minutes before Doyle pulled me out of the water."

"What knocked you unconscious?" Melody asked with a frown.

Violet shrugged. "I didn't get a good look at it. But it was probably just a shark bumping me to figure out what I was doing there." Her grin widened at Melody's troubled expression.

"Well, I was probably swimming in its living room or something. Wouldn't you want to know what I was doing there if you were it?" she joked.

Melody didn't laugh. "That's very scary, Violet. Especially after what happened with…" she trailed off, looking even more apprehensive. "I think you are far more courageous than I am," she admitted in a small voice.

"I'm not so sure about all that," Violet replied with a chuckle. "But please don't feel like you have to walk on eggshells around the topic of my parents. They loved the ocean, and they taught me to love it as well. They wouldn't have wanted me to allow their deaths to ruin that."

Melody blinked at Violet as if she wanted to argue, but then decided against it. "I think it's very admirable that you don't allow fear to control you," she said. "But I hope you will be more careful from now on."

Violet smiled. "I intend to be. Do you want another cup of coffee?"

Melody shook her head. "No, that's alright. Manny's picking me up after his last tour, and I should probably go get ready. But thank you very much for inviting me in. I enjoyed talking to you."

"Me too," Violet agreed, feeling genuine affection for the other woman as she stood and followed her to the door.

Melody paused on her way out. "I'm only three doors down. Please let me know if you need anything."

"I will," Violet affirmed with a chuckle. "And I'll let you know about those hats too."

"Please do. And next time I'll make the coffee." She waved and disappeared down the cobblestone path.

Violet closed the door, feeling a little better for the company and deciding she'd been cooped up inside for long enough. She headed toward the bedroom to change into her swimsuit. While grabbing a fresh towel from the dryer, she grinned to find the clothes Doyle had forgotten to take home. At least she had a good excuse to see him again.

She stuffed the towel and a bottle of water in her backpack, donned her sunglasses, and began a leisurely stroll down to the beach. The sun's warmth sank into her bones as she walked, and a light breeze blew off the ocean to gently tousle her hair. She couldn't help slowing as she passed the docks, her eyes scanning for the *Ocean Magic*, but it wasn't yet back in its slip.

Ignoring her flash of disappointment, she continued on for another block until she reached a small, local stretch of beach. She slipped off her sandals and stepped onto a sandy path leading beneath a shady forest of towering sea-grapes. The trail continued through a gap in the dunes, bordered by thick, wiry clumps of beach grass.

Eventually the path widened into a broad, white expanse and Violet had to quicken her step as the dry, powdery sand became hot enough to scald the bottoms of her feet. With a sigh of relief, she reached the cooler sand near the shore, damp and compressed by the endless rush of waves.

She slipped off her t-shirt and shorts, stuffing clothing and sunglasses inside her bag before venturing to the water's edge. As the foam swirled around her feet, she felt a tiny prickle of unease creep down her spine. She waded up to her knees, and to her annoyance the feeling grew into a full-fledged tingle of fear. Her muscles tense, she gazed around uneasily, trying to pinpoint its source.

Nothing appeared to signal danger. The sun was shining down to glint enticingly off calm turquoise water, so clear she could see the sandy, shell-scattered seafloor beneath. Steeling herself, she waded up to her waist, her inner alarm bells going off so loudly that she couldn't force herself to go any deeper.

Aggravated, she took several slow breaths and tried to calm down. This irrational fear was exactly what she had been trying to avoid. She refused to allow her parents' accident, and one stupid snorkeling mishap, to ruin something she enjoyed so much.

Without warning, she broke out into a sneezing fit. Exasperated, she dunked her head beneath the water, hoping the salt would clear her sinuses. When she emerged, her nose still tickled, but it seemed to have helped.

Focusing her resolve, she began a steady breaststroke parallel to the shore, thinking maybe she would venture deeper as the unfounded fear subsided.

∞∞∞∞∞∞∞∞∞

Several miles away, Hagar cursed at the interruption to his meal. The meddlers' female spawn was in the water again. He had spelled her strand of silver jewelry to alert him to her presence. Had it not been for the interference of that human-loving sidhe, the girl would have been taken care of two days ago. He was fairly certain the warrior hadn't seen him, and he was going to have to be careful to keep it that way.

At least he had found a more personal item to track the girl with than the water-logged picture he had taken from her parents' sunken vessel. The piece of silver had fallen off of her as he'd pulled her beneath the water. Being something she owned and wore against her skin, it was more in tune with her energy than the picture, and therefore easier to use as a tracer.

He slipped out through the cave entrance of his underwater grotto and sped off toward the shore. He regretted the need to end the girl's life. It was more of a nuisance than anything else. But when he'd discovered that she was in the area to retrieve her parents' possessions, he'd realized what a liability she could be.

He'd found the most incriminating evidence of his people's existence on their sunken boat—the stolen chart, drawn in his own hand, and spelled to reveal the hidden merrow city in which he lived. But he couldn't be sure the meddling couple hadn't left something behind on the land. And if they had, their daughter would most likely be the one to find it and start asking questions.

He was sure any other human would laugh at their claim to have discovered a race of mer-people. But the meddlers' own spawn might begin to believe. She might realize that her parents' deaths hadn't been an accident. And that could bring all sorts of unwanted attention down on him.

And then there was the other coveted object he'd been counting on recovering. Truth be told, it was the humans' refusal to return that item to him that had sent him into a killing rage. He hadn't believed they didn't have it with them until he'd searched their sunken vessel for himself. Was it still tucked away in the humans' home on the land, and if so, had the girl found it? His only comfort was the fact that he could sense it had not yet been destroyed.

But first things first. He was less than half a league from shore, and in the distance he could just make out the outline of a human swimming alone along the surface...

Chapter Six

Eleanor was frantic.

She had done her best to warn Violet away from the water, but her stubborn charge had ignored both her strongest anxiety spell and the sneezing fit Eleanor had produced with her wing dust. This time she had sensed the approaching danger, but she was helpless to do anything about it. Faerie guardians were sworn not to harm any living creature, and a merrow would be powerful enough to overcome any of the obstacles that she could come up with.

Where in the realm was Doyle? He was supposed to be protecting Violet! Beside herself with fear for her charge, she blinked out to find him.

∞∞∞∞∞∞∞∞

Distance from Violet hadn't been quite the remedy Doyle had hoped for. He'd slept fitfully, unable to stop torturing himself with images of her lush body stretched out beside him, barely concealed by those filmy scraps of white lace. All day long he'd been distracted by thoughts of seeing her again.

Poor Manny had been forced to pick up his slack, taking over the safety presentations for the remainder of the day when—two tours in a row—Doyle stopped midway through, forgot what he was saying, and began repeating himself. His first mate had also ended up having to pacify an insulted female customer who Doyle had inadvertently snubbed, first by ignoring her attempts at conversation, and then by walking away from her as she leaned against him to put on her flippers.

Grateful the day was almost over, he watched the last passengers file off the boat and swiftly followed after them to grab the hose. He was eager to pay Violet a visit and ask her out to dinner. His infatuated mind had even imagined he'd seen her walking past the docks as they'd been coming in. He yanked impatiently at a kink in the tubing and began quickly sluicing the deck with water.

A hazy patch of purple sparkled in the sunlight before him, a split second before Eleanor darted at his face and began babbling at him in incoherent, high-pitched alarm. He stopped and stared at her, trying to make out her jumbled words, unmindful of the water spilling down onto his feet.

"Violet…beach…swimming… Merrow!" she gasped.

Doyle dropped the hose and started to run.

"Hey, *hermano*! Where are you going?" Manny's voice rang out behind him.

"Sorry, Manny, it's an emergency! I'll make it up to you later, man, I swear!"

Doyle skidded down the dock ramp and tore off up the sidewalk at breakneck speed, Eleanor keeping pace at his shoulder. "Couldn't you have kept her out of the water for ten more minutes?" he demanded angrily.

"I *told* you that wasn't going to work, you overgrown lump of ogre meat! That was why you were supposed to be watching her, remember?" Eleanor retorted.

Doyle grunted in irritation as he leapt onto the beach access path, his boat shoes kicking up showers of sand as he ran. He exploded past the dunes, his eyes scanning the shoreline as he sprinted for the water. There she was, a lone swimmer, arms pumping gracefully as her face tilted up to take in measured breaths.

He veered diagonally toward her position, relief slamming into him at finding her unharmed, when the unmistakable 'V' of a merrow's tail broke the surface several hundred yards away. Panic gave him an extra burst of speed as he raced to get to her first. He was almost there, when he saw a pause in her flowing strokes, and she suddenly sank beneath the waves.

"Violet!" he shouted, wading past the shallow breakers and diving after her.

Squinting against the saltwater and clouds of disturbed sand, he saw a solid mass, large enough to be a human body, and made a grab for it. His hands made contact with warm, soft skin, and he held tight, pulling the flailing form against him as he brought them both to the surface.

Violet let out a stilted scream, swallowing saltwater as she struggled to free herself from her attacker and scream again. She fought harder, knowing that just moments earlier, there had been no one on the beach to hear her. She heard a grunt as her elbow made satisfyingly solid contact with firm flesh, and jabbed for the same spot again, when she realized it was Doyle's voice yelling in her ear for her to stop hitting him.

She forced herself around, his arms still clamped about her waist. "Doyle!" she gasped in shock. "Just what the hell do you think you're doing? You scared me to death, grabbing me like that!"

Doyle's face was mere inches from her own, his sea-green eyes swirling with a tangle of fear and confusion. "Are you alright?" he demanded.

"Alright?" she exclaimed, her expression turning incredulous. "I was fine until you almost drowned me! Would you let go? I can't breathe!"

He loosened his grip immediately and she slid several inches down his water-slicked body, so that she had to crane her neck to look him in the eye. But he didn't release her. "I thought I saw..." His eyes scanned the sun-speckled water, finding no sign of the merrow he thought he'd spotted. "You were swimming, and then I saw you get pulled under," he said, a hint of doubt entering his voice.

She glared at him. "I was practicing my breaststroke, and then I dove down to swim underwater for a bit."

His gazed roved her face, as if he was assuring himself that she was unharmed. "I thought you were in trouble," he muttered softly.

She certainly seemed alright, if her fierce expression and that wicked elbow to his ribs were anything to go by. He studied her more carefully, trying to convince his hammering heart to return to normal. But looking at her seemed to have the opposite effect of what he'd intended. His pulse pounded harder and his blood heated as he hungrily absorbed the details of her face.

Crystalline droplets of water clung to her thick lashes, as if paying homage to the amethyst depths of her eyes. Her lips were rosy from salt and sun, slightly parted as she raised her small chin to stare back at him. Her cheeks were flushed with exertion, and her full breasts pressed against his bare chest through the thin material of her bathing suit, swelling captivatingly with each breath she took.

The length of her alluring body rested firmly against him, the smooth expanse of her legs entwined with his as he held her in the circle of his arms. He felt himself stir with need, and he reached up to brush the damp hair from her face, his hand gliding to the back of her neck as he gathered the dark strands away from her cheek.

Violet took an unsteady breath, becoming intensely aware of Doyle's proximity. She moistened her lips as her eyes became riveted by the stray droplets of water trickling down the rugged planes of his jaw. Her palms rested against the contours of his muscular shoulders, and his warm, unyielding body seemed to welcome her softness as he clasped her to him. The ocean stirred around them, its current causing her to sway gently in his embrace, the minute friction building into an endlessly erotic dance.

When he reached up to touch her cheek, his fingertips moved in an enticing path back along her neck to brush against the sensitive skin at her nape. Desire flared sharp and needy along every nerve-ending in her body.

"I'm fine," she whispered, unable to look away from the rising heat in his eyes.

But she wasn't fine. She was in trouble—*so* much trouble—with this man.

"Violet," Doyle's brogue thickened and turned rough, transforming her name into a jagged plea as his mouth descended toward hers with relentless purpose.

Her eyes fell shut and she was lost in a torrent of sensation as his lips began to move over hers, teasing and tasting, nibbling softly, coaxing her to open to the seductive exploration of his tongue. His fingers stroked her neck where his palm rested against her nape, while his other hand glided unhurriedly up her ribcage to curl beneath her breast, gently testing its weight.

She arched into him, releasing a quiet moan as his thumb brushed across her taut nipple, straining against the tight, wet fabric of her suit. He groaned and his hands moved restlessly down her body, cupping the curves of her bottom as he lifted her weightless form beneath the water, pulling her legs around his hips so that she rested against his rigid length.

He deepened the kiss, shifting his body against hers in time to the shallow thrusts of his tongue, the friction building her up into a mindless frenzy that left her edgy and aching for completion.

Doyle broke away, his breathing heavy as he cradled her against him. He squeezed his eyes shut as he prayed for the strength to stop himself from loosing the flimsy scraps of cloth between them and taking her like an animal right there in broad daylight. He didn't want to do it that way. He wanted her in the privacy of a bedroom, where he could make love to her properly, the way she deserved.

Violet's eyes drifted open, cloudy with passion, and confused at the abrupt end to their kiss. She gazed at him questioningly, and he nearly lost his resolve.

"Not here, *a thaisce,*" he rasped, his voice rife with apology and regret. "Not like this. I want you in a bed, where I can give you my full attention."

Her muscles clenched and liquid need pooled low inside her at the raw promise in his words.

"Let's go to my parents' villa." Her tone was quiet and intense, bereft of any doubt.

Doyle gave her a scorching smile and kissed her slowly once more before releasing her so they could swim, side by side, back to shore.

His little schoolteacher was a more passionate creature than he could have dreamed. And he swore to himself that he was going take his time with her, stoking her fire until it burned higher and brighter than it ever had for anyone before. Even if it killed him.

∞∞∞∞∞∞∞∞∞

Hagar watched from a distance as the sidhe came to the girl's rescue once again. If only he'd gotten to her a few minutes earlier. His face contorted in a humorless smirk as the couple fell into an intimate embrace. So that was the sidhe's interest in her. Well, he supposed she was somewhat attractive, for a land dweller.

His temper flared as they remained together in the water, *his* domain. He itched to take action, but knew that, weaponless, he was no match for one of the immortal warriors of faerie. Hagar's people, though long-lived and possessed of magical abilities, were not immortal. They existed somewhere between the human and faerie realms.

But the sidhe's continued interference galled him to no end. He fingered the small cowrie shell he wore around his neck, abruptly deciding it was time to take matters a step further. He hated to waste his coin on high-priced mercenaries, but he needed the girl taken care of quickly, and he couldn't be expected to camp out by the shore waiting for her to enter the water alone again.

The girl's lack of awareness that she was in danger, combined with the stealth of the mercenaries Hagar had in mind, would give him an added advantage against her warrior protector.

He flipped his tail and sliced smoothly through the water as he made the return journey to his lair. He would summon Ligan and Lagan, two infamously unpleasant nixes, who purportedly could be counted on to sell their services to the highest bidder. He'd never hired the water pixies before, but their felonious reputation preceded them.

He was certain he could come to some agreement with the pair, especially since the work would be done outside the faerie realm, and therefore far from the watchful eyes of the Seelie Court. If they were careful, they should be able to slip in and out without notice, making the girl's death appear accidental. Hagar would, of course, be sure he had an alibi in case the interfering sidhe suspected something and came snooping around afterward.

Perhaps he'd even be able to get a reduction on the nefarious nixes' fee, since their target would be a non-magical human.

He smiled grimly at the thought as he swept past his blooming garden of anemones and entered his grotto. He immediately put out the call to the faerie realm that would summon Ligan and Lagan.

As he awaited their arrival, he mentally outlined how he would present his proposal and negotiate the lowest price for the girl's death.

Chapter Seven

"I think you should tell her," Eleanor insisted obstinately.

Doyle shifted Violet's backpack higher onto his shoulder and squeezed her hand lightly as they made their way up the sidewalk toward her villa. The sun, although headed for the horizon, still gleamed brightly off the long, spiky palm fronds and the wide, green paddles of the birds of paradise. Dragonflies hovered and darted in the shimmering afternoon haze, their jewel-toned bodies bright against the softer vibrancy of the flowers overflowing the neighbors' front yards.

Doyle attempted to enjoy the lush scenery, and the arousing prospect of the things he was about to do with Violet. But he was finding it difficult to ignore the increasingly discordant buzz of agitated faerie wings.

"I think you should tell her!" Eleanor repeated. "And not only because you're about to do the horizontal mambo." She darted forward to glare at him in reproof, making him feel like he'd been caught with his hand in the cookie jar. "Although that ought to be reason enough," she accused darkly.

"You should tell her because she needs to know what kind of danger she's in every time she goes in the water. That little episode at the beach just now was far too close!"

She hovered backward in the air before him, tiny hands propped on her pastel-clad hips. "Doyle, you nod your head yes that you'll tell her before you take things any further with her, or I swear to Titania I'll sprinkle your *specimens* with fire dust at the first opportunity," she warned in a dangerous tone.

Doyle scowled at her, his eyes shooting daggers, as he nodded irritably. He ran his hand through his damp hair, using the gesture as an excuse to make a flicking motion with his thumb and middle finger, telling the pint-sized pain in his ass to buzz off.

Her threat was no joke. Faerie fire dust had the effect of a miniature explosion. It was a colorful blast of sparks, generally used to wake a human charge if there was imminent danger. The humans might not be able to see it, but they could certainly feel it if it came into contact with their skin. And he had no doubt the tetchy sprite would use it on his most sensitive parts, if it came to that.

Eleanor pointed a finger at him. "And I'll hold you to it, big boy." She shot him a blithe grin and blinked out, leaving him with the suspicious feeling that his agreement to reveal himself to Violet had been her aim all along.

But how in the realm was he going to convince Violet of the truth without sending her into a panic? He frowned at the prospect, his romantic hopes spiraling down the drain.

Violet stole a nervous peek at Doyle's handsome face as they traversed the sidewalk, hand in hand. She couldn't believe she was actually going to go through with this after only knowing him for two days. Somehow it was enough, though. Her body ached for his touch. And her heart, well, she might be setting herself up for that to ache also. But she wanted him too much to worry about it right now.

He reached up to run his fingers through his honey-brown hair in an unconsciously sexy gesture that sent his muscles rippling beneath the bare, tanned flesh of his shoulder and chest. But for some reason he was staring straight ahead and frowning ferociously.

"Doyle?" she ventured uncertainly.

He tipped his head to look over at her, his expression immediately softening into an intimate smile. "Yes, *a thaisce*?" he answered, bringing her hand up to brush his lips against her knuckles.

The soft caress made her catch her breath and sent shivers cascading through her. "Is that Gaelic?" she asked, a husky note entering her voice.

"Yes." He looked away, his smile widening and turning abashed, as if he knew what she would ask next, but didn't intend to volunteer the information.

Violet laughed on a quick exhalation. "And what does it mean?"

"It's an endearment," he said with an evasive grin.

Violet threaded her fingers through his and leaned her head against his shoulder. "As I'd gathered and hoped," she sighed.

She felt him relax and added, "But what's the translation, Doyle?"

He let out a derisive chuckle. "Not going to let me off the hook so easily, are you?"

She shook her head, her lips twitching in amusement.

"I'll warn you then, it's fairly corny sounding in English."

"I'll bet it's sweet," she insisted.

She smiled up at him, her amethyst eyes expectant and trusting, drawing him in so completely that he almost stumbled.

"You're sweet," he whispered, regaining his balance and swooping down to take her lips in an unexpected kiss.

He pulled her against him, placing the threaded fingers of their hands above her hip, stroking her side in a slow, tandem caress that seemed to polarize all of her body's awareness into that one zone of pleasure. He teased the seam of her lips with his tongue, moving his other hand up to cup her cheek, his thumb brushing across the small indention in her chin, just below her mouth.

All Violet's thoughts were swept away, nothing existing beyond the tantalizing exploration of his hands and lips. His tongue slipped into her mouth, stroking and caressing hers, and she melted against the warmth of his chest as she surrendered to the heady sensation.

He drew back slowly, grinning down at her as he held her to him. "We're here."

She looked around, surprised to find that they had indeed stopped at the white picket gate in front of her parents' villa. "So we are." *The man was so intoxicating he should be illegal*, she thought with a smirk.

He reached around her to unlatch the gate, draping his arm over her shoulders as they walked up the cobblestone path, hemmed in by the increasing jungle of bougainvillea and trumpet vines. "They're starting to take over," he commented, indicating the teeming blossoms.

"Yeah." Violet frowned. "I meant to ask Melody if she knew of a good yard service. I think my dad probably cut them back himself, but I'm not much of a gardener."

"I'll do it," Doyle offered.

Violet blinked at him doubtfully. "You will?"

"Sure." He nodded. "I'll bring over the hedge clippers on my next day off."

She beamed at him. "You're the best." She stood on her tiptoes and gave him a quick peck on the lips, oddly elated at his offer of domestic assistance. It implied that he was going to stick around, at least for a while. Not that she expected him to turn tail and run as soon as they got intimate, but still.

She turned to unlock the door, suddenly nervous as they stepped into the cool, empty interior of her parents' villa. Now they were truly alone.

Doyle followed Violet inside, still feeling a little punch-drunk from her kiss of gratitude. It had only been a brief touch, but she had initiated it with a sweetness that left him giddy. Just what ruddy kind of men had she been spending time with that she was so excited by his offer to help with a little yard work?

The thought of her with anyone else made his insides churn with ire, so he put it from his mind. He wondered, instead, how he was going to break the news that he was an immortal from the faerie realm. And that a merrow was apparently trying to kill her. And that her faerie guardian believed her parents' deaths hadn't been an accident.

What a perfectly good way to ruin his plans for making love to her all afternoon, he thought sourly. Bloomin' faerie.

"Would you like something to drink?" Violet's voice broke through his ill tempered musings.

She was standing halfway between the bright assortment of living room furniture, and the softly lit kitchen nook where they had eaten breakfast. She twisted her hands together in front of her, seeming unsure what to do with them. Doyle realized she was nervous at the prospect of what they were about to do together.

He gave her a warm smile as he approached, careful not to crowd her.

"I don't suppose you'd want to crack open that bottle of red wine I found in the cabinet yesterday? I left a couple of wine glasses and a corkscrew unpacked, just in case."

Her eyes lit up. "That sounds perfect. I didn't know I had anything other than yogurt and water, and the coffee you left. I was extremely grateful for that again this morning, by the way."

"Let's not forget your ever versatile jar of mustard," he joked. "And I'm glad you're enjoying the coffee. I believe I left my t-shirt and shorts here as well. Do you mind if I go change into them?"

"Sure. They're still in the laundry room. And I need to get out of this damp suit. I'll meet you back here in a few minutes?"

"It's a date," he agreed with a soft smile.

Doyle changed and returned to the empty kitchen to retrieve the wine and glasses from the cabinet. It took opening a couple of drawers to find where he'd left the corkscrew, and then he moved everything onto the coffee table in the living room while he waited for Violet.

He was glad she had agreed to the wine. He had a feeling they were both going to need it in order to survive the upcoming conversation. For a little while longer, though, he would pretend that he was simply a mortal tour boat captain enjoying the afternoon with a beautiful young schoolteacher, who was well on her way to stealing his heart.

"Red couch or blue couch?" he asked in a mock serious tone as she exited the bedroom.

Violet tilted her head as she considered the furniture. "Red," she answered with certainty. "It'll match if we spill."

"Aha," Doyle agreed sagely as they settled onto the thick cushions. "So that's the brilliance behind the mix and match colors. You can coordinate them with whatever you're eating or drinking at the time. Red for wine and strawberries…"

"And spaghetti sauce," Violet chimed in with a grin.

"Mmm," Doyle intoned appreciatively. "And green for pesto sauce and…"

"Avocados," Violet offered.

"Of course. And then there's blue for…" He frowned. "I think I've found a hole in my theory."

Violet rolled her eyes. "Blueberries," she supplied in an obvious voice. "And grape juice," she added.

"I'll give you blueberries," Doyle agreed charitably, "but I'm afraid that grape juice is purple."

"Blue and purple are close enough," Violet argued, attempting to hide her smile in her wine.

He regarded her from beneath a single raised eyebrow for a moment, pretending to consider her words. "I concede, due to the undeniable evidence before me."

She laughed. "Other than the fact that you can't deny I'm right, what evidence might that be?"

"Your eyes," he said softly, giving her a heated look over the rim of his wineglass, "happen to be a rather lovely shade of purplish-blue."

Violet's heart sped up, but her answering smile was unhurried. "See, that's exactly the sort of thing I was talking about before."

"What do you mean?" he asked with a chuckle.

"You say the sweetest things. That's why I want to know what that word means."

"What word?" he inquired innocently.

Violet snorted in mirth. "I think it was something like…ah-hash-keh."

"Ohhh, you mean *a thaisce*." His sea-green eyes sparkled with barely contained laughter. "The translation escapes me at the moment."

"I *will* find out what it means," she informed him.

"This wine is lovely. Are you enjoying it?"

Violet sputtered with amusement. "Is this the sort of avoidance technique I can look forward to whenever you don't want to discuss something?"

"Some music would be nice, don't you think?" Doyle suggested in a pleasant tone. "Do you mind if I have a look at the stereo?"

Violet lifted her wine glass and curled her lip at him before drinking.

He rose and planted an affectionate kiss on the top of her head, then walked over to the small stereo unit, situated on a low wooden stand against the back wall. It looked fairly new, with a shiny red plastic casing and two speakers flanking it like bookends. The speakers obviously predated the stereo, with rivulets of melted candle-wax hardened to their tops and dust flecking their covers.

Doyle knelt and picked a CD at random from the glass-fronted cabinet below. "How about some Van Morrison?"

"Sure," Violet answered with a sigh that succinctly expressed her refusal to be diverted from their previous conversation.

"What's the matter, *a thaisce*," he asked silkily, "wouldn't you like to share little *Moondance* with me?"

His voice was charged with such raw sexuality that her throat went slack in the middle of a swallow and she almost choked on her wine. She shot him a bemused look over the back of the couch. "I take it you intend to charm your way back into my good graces."

Doyle pressed the disc into an empty slot in the CD changer and forwarded to the track he wanted. Then he stood and stalked back toward Violet, extending his hand to her as the strains of *Into The Mystic* filled the small villa. "Nothing would please me more than to charm you, Violet. At this moment, however, I would like to dance with you."

Captivated by his seductive invitation, Violet set her wineglass on the tiled coffee table and took his hand. He pulled her effortlessly to her feet and led her around to the clear section of wood floor between the couch and the stereo. One warm palm engulfed her hand, while the other gathered her closer, moving to rest against the curve of her lower back as he started to move in rhythm to the music. It was a provocative mix of formality and intimacy, fueling her desire with a delicious, leisurely anticipation.

"This isn't *Moondance*," she commented in a throaty voice, lulled by the unhurried sway of their bodies and the enticing promise glowing in the depths of his eyes. He smelled of the sun and the ocean, with the clean fragrance of her fabric softener lingering softly beneath.

"No. But this tune is better suited to the type of dancing I have in mind." His words came out in a low, husky rumble that resonated through her chest, their dual meaning infusing her blood with heat.

"There is something I have a need to discuss with you first, though."

The reluctance lacing his tone shook Violet from the drowsy seduction he had begun to weave around her, and she stiffened. "You're not married." It fell somewhere between a disbelieving question and a statement of fact.

Doyle's eyes widened and he let out a shocked gust of laughter. "Absolutely not. Nor am I engaged. And as far as that goes, neither have I ever been divorced."

Violet sagged with relief. She was relatively sure she could deal with anything else he might have to tell her. But it would have been horrible to find out that he was married. "What is it then?"

Doyle took a fortifying breath. "This is something about me personally, which I don't tell people as a rule. I'm only telling you now because I feel we have a genuine connection and you have a right to know before we take things any further." He hesitated, as if unsure how to continue.

Understanding surged through Violet. She thought she knew exactly where this was going. It wasn't a pleasant idea, but she liked Doyle too much to write him off over it. "Do you have something transmittable?" she prodded softly. "Because I was going to insist that we use protection anyway."

He looked confused for a moment, then his mouth dropped open and he made a strangled noise. "Uh, no," he answered when he regained the ability to speak. "That's not it either."

A flush of mortification crept up Violet's throat to suffuse her cheeks.

"Violet, there is nothing about me that troubles my conscience with regard to us being together sexually," he told her in a frank tone. "There is, however, something about me that makes me different from other people." He closed his eyes briefly before he continued. "Do you remember yesterday, when I was going through your parents' books, and I got a little testy when you said you didn't believe in magic?"

Violet nodded mutely.

"Well, I do believe in magic." Doyle gave her a searching look. "And the reason I believe in it, is that I have seen it and been a part of it. I grew up around it. I'm..." A pregnant pause fell between them as Doyle struggled to finish his sentence.

Violet's mind raced with the compulsive instinct to complete the thought. He was what? "Wiccan?" she blurted, just as the CD began to skip loudly on the last syllable of a lyric.

Doyle cursed beneath his breath in Gaelic and released Violet to stop the grating noise that was now pulsing from the speakers. He pressed a button and there was sudden, blessed silence, followed by the quiet click of the CD changer revolving. He stood to face her once more and rubbed an agitated hand over his face.

"No. Not Wiccan. This goes a bit deeper than religious differences. I'm sidhe."

"Shee," Violet repeated the word slowly, pronouncing it as he had, searching for its meaning and only coming up with the confounding thought that there was some gender issue here that she had obviously missed.

"Sidhe are a race of immortal warriors from the..."

But Violet was no longer listening. She was staring, arrested, at the stereo. A man's voice was coming through the speakers, unaccompanied by music, simply talking.

"That's my dad," she whispered, her words layered with a painful blend of joy, bewilderment and grief.

Doyle's eyes shot to the source of the sound, his attention zeroing in on the excited male voice.

"...Hendrickson here. Er, Vicki came up with the clever idea to make this recording since we promised not to leave any written evidence. ('Hello!' chirped a friendly female voice.) Anyway, for posterity's sake, we would like to record our findings with regard to the existence of a magical race of people from whom we believe the legends of mermaids stem.

"These people live beneath the oceans of our world, in great underwater cities, magically hidden from the sight of humans. They call themselves 'merrows'. The one we have seen looks very like the mythical depiction of a mermaid, being human in appearance from the waist up, and having the proportional body and tail of a large fish with silvery green scales from the waist down.

"We were fortunate enough to acquire the location of a nearby merrow city, in the form of one of their hand-drawn nautical charts. We have been told that possession of this map is one of the only ways in which the location can be revealed to human eyes.

"Therefore, with great excitement, Vicki and I are planning a diving trip using the merrow chart to guide us, so that we can observe this amazing phenomenon for ourselves. We will give the coordinates at the end of this recording, solely for our personal archival information. The coordinates will not reveal the city to human eyes without possession of the chart."

"And we've promised to return the chart to its owner after our dive," Vicki chimed in.

George Hendrickson said a few additional words, rattled off some coordinates, and the recording ended. It left a silence in its wake that was more deafening than sound.

Violet appeared to be having trouble focusing, and Doyle hastily led her to the couch. Her eyes were huge and bruised-looking in her pale face as she stared at him in shock.

"What your parents discovered is true, Violet," Doyle told her gently. "There is a magical underwater race of people called merrows. They exist somewhere between the human realm and the faerie realm, where I come from. That's what I've been trying to tell you. I belong to an immortal race of faerie warriors called sidhe.

"There are magical beings that you've heard of only in myth and legend, but they really do exist in my world," he continued, unable to stem the flow of words now that he was finally telling her the truth. "There are pegasuses and dwarves and sprites, and many more. You don't know it, but there's a sprite named Eleanor who acts as your faerie guardian and watches out for you.

"She asked me to help protect you and keep you out of the water because, when you almost drowned on my tour the other day, she knew it wasn't an accident." He paused, giving her an anxious look. "A merrow pulled you under. We don't know why, but Eleanor thinks it may have caused your parents' deaths as well. And the recording we just heard only confirms it…"

"Get out."

She said it so softly he thought he'd misheard her.

"What?" he asked in confusion.

"Get out!" she cried, tears looming heavy in her eyes before they began to spill in fat droplets down her cheeks.

"Violet, I'm sorry," he stuttered in a bewildered tone. "I didn't mean to frighten you, or…"

"Just go, Doyle," she pleaded on a sob. "I want you to go. I need to be alone right now."

He reached for her and she shied away as if the idea of his touch terrified her. "Violet…"

"Go!" she screamed.

Jaw tight and chest heavy, he stood and walked out the door, shutting it softly behind him. He didn't know what else to do. But he couldn't make himself leave her like that. He hovered outside the opaque glass panes of the front door and listened.

No sound came from within. Behind him, birds chirped in the dying afternoon light, accompanied by the occasional hum of a car passing on the main thoroughfare beyond. But inside the villa it was still and silent as a tomb.

His fists clenched at his sides, gradually tightening, until his knuckles cracked. Damn the merrow that had done this. He was certain now that Eleanor was right. Violet's parents had been killed because of the information they had uncovered. And somehow the bastard had found out about Violet and had decided she was a threat as well.

And damn Eleanor. If the ruddy sprite hadn't blackmailed him into telling Violet what he was, he'd be inside making love to her right now. The faerie appeared at his shoulder as if summoned.

"Go home, Doyle," she told him quietly. "I'm going to try to talk to her."

He opened and closed his mouth in mute fury. Then he swore in a low voice and blinked out. It wasn't until he found himself in his living room, standing next to his battered leather recliner, that he realized he had violated his vow not to use magic while living in the human realm. Bruno gave a grunt of surprise and lifted his head from his mattress in the corner. Then he bounded over in eagerness to greet his master.

Doyle scowled as he absently began rubbing the dog's ears, earning a rapturous canine gaze.

At least someone was happy.

Chapter Eight

Violet sat on the couch and stared blankly into space, her vision blurred by steadily streaming tears. She felt like she was losing her mind. It had undoubtedly been her mom and dad's voices on that CD, going on about mermaids and hidden underwater cities as if it was the most natural thing in the world. They had sounded so sure of themselves.

And then, before she could even begin to digest what she'd heard, Doyle had started in with the magic thing. He had actually insisted that her parents' story was true, and that not only did mermaids exist, but all manner of other fantasy creatures as well. Her brain had been reeling, but she thought he'd named pegasuses and sprites among them. He'd claimed *he* wasn't human.

And as if that wasn't enough of a cruel joke, he'd proceeded to suggest that her parents might have been killed by one of the mermaids they'd been so determined to find. What had they called them? *Merrows.* Doyle had said that one was trying to kill her as well, and had almost succeeded while she was on his snorkeling tour.

He appeared to be under the delusion that it was his mission to save her. That must have been why he'd come home with her the other night, and tried to 'rescue' her at the beach today. And she'd actually begun to believe that they had something special together. She'd been about to go to bed with him!

How desperate she must have seemed, showing up all alone for his tour and nearly drowning. Telling him about her dead parents and getting so drunk she couldn't make it home alone. She must have fed right into his psychosis—the weak, pathetic female in need of a hero.

She dropped her head into her trembling hands. How could she have been so wrong about him? He didn't seem unstable. He made her feel safe. And loved. And what was she supposed to make of that CD? She knew her parents had always been a little eccentric. They had always believed that magical forces existed all around them, just waiting to be tapped into.

And when she was younger, she had believed it too. But then she'd grown up and magic had taken a backseat to reality. It was hard to concentrate on how magical life was when you were trying to make it through college on student loans, graduate with decent grades, and find a job that paid enough so that you could scrape by on your own.

Still, her parents had been intelligent people. She couldn't accept that they were insane, or that they had allowed themselves to be taken in by such a ridiculous con. They must have truly believed that they had discovered the existence of an underwater race. They claimed they'd seen, and spoken to, one of these merrows.

It couldn't be true, could it? It was madness to even consider it. It was just easier than accepting the fact that her parents had been so completely duped. And that Doyle might be deluded to the point of being dangerous.

Sweet, sexy Doyle, with his amazing sea-green eyes and his gentle touch that set her on fire. He'd been so wonderful, taking care of her and helping her with the villa these past couple of days. He'd teased her and made her laugh, put up with her temper, and stuck around to make her breakfast.

She realized that was what hurt most of all, thinking that their time together hadn't meant the same thing to him that it had to her. But it wasn't his fault if he was mentally unstable. How did he manage to run his own company, though? And wouldn't Manny have noticed a problem by now, as a long-time partner and friend? The other man seemed so grounded and down-to-earth.

Doyle had claimed he was an immortal warrior. What if, for the sake of argument, she considered it? Maybe there was a way he could prove it. She could certainly picture him wielding a sword, with his broad chest, muscular shoulders and thick, solid arms. Maybe wearing tight leather armor…

Her head jerked up at a small sound, like the rustling of a wind-chime, and all coherent thought ceased. There was a creature hovering in midair before her. A winged woman, mere inches in height, with shining dark hair that cascaded down the length of her body. She wore an eye-befuddling dress that shimmered between shades of pink, blue and yellow, ending at her knees above tiny, bare feet.

Her eyes were tilted, and almost the same color as Violet's, in a delicate face that drew down into a pointed chin. A silvery aura bled from her skin, and her translucent, glittering wings began to flutter faster as she smiled tentatively at Violet.

"You can see me now, can't you?"

Her voice was soft and musical, uncertain yet immensely soothing. Violet found herself relaxing into the couch, her muscles going blissfully limp as her eyes swam dreamily out of focus. The corners of her mouth lifted in a rapturous smile and a giddy giggle spilled from her lips, echoing in her ears as if it came from a great distance.

The creature's tiny brows drew down in a frown and she muttered something that Violet couldn't quite make out. But Violet didn't care. She was content merely to gaze at the lovely little winged woman.

Suddenly the creature swam closer into Violet's field of vision and snapped her fingers. There was a miniature explosion of sparks, and Violet's eyes popped into focus, her body coming out of its lull as if she had received an intravenous shot of caffeine. She blinked and gasped at the impossibility of what she was seeing.

There was no disputing it. She was looking at a faerie.

Violet was speechless with wonder. Her heart felt strangely light, and not only because she was witnessing something so clearly magical, but because Doyle had been telling the truth. Either that, or she was as crazy as he was.

"Violet?" asked the tinkling voice.

Violet breathed a hysterical little laugh, the sound emanating from deep within her throat.

"Just relax," the faerie cooed gently. "It'll probably take a minute for you to come around. I'm afraid faerie magic can make you humans a little loopy, especially the first time you're exposed to it." Her rosebud mouth bloomed in a kindly smile. "I'm Eleanor. I believe Doyle mentioned me. I'm your faerie guardian."

"Incredible," Violet managed on a cracked whisper.

"Yes," Eleanor agreed with a grin. "I realize it's a bit of a shock. Especially after the way that dolt of a sidhe threw everything at you with no warning," the faerie grumbled as she sank gracefully down to stand on the tiled edge of the coffee table, her wings slowing to a dainty flutter.

"I'm very sorry about your parents," she added in a pained voice. "That immortal imbecile should have known better than to blurt out that their deaths might not have been an accident."

Something tightened defensively in Violet's chest and she shook her head in denial. "He was just trying to help. I shouldn't have reacted the way I did."

Eleanor gave her a considering look from beneath glittering eyelashes. She seemed almost on the verge of a smile as she looked down and pulled a thimble-sized mug from somewhere within her color-shifting dress. "Do you mind if I help myself?" she asked, indicating Doyle's abandoned glass of wine.

"No, please do," Violet mumbled, unable to deflect the unhappy turn of her thoughts.

Now that her mind was beginning to wrap itself around the faerie's existence, the full extent of the mess that the afternoon had become began to crash over her. Not only did she have this terrible new information about her parents' deaths, but she had also been unbearably nasty to Doyle, screaming for him to leave like that.

"I suggest you have some as well," Eleanor recommended as she lowered herself to sit on the edge of the coffee table, legs swinging over the side. "I need to talk to you about the merrow, and a drink might help take the edge off."

Violet retrieved her own glass from the table and added a liberal pour from the bottle before sinking back into the couch cushions. Her head spun with awe. "Why have I never seen you before now?" she blurted.

Eleanor snorted softly. "You have seen me before, you just don't remember. You saw me when you were a child. But you stopped believing Violet.

I needed Doyle to convince you to believe again."

Violet shook her head as if to clear the cobwebs from her muddled brain. "I saw you when I was a child," she whispered, reaching for an elusive wisp of memory that wouldn't solidify. Her eyes narrowed on Eleanor. "But if Doyle's not human, why could I see him?"

"Because he appears human." Eleanor's tiny lips curved in a smile. "It's only the obviously non-human beings that humans can't see, unless they already know we exist."

Violet's mouth dropped open as she played that revelation out to its conclusion. "So I'll be able to see other kinds of magical beings now? Doyle said there were pegasuses!"

Eleanor chortled into her mug at Violet's surge of excitement. "You could see one if you came across it, but most magical beings, pegasuses included, don't venture into the human realm. The Seelie Court frowns upon it."

"Seelie Court?" repeated Violet, feeling letdown that she wasn't going to walk outside and see a pegasus swooping by overhead.

"The Seelie Court is the ruling body of the faerie realm. They work to keep the balance between good and evil in check." Eleanor gave a rueful sigh. "Many years ago, there was much more contact between our realms. But as humans lost their belief in us, they lost their ability to see us. The Seelie Court enforces the separation because they're afraid it would cause mass chaos for humans to rediscover our presence."

Violet absorbed that in silence. "So Doyle's really immortal?" she mumbled after a moment.

Eleanor gave a smile of confirmation.

"And you asked him to protect me from the merrow, which is why he's been sticking so close to me." She tried to make the statement casual, but the thought of him only being with her because of a secret assignment made her heart twinge painfully.

Eleanor's eyes held a knowing twinkle. "That, and he cares for you, Violet. Maybe more than he's willing to admit so soon after meeting you."

Violet's heart swelled. Eleanor had just voiced the secret hope that had been kindling inside of her. But although she felt curiously comfortable with the faerie, she wasn't ready to examine her feelings for Doyle aloud. She took a bracing breath and returned to the more pressing topic.

"You really think my parents were killed by one of these merrows? And that it's coming after me now?" she asked incredulously.

Eleanor gave an apologetic nod. "I do, Violet. I know for a fact that you were attacked by a merrow before Doyle pulled you out of the water the other day. I saw it." She took a sip of wine, watching Violet over the rim of her mug before speaking again. "You didn't see anything unusual before you went under?"

Violet nibbled her lip, trying to remember. "I saw a shadow in the water," she answered slowly. "And then something hit me in the head hard enough to stun me. Before I knew it, I was being dragged down. There was water in my mask and I couldn't see anything, and I kicked and struggled, but I couldn't get back to the surface. When I couldn't hold my breath anymore, I passed out."

She looked at the faerie with haunted eyes. "I thought I'd imagined the part about being dragged down."

"You didn't," Eleanor denied in a grim voice. "And when I started to wonder why a merrow would attack you, I was hit with the feeling that it had something to do with your parents' deaths as well. That recording they made, the fact that they discovered the existence of the merrows, and were probably looking for one of their hidden cities when their boat went down; it's all too much of a coincidence not to be connected.

"You need to stay out of the ocean, Violet," she warned anxiously. "Doyle got to you just in time at the beach today. The merrow was coming for you again. It was so strong, even I could sense it. That's why I insisted that Doyle tell you what was going on. I tried to keep you from going in the water myself, but you ignored me. You had to know the truth for your own protection."

Violet gaped at her. "The fear as I was getting in the water, the prickles down my spine—that was you."

Eleanor nodded. "It's one of the ways that faerie guardians warn their charges away from danger. But you were too stubborn to listen." She gave Violet an exasperated look.

"I thought I was just reacting to what happened the other day, and the fact that my parents died in the ocean. I didn't want to let the fear control me," she mumbled, her mind racing as she brought her glass up to her numb lips. "So, you think a merrow sabotaged my parents' boat and killed them to prevent their race from being revealed to other humans?"

The thought filled Violet with anger as well as sorrow. If it was true, her parents' lives had been ended needlessly. Vicki and George Hendrickson had always kept their word. And it was clear from the recording that they'd intended to give the map leading to the merrow city back, as soon as they saw it for themselves.

Eleanor's expression turned sad. "I'm afraid so. I believe that the merrow made sure he retrieved the nautical chart your father spoke of, and then killed your parents, probably in order to ensure their silence. Now he's coming after you for one of two reasons. Either he believes your parents' told you something before he got to them, or he believes they left something behind that you might find."

"That's completely senseless!" Violet's face screwed up in helpless fury. "No one in their right mind would believe that recording was true, and even if they did, the chart would have been the only proof. So he killed them for nothing!

"And now what?" she demanded, angry tears spilling down her cheeks. "He's going kill everyone who goes through their belongings, on the off chance that his precious secret might be revealed? Shouldn't your Seelie Court, or whatever, be doing something to stop this?"

Eleanor tensed, her hands clutched tightly around the mug she held in her lap. "I'm sorry, Violet," she said softly. "I wish I had an easy answer for you, but this is a very unusual situation. As magical beings, the merrows are technically policed by the Seelie Court. But they exist outside the faerie realm, so there's never been much official involvement with them. The merrows have always been trusted to govern their own affairs."

"Well maybe it's time someone looked in on them, seeing as they've begun murdering people!" Violet retorted.

Eleanor's forehead fell into a sympathetic frown. "Unfortunately we don't have any proof that a merrow caused your parents' deaths. And it's going to be hard to convince the Seelie Police that one of them is after you. The merrows are known to be a reclusive and peaceful race."

"So what are we supposed to do," Violet asked incredulously, "wait until a merrow kills me so they can examine my body for foul play?"

"Well, I've been thinking about that," Eleanor hedged. "We're going to need to draw the merrow out without putting you in danger again. What I'd like to know, is how in the realm is he tracking you? He's come after you twice now within moments of you entering the ocean."

Violet's face hardened. "However he's doing it, that's how we'll draw him out. I'll go back in the ocean and wait for him to come after me. Then Doyle can grab him, if he's still speaking to me, that is," she added in a dismal voice.

"Absolutely not!" Eleanor disagreed firmly. "I said we need to do this *without* putting you in danger again. And it's suicide to give the merrow the upper hand by letting him find you alone in the water.

"Besides, we've proved twice now that the merrow will retreat rather than challenge Doyle. It won't be worth his while to come out into the open unless he thinks we have something to offer him. Which brings me to my next question. Other than that recording, have you found anything at all that seemed unusual as you were going through your parents' things?"

"Like what?" Violet asked, throwing her hands up in frustration. "They said that they weren't leaving behind any written evidence. That's why they made the CD."

"I don't know," Eleanor muttered. She set her empty mug on the tile top of the coffee table and clasped both hands behind her head, staring up at the ceiling as if something might appear there if she looked hard enough.

"I just can't seem to get past the feeling that there's something more to this than a map and the fear of discovery." The faerie shook her head and met Violet's gaze. "I'm not sure what you should be looking for. Just take note of anything that seems out of the ordinary."

"Alright," Violet grumbled, feeling defeated by the prospect of not taking more decisive action. "I haven't seen anything so far, but I still have their office papers to finish going through." She grimaced. "Actually, I was just saying to Doyle yesterday that I thought it was odd how much they'd been spending on gas. I assume it was for their boat."

Eleanor dipped her chin in a sharp nod. "That's the sort of thing I'm talking about. If you find anything else that seems strange to you, flag it and let me know."

"Fine." Violet paused, concern marring her forehead. "Do you think the merrow will target anyone else that had contact with my parents?"

"I hope not," Eleanor replied with a sigh. "He has to know that most humans wouldn't believe he exists. But as their daughter, you pose a greater risk of believing, discovering the truth about their deaths, and doing something about it."

"Damned right I'm going to do something about it," Violet growled. She reached forward and pulled the wine bottle toward her, tipping more of the ruby liquid into her glass. She swallowed, vacillating between grief and growing thoughts of revenge.

"If the merrow was so concerned about being discovered, why would he give my parents the stupid chart to begin with?" she muttered.

"That's a good question," Eleanor replied, "and part of what makes me think there's something more to this. Anything we can find out about what sort of contact your parents had with the merrow, and how they ended up with that chart, could help us both solve their murder and draw the merrow out into the open."

The last rays of the setting sun stole through the west-facing box window by the kitchen nook, shining into the living room to gild Violet's expression with its fiery glow. "Promise me we're going to get this bastard."

Eleanor's answering smile held no humor. After twenty-seven years of watching over her charge, she knew that look. It meant that Violet had just made up her mind. And when her headstrong charge committed to a course of action, she let nothing get in her way.

"We'll get him, Violet, one way or another," the faerie promised grimly.

She only hoped that Violet's stubbornness wouldn't get her hurt in the process.

Chapter Nine

Doyle spent a restless night dreaming about a dark-haired temptress, but her violet eyes stared at him with such betrayal, he woke feeling as if his heart had been ripped out with a pair of pliers. He lingered beneath the scalding shower spray to wash away the image of her face, and downed two extra cups of coffee before setting out on his walk to the docks.

It promised to be a perfect day, bright and hot with a clear, cloudless sky. Sunlight gleamed off the white-washed hull of the *Ocean Magic,* silvering the glassy surface of a calm sea. But despite his efforts to the contrary, Doyle's mind refused to stray from Violet. Was she grief-stricken over his suggestion that her parents' deaths weren't an accident?

Of course she was. He was a tactless fool. He never should have bombarded her with all that information at once. It would have been too much for anyone to deal with. It had been selfish of him to tell her about his world right after the shock of hearing her parents' voices on that CD.

She must be angry that he'd been so insensitive. Or was she afraid of him now that he'd told her he wasn't human? Maybe she thought he was a madman. Or perhaps she believed him, and the idea of being with a non-human repulsed her.

The heaviness weighing on his chest since she'd screamed for him to get out yesterday became a crushing pressure against his heart. Her anger he could deal with. He knew he deserved it, and he would do everything in his power to make it up to her.

But he wasn't sure if he could survive looking into her luminous eyes again, and finding only fear and revulsion there.

"Morning, *hermano*," Manny greeted from the *Ocean Magic*'s bow. A large Styrofoam cup of coffee glowed white between the tanned fingers of one hand, and he'd already tossed his t-shirt aside in preparation for the morning's work. "What happen to you yesterday? You ran outta here like your *cajones* were on fire."

Doyle worked up a penitent smile for his friend as he jogged up the gangplank. "I'm sorry brother. I promised Violet I'd be by her place at 4:30 to help her pack up some stuff that she didn't want to go through alone," he lied, feeling lower than the dirt on the bottom of his boat shoe as he said it.

"I don't know what I was thinking. I should have known we wouldn't get back early enough for me to meet her by then. When I realized I was late, I panicked. I didn't want her to think I'd forgotten. So today, you can leave all of the cleanup to me."

Manny gave him a friendly slap on the shoulder and his brown face split into a round-cheeked grin. "You been spending a lot of time with this *lindita, hermano*. Even when you not with her, I think you with her. Your head was somewhere else all day yesterday. I think maybe your *cajones were* on fire. For her."

Doyle snorted. "Yeah, they've been that way for three days straight," he muttered.

Manny barked a sharp laugh. "You got it bad, *hermano*. Almost as bad as I do for my Melody. You think she feel the same?" he asked.

Doyle couldn't help smiling. The Costa Rican's candid manner was one of the things Doyle had always loved about him. "I'm afraid it's not looking that way, man." He shook his head, his smile fading. "We had an argument yesterday and she asked me to leave."

Manny clicked his tongue. "You shouldn't worry so much. All lovers quarrel. I see the way she look at you the other night in the bar. She'll come round. You just gotta give her time to cool off, then you go by and tell her you was wrong and how sorry you are. With those big muscles and that handsome face, you almost as sexy as me, *hermano*. The *lindita* won't be able to resist for long. Too bad you have that silly accent, though."

Doyle barked out a laugh. "Oh, I'm the one with the silly accent, am I?"

"Yeah. Maybe I give you lessons to help you sound more like me. Whenever I open my mouth, the ladies go wild with desire," Manny called over his shoulder as he started pulling out the snorkeling equipment.

"The desire for you to shut up, maybe," Doyle commented dryly.

"Every wise man knows there's a time for talk and a time for action, *hermano*," Manny quipped, deliberately ignoring Doyle's insult.

They continued their friendly banter as Doyle began testing the radio equipment, his heart a little lighter. But he wished to the devil that Eleanor would come and tell him what had happened with Violet after he left. Apparently the blasted sprite only deigned to appear when he didn't want her around.

∞∞∞∞∞∞∞∞∞

Violet yawned and rolled out of bed, determined that she was going to find something useful in her parents' things today. Some sign of what had really been going on before their last fateful boating trip. She believed that they would have kept their word and not saved anything about the merrows in writing. But maybe there was something revealing about the underwater race in one of their many books, or maybe they had come across some sort of merrow object or artifact. She didn't know. But if it was there, she was going to find it.

She padded across the thick bathmat and blinked against the reflected brightness of the mirrored row of lights above the sink. She splashed water onto her face and brushed her teeth. Then she exchanged her soft nightshirt for a t-shirt and shorts, pulled her hair back into a careless ponytail, and headed for the coffeemaker.

She felt a renewed tug of guilt as the heavenly aroma of Doyle's leftover coffee wafted through the villa, and she pulled his milk and sugar from the fridge. She was definitely going to have to apologize for yesterday. If he'd even hear it after the way she'd spoken to him.

She pushed the alluring memory of his kisses from her mind, reminding herself firmly that today was not for dwelling on her personal problems. Today was for working on a way to catch her parents' killer.

Two hours, one yogurt cup and an empty pot of coffee later, Violet sat on the creaky chair in her parents' office, fuming over her lack of success. She had poured through every mermaid legend on their considerable shelf, with nary a mention of a merrow in sight. All she found were contradictory references to various mer-people in literature throughout history.

Some stories claimed they drowned humans out of spite. Others said they fell in love with humans and sometimes drowned them by accident, forgetting that they couldn't breathe underwater. Some legends claimed they could grant wishes or heal people; or conversely, that they had no interest in humans at all.

And then there were the theories on split tails versus single tails, and the arguments over whether they became human when they walked on land, and returned to mermaid form when their feet touched the water.

It was enough to make her head spin.

She sighed in defeat and got up to walk off the coffee jitters, peering around the remainder of her parents' unpacked belongings, in the hope that some mermish object had been staring her in the face for the past three days. She studied the paintings on her parents' walls as if she was at a museum admiring the Monets.

Her mom had been partial to vivid colors and soft, rounded strokes depicting dreamlike nature scenes. But although some of the artwork was reminiscent of the ocean, Violet found nothing suggesting that a magical race of beings lived beneath it. Disheartened, she grabbed a bottle of water and returned to the office.

Weary of flipping through pages, she eschewed paperwork for her parents' old computer. She spent another two hours searching through all their saved documents, which turned out to be mostly from their teaching days—lesson plans, worksheets and research papers for continuing education courses they'd taken.

She checked their email, which was surprisingly empty. Hers would have been overflowing with a mountain of spam if she left it alone for two months. But her parents had never been particularly keen on using email, so she didn't think it qualified as the sort of unusual thing she was looking for.

She proceeded to go through their list of favorite websites and sleuthed her way through the history of the last sites they'd visited. They hadn't bookmarked very many, and she saw why as she impatiently joggled her foot beneath the desk, suffering through the archaic download times of their dial-up connection.

She got excited when she found a page referencing the merrow as a race of underwater people originating in Irish folklore. But that was the one bright moment in an otherwise dull and fruitless search. By the time she shut down the outdated computer, she was relieved to be returning to paper pages that she could flip manually at her own speed.

She made a pile on the floor and started to go through bank statements, most recent first. She found something strange immediately. The week before her parents died, they withdrew an even $3500 in cash from their account. And unlike the credit card charges for gas, Violet had no way of knowing why they had withdrawn such a sizable chunk. It left them with a low balance, as if they had purposely taken out the most they could spare at one time.

She stared at the page in frustration, as if willing it to reveal the answer.

"How's it going?" Eleanor's voice spilled into Violet's ear, making her jump with a startled jerk.

"Sorry, didn't mean to scare you." The shimmering, pastel-clad faerie hovered over her shoulder, pointed face screwed up in chagrin.

Violet puffed out a loud breath and rubbed her fingers over her stinging eyes. "It's alright. I was just thinking. I've been pouring over books, computer files, and even the pictures hanging on the walls for hours, and I haven't found one useful thing. But then I started looking at bank statements and this jumped out at me."

She jabbed her finger at the line showing the $3500 cash withdrawal. "This was the week before my parents died, Eleanor. And I have no idea what they'd need that much cash for."

The faerie flitted forward to study the page, her tilted eyes alight with curiosity. "Is that a lot?" she asked, glancing back at Violet. "This doesn't tell you what they spent it on?"

Violet let out a mirthless snort. "Afraid not. That's the beauty of cash. It's pretty much untraceable. And yes, $3500 is a good chunk of change for most people. That's a respectable down-payment on a car; or first, last and security on a nice apartment. But I can't think of anything my parents would have needed it for. Maybe diving equipment? I have no idea how much that stuff costs."

Eleanor gave an unhelpful shrug.

Violet sighed. "It could be nothing. I'll have to dig through more paperwork to see if I can find any receipts for a big purchase."

"Do you want company?" Eleanor asked hesitantly.

Violet smiled. "I'd love company. And maybe if you fly around you'll see some evidence of the merrows that I missed the last twelve times I've looked." She made a discouraged gesture with her hand.

"But I'm going to pass out if I don't get some food. The place up the street has good fish sandwiches. Do you want anything?"

Eleanor made a disgusted face. "I definitely don't want anything that used to be alive. And especially not if it was covered in slime and scales and swam in its own filth."

Violet let out a startled laugh. "You make it sound so appetizing. I take it you're a vegetarian."

"Sprites don't eat living creatures," she said, her expression as sour as if she was sucking a lemon. "It fouls up the digestion and poses disturbing ethical issues. As faerie guardians, we take a vow to never harm another living creature. I think ingesting something pretty much qualifies as causing it irreparable harm."

Violet gave a bemused nod. "I agree with you on principal. And if I had to kill and gut my own food, I probably wouldn't eat meat either. But I like it too much to give it up. I guess I'm just hypocritical that way." She lifted her shoulders in a self-deprecating shrug. "So what *do* you eat?"

"Fruits, vegetables, flowers, stuff like that," Eleanor replied, alighting on the computer desk with a curious glance at the keyboard.

"Flowers?" Violet asked with a grin, trying to picture the faerie flitting from blossom to blossom like an overgrown butterfly, munching on the petals.

"Mmhm," Eleanor sounded, as she distractedly tested the long rectangle of the space bar with the weight of her bare toes. "Honeysuckle is my favorite."

"Well, I'm not sure they have any honeysuckle on the menu, but I'm sure I can get you a fruit salad."

"I've always wanted to try one of these things," muttered Eleanor, now jumping from letter to letter in fascination, as if playing a game of hopscotch.

Violet snorted in amusement. "Here, I'll turn it on for you." She reached over to press the button on the CPU, the small motor whirring to life inside as the screen warmed up and proprietary words flashed across it. Eleanor stared as if mesmerized.

"If you've been watching me my whole life, you have to have seen a computer before," Violet said with a chuckle of disbelief.

"Sure I've seen them, but it's not as if I spend all my time staring over your shoulder," Eleanor replied without taking her eyes from the screen. "I mostly only come around when you need help. I've thrown some dust at your computer once or twice, to keep you from losing something you spent a lot of time working on. But I couldn't very well practice typing on it." She snuck a guilty glance at Violet. "Well, I might have stood on one letter. But you just thought it was stuck."

Violet laughed outright. "So that's why I always seem to get the keyboards with the sticky E's."

Eleanor shot her charge a mischievous grin as Violet rose from the floor and plunked herself onto the rickety office chair in front of the computer. She reached for the mouse and opened a word processing program. "There. Now you can type to your heart's content. That long one's the space bar," she instructed, pointing to the key Eleanor had stepped on first.

"Caps Lock will make the letters go between upper case and lower case. Or you can step on the Shift key and the letter you want to capitalize at the same time, but you won't be able to reach all of them unless you're planning on playing keyboard Twister. Holding Shift also gives you the upper symbols on the keys with two symbols."

Eleanor rubbed her small hands together in anticipation, giggling gleefully. Violet smirked.

"Knock yourself out; I'm gonna order and go pick up lunch. I'll get you a fruit salad. Whatever you don't eat, I'll finish later." But Eleanor was already busy hopping from key to key, eagerly watching the screen as she experimented. Violet shook her head as she went to retrieve the lunch menu.

"If you get stuck, try the E-S-C key to escape," she called as she walked out the door a few minutes later. "And if you get bored of that, maybe you can take a look around for any merrow artifacts I missed. I'll be back soon!"

She donned her sunglasses and stepped into the bright, cloudless afternoon, enjoying the heat against her skin. Her mind drifted to Doyle, out on his tour boat, and she wondered what he was doing right now. *Probably hanging out with his shirt off and flirting with a couple of gorgeous, half-naked women*, a maddening voice inside her head needled.

She looked over to see a white-haired woman in a floppy-brimmed hat, and an embroidered sundress, glance at her in alarm. The woman quickened her step down the sidewalk. Violet realized that her face was pinched in a ferocious glower, and hurriedly smoothed her expression. She would simply have to go apologize to Doyle after his final tour today. That was all there was to it.

And maybe they could pick up where they'd left off. She remembered they way he'd held her in his arms as they danced, and a heat that had nothing to do with the summer sun moved through her. And that kiss they'd shared in the water at the beach. Sweet heaven the man knew how to kiss. It had been slow and masterful, a sliding penetration of lips and tongue, heightened by the unhurried caress of his hands on her body. A sensual promise of the way he would make love to her later, when he had her alone.

Violet felt shivery and flushed as she entered the air conditioned interior of the restaurant, self-conscious that anyone who looked at her would guess exactly what she'd been thinking only moments before. She paid and walked back to the villa in a dreamy state of semi-arousal, as she allowed her mind to continue replaying intimate scenes from the previous day.

She opened the front door to the faint, tinkling sound of faerie laughter, and dropped the food bag on the kitchen table, before making her way back to the office. The keyboard was abandoned and Eleanor was nowhere in sight. Then her eyes spotted movement beneath the computer desk, and she looked down just as a small faerie child came bouncing around the side of the CPU, his tiny wings flickering in a tottering parody of flight. He wobbled to a halt when he saw Violet, his eyes growing wide in his chubby pink face.

"I'm coming to get you, Obie," Eleanor teased in a high-pitched voice, laughing as she darted into view behind the boy. She swept him up in her arms, tousling his feathery black hair. "Oh, Violet, you're back!" She gripped the child tighter and flew up to hover in front of Violet. The tiny boy's face erupted into a shy smile beneath eyes the exact same color as Eleanor's.

"Who is this adorable little chunk?" Violet demanded, instinctively reverting to baby talk and earning a gleeful chortle from the child.

"This is my son, Oberon. My sister was watching him, but her human charge has been having some trouble lately. Death djinns," she added on a whisper, leaving Violet blinking in confusion.

"Bad business. Anyway, she had to leave unexpectedly. And I didn't want to just disappear on you, so I thought I'd bring Obie by to say 'hi'. Say 'hello' to Miss Violet, Obie," she instructed, reaching down to playfully shake his pudgy fist in greeting.

"Hello, Mith Violet," Obie repeated with a soft lisp.

Violet's smile widened. "Hello Obie. You are just the cutest thing ever. How old are you?"

Obie's wide purple eyes rose inquiringly to his mother's face and she laughed as she held his fist up with three fingers showing. "He'll be three next Monday."

"Thith many!" Obie insisted gleefully, holding his fingers up higher.

"How exciting!" Violet exclaimed. "And what do you want for your birthday?"

Obie tittered happily. "Wingleth peg," he answered in a chuckling voice, as if this was the funniest thing he'd ever heard.

"Wingless peg?" Violet repeated with a grin, shooting a questioning glance at Eleanor.

Eleanor snorted. "He wants a rocking horse. We don't have horses in the faerie realm, we only have pegs—that's short for pegasus," she clarified. "Obie's auntie Lori told him that the pegs in the human realm don't have wings and he thinks it's hilarious. Guess what, Obie?" she asked the boy.

His eyes sparkled up at her and her lips twitched with humor as she smiled back at him. "Miss Violet has never seen a pegasus with wings. She's only seen them without!"

Obie's eyes jerked back to Violet in disbelief and he let out a crowing peal of laughter. "See what I mean?" Eleanor chuckled.

Violet shook her head in amazement. "Do you want to bring him to the table for some fruit salad?"

"Are you kidding? He's *always* hungry," Eleanor said dryly as she followed Violet back to the kitchen, making little swooping drops in the air that sent Obie into raucous fits of giggles.

Violet unpacked the food, plastic ware and paper napkins. "Uh, do you need anything special?" she asked uncertainly as she propped open the lid of the fruit salad container.

"Nope, we're good," Eleanor answered.

Violet sat and gratefully tucked into her sandwich, watching in amazement as Eleanor pulled faerie-sized cups, plates and a tiny knife from her shimmering dress. She scooped up some juice from the bottom of the fruit salad container, cut off some crumb-sized pieces of fruit and arranged them on the plates, then ripped off two corners of a napkin, before seating herself and her son down to their neat little lunch.

"Do you have any other children?" Violet asked. She snorted into her water bottle as Obie shoved a fistful of melon into his mouth, making his already chubby cheeks bulge like a miniscule chipmunk's.

"Nope. Obie's my spoiled baby," she answered with a fond grin. "The whole family dotes on him. I only have one sister, Lorien, and she hasn't bonded yet."

"Is that like marriage?" Violet mumbled around a fry.

Eleanor gave a sideways nod. "Sort of. Sprites bond for life, though. Which is a serious commitment, seeing as we're immortal," she added with a chuckle.

"What's Obie's father like? Is he a faerie guardian too? *Are* there male faerie guardians?" Violet asked in fascination.

Eleanor smiled, a soft light coming into her clear, purple eyes. "Yes, there are male faerie guardians, but Firien holds a seat on the Faerie Council. They're the ruling body of the sprites and our representatives within the Seelie Court."

Violet expressed a food-muffled, "Wow."

"It's a very important job," Eleanor agreed with pride in her voice.

"How long have the two of you been bonded?" Violet asked.

"Firien and I were bonded the same year we met, so it's been about," she paused to count silently, "seventeen years now."

Violet choked. "You made an immortal lifetime commitment after knowing each other for less than a year?"

Eleanor laughed. "It's often like that with sprites. We go through our lives unbonded for however long it takes until we meet our lifemate. But we know them immediately. It's an undeniable connection."

Violet digested that in wonder. "It must be amazing to be so certain you'll love someone forever, and that they'll spend forever loving you in return."

"Love is always a gift," Eleanor said softly, "and there are always uncertainties, but a steadfast heart will recognize its mate and rise above them."

Her words caused Doyle's image to appear in Violet's mind, warm and unwavering, solidifying her earlier decision to meet him at the docks to apologize. She glanced at the clock and began eating faster. She wanted to finish looking through a few more bank statements, and then shower and change, before she went looking for him.

Eleanor watched the preoccupied look come over her charge's face, and hid a pleased smile as she bent down to wipe some dribbling fruit juice from Obie's chin. She'd bet her sweet wand that Doyle would soon be thanking her for making him tell Violet the truth.

Chapter Ten

"The human approaches," Lagan hissed. "We have a job to do, even if that cheapskate Hagar is paying us less than we deserve. Have done with your games and get over here."

Ligan released the struggling stingray he was tormenting and bared his green teeth at his twin brother, as he glided toward him through the sand clouded water with a flick of his flipper-like feet. His shoulder length mane of gray hair, usually soft and supple as a tuft of waving sea grass, felt as brittle as dried seaweed in this human realm ocean. No doubt it was all the pollution they so carelessly dumped into their waters.

"We should have never taken this job," he growled. "We should have stayed in our own realm and bid on that Undine job. This human ocean stinks of chemicals and filth. I can feel the grit of it burning in my gills."

"Pah!" Lagan snorted in disgust, water gusting from the sides of his neck though his own gills. "Don't be such a whiny fry. Too many of us knew about that job. The bidding war alone would have ruined our chances at earning a decent fee."

"It still would have been more than what Hagar is colt-pixieing our services for. And at least then I wouldn't have had to worry about coming down with a case of scale rot." Ligan brushed the webbed fingers of one hand over a flaky patch on his long, spindly arm. A few dry, grey-green scales came off and dissipated into the surrounding water.

Lagan's round black eyes narrowed, their green rims constricting in annoyance. "We would have been paid less than twice as much for a job that would have been three times as difficult. And even if we'd gotten it, we'd likely have had jealous bidders trying to sabotage us. It wasn't worth the trouble and the possibility of the Seelie Court getting involved.

"This is a kelp-cake job," Lagan continued with a sneer, his nostril slits flaring. "Taking down a non-magical human, a realm away from the prying eyes of the Seelies. What could be easier? And you've had that rash for a week," he added sourly. "You ate too much dulse. You know you're allergic."

Ligan sent him a sullen glare. "I'm sure this water isn't helping it, though," he muttered.

Lagan ignored him, studying the thin, heavily tarnished strip of silver with the tiny silver orbs worked into it. Hagar had spelled it to track the human and it vibrated with her approach, pointing him in her direction like a compass. The plan was to remain near land until she ventured into the water again, and right now she appeared to be heading straight for the shoreline.

Hagar had warned them of the presence of a sidhe warrior, but Lagan wasn't overly concerned. He and Ligan didn't intend to engage in battle; their specialty was stealth. A cleverly placed illusion spell and a well-timed distraction would have the human in their clutches, and beyond the sidhe's help, before he even realized the girl was gone.

"Come on," he barked at his twin, streamlining his arms against the sides of his rangy body, and carving a swift path through the water toward the point where the human approached. His rubbery lips brushed the algae-coated surface of his teeth in a grim smile as he felt Ligan fall in behind him.

He didn't completely disagree with his brother. The sooner they finished this job and left this Triton forsaken realm, the better.

∞∞∞∞∞∞∞∞∞∞

Violet's stomach fluttered nervously as she approached the docks. A group of people filed toward her in chattering clusters, their mismatched footsteps clunking against the wooden planks. They looked wind-swept and damp, their faces brightened by sun and saltwater. She stood aside and smiled politely as they trundled past, then started up the gently sloping timbers.

Ocean Magic rested in her slip and Violet could see Manny's coffee-brown form circling the deck as he collected the neon orange snorkel vests and looped them onto his lean, corded forearms. Doyle's bulkier, golden-tan figure appeared around the side of the covered area that housed the bathroom. He leapt lightly down the gangplank, not yet aware of her presence, and began unwinding a length of hose.

The butterflies in her stomach increased their frantic winging, and her step quickened. She was about to call out to him when, from the corner of her eye, she saw a stack of wooden crates begin to teeter dangerously. She leapt out of the way with a muffled shout, barely in time to avoid being knocked into the murky depths below.

One of the crates hit the water with a resounding splash just as a pair of large hands steadied her shoulders. She looked up to find Doyle hovering over her, his face tight with anxiety. Her hammering pulse jumped at his touch.

He lifted his palms away from her in a jerky motion, curling them into loose fists at his sides, as if uncertain what to do with them. "Are you alright?" he asked, his voice oddly hoarse.

She nodded. "Yeah, thanks. I'm not sure what happened there." She laughed nervously.

He scowled as his sea-green eyes traveled to the tumbled crates, but his expression smoothed when he looked back at her. "The people around here aren't always the smartest, most safety conscious lot."

Sunlight glinted in his hair, bronzing his skin. He continued to stare down at her with a remote, unreadable look, his muscles tense.

She sucked in a breath. "Doyle...about yesterday..." His gaze grew shuttered and she could practically feel him trying to distance himself from her. The fear that she had ruined things between them grew into an icy lump of certainty inside her chest.

"I'm so sorry," she whispered. She looked down, unable to stand the chill in his eyes. Only yesterday they had been filled with such heat.

Doyle was silent for an unbearable stretch of moments before his voice washed over her in a tone that was as dispassionate as his gaze. "Why are you sorry, Violet?"

Her heart constricted. Eleanor was wrong. He didn't sound as if he cared whether they straightened things out or not. She swallowed painfully and lifted her chin. "I regret the way things ended between us yesterday, and I'm apologizing for the way I spoke to you," she said, struggling to sound dignified. "But if you have trouble accepting my apology, I understand."

Doyle gazed intently at her face, trying desperately to read what she was feeling. He could barely breathe for the fear that she had come here to end things between them. He'd been sure that's what she was about to say when she told him how sorry she was. She hadn't even been able to look at him as she said it.

But a glimmer of cautious hope pierced his despair with her words. She looked almost as miserable as he felt. She either thought there was still a chance for them, or she was being overly polite.

He wished to the devil he knew whether she trusted him or thought him a madman. Had that confounded sprite gotten through to her? He needed to apologize for breaking the news to her about her parents the way he had. But he needed to know whether she'd accepted the truth before he put his foot in his mouth again.

"There's no need for you to apologize; you didn't do anything wrong. I'm the one who's sorry, Violet," he ventured carefully. "I was thoughtless. And I don't blame you for thinking I was mad."

Violet stared at him in confusion, trying to reconcile his closed expression with his words. "So, you're not angry with me?"

"Angry with you?" he echoed in disbelief. "Violet, no. I have no call to be angry with you. You must be angry with *me* about those things I said to you."

Violet shook her head, denying his words in a rush of her own. "No, Eleanor showed up after you left and explained everything. How she tried to keep me out of the water but it didn't work. How you'd been trying to protect me. But I wasn't sure if that was the only reason you were hanging around."

She snapped her mouth shut, realizing she'd just babbled her deepest fear aloud.

Doyle's expression thawed and a jumble of emotions flitted across his face as he watched her. "You believe me?" he whispered, needing to make sure he understood her correctly.

Her eyes widened with sincerity, devoid of the haunting accusations they'd held in his dreams. "I do," she said quietly, looking around to make sure no one else could hear. "It was a little hard to take it all in at first, but then Eleanor appeared, and…"

"And it doesn't bother you that I'm not human," he plowed through her explanation, his voice gravelly and intense.

She gave him a blank look, as if the question was in a foreign language. "Doyle. No," she refuted, sounding confused.

He stood before her, paralyzed with a tangle of fear and hope.

"I hadn't even thought about that," she said slowly. "Is it a problem?"

A muscle ticked in his jaw. "It isn't for me if it's not for you."

Her smile was like the sun coming out from behind a cloud. They stared at each other, the space between them thick with mingled relief. Then relief melted into need. Doyle stepped forward, one hand splaying at Violet's back to urge her against him, the other coming up to cup her cheek as he lowered his mouth to hers.

"I'm crazy about you," he breathed, the soft words like a balm to her senses. And then he was teasing her lips with fluttering kisses, unhurriedly exploring their fullness, savoring them.

Violet's hands slid past his hips and up his firm, sunwarmed flesh, smoothing over the rippled contours of his stomach, and traveling higher in discovery of the broad expanse of his chest. They curved across the solid slopes of his shoulders and snaked around his neck as she rose onto her toes and tangled her fingers in the softness of his hair, fitting her body to his.

Lightning crackled along Doyle's nerve endings with Violet's touch. When she pressed herself against him, the length of her body molding itself to his and the rounded curves of her breasts cushioning his chest, it was as if a storm broke within him. He crushed her to him, his hunger for her spreading like wildfire. His hand moved lower, urging her hips to grind against his, as his tongue penetrated the seam of her lips to plunder her mouth with deep, sweeping strokes.

Flames licked through Violet's veins as Doyle engulfed her senses, the strength and warmth of his body surrounding her, his mouth claiming her, his hips moving against hers in an insistent promise of wicked pleasures. She needed him so badly she ached.

"Hey, *hermano*, you think the ocean want more water?" Manny's voice was an unwelcome reminder of where they were.

Doyle reluctantly gentled the erotic friction between them and slowly retreated from her mouth. One hand rubbed the length of her back in a soothing caress, the other moving to brush some silky strands of hair from her temple as he pulled away.

He turned to find his first mate holding the running hose that Doyle had abandoned when he'd heard Violet's yell. Manny was beaming at him with unabashed glee, his teeth gleaming white in his wide smile.

"Sorry to interrupt, *hermano*," Manny said in an undertone, "but you was gathering an audience." He nodded his close-cropped head at a couple of the other boats docked nearby, and Doyle glanced around to find several men looking conspicuously busy and two women grinning openly at him.

Violet's cheeks heated. She'd completely forgotten their surroundings, the presence of other people, pretty much everything except for Doyle's body moving against hers. Doyle put his arm around her shoulders and pulled her into his side, his touch easing her discomfort.

"Good to see you again, *lindita*," Manny greeted. "Your boy here been moping around all day, worried you mad at him," he confided, his cheeks bunching up in an impish expression of merriment.

Violet bit her lip to hide a smile.

Doyle glared at his busybody friend, but before he could fire back with a retort, Manny tossed him his t-shirt and said, "Go home, *hermano*, I'll finish up here."

Doyle frowned. "No, man. I was supposed to do the cleanup today. I can't leave it all to you for two days in a row."

"You can owe me, *amigo*. You two go on and work things out. Then maybe when we come back on Friday, you be back to your old self." Manny winked at Violet. "You take care of him, *lindita*, he been mooning around like a lost *perrito* ever since he met you."

Violet giggled. "Thanks, Manny. Tell Melody I said 'hi'."

"Will do," Manny agreed with a quick salute. "*Hasta luego*." He turned and strode back across the gangplank, dragging the length of streaming hose behind him.

Violet couldn't stop smiling as she threaded her arm behind Doyle's back and pulled him toward the parking lot.

Doyle scowled as he allowed her to lead him away. "Mooning around? Lost *perrito*?" he grumbled, stopping to yank on his tour t-shirt. "I'll give that loud mouthed Costa Rican a lost *perrito*," he muttered as his honey-brown head popped through the neck hole.

"I think he's sweet," Violet piped up in Manny's defense.

Doyle's scowl deepened and he gave Violet a disgruntled glance. Her lips were trembling and he realized that she was holding back laughter. His ire faded as he watched her joy bubble to the surface, and he smiled at the thought of finally having her alone, with no secrets to foul the air between them.

"Let's go to my place," he suggested, pulling her to a halt as she started to turn toward her parents' villa. "I didn't get a chance to let my dog out today. And I want to show you my house."

Violet's heart did a little flip at the boyish excitement in his voice. "I'd love to," she said softly.

Doyle gave her shoulders a squeeze as they started walking again, everything looking brighter than he remembered. The sun's heat was cut by a cooling ocean breeze. The birds twittered musically from their hidden perches in the trees. And he'd never noticed how nicely landscaped this section of road was, its thin strip of median overflowing with a profusion of purple and red blooms. He had no idea what they were called, but they really spruced up the place.

He smiled in anticipation as he thought about showing Violet his home. It wasn't fancy, but he was proud of the improvements he'd made over the years, while still managing to preserve its old Florida charm. The huge yard with its backdrop of tropical palms and sea grapes, the updated kitchen and its shiny stainless steel appliances juxtaposed with its original countertops, the expanded master bath with its vintage glass-bricked shower and state-of-the-art Jacuzzi tub.

His blood seared his veins as he thought about bringing her into the private sanctuary of his bedroom. He imagined Violet lying naked in his bed and nearly groaned aloud. He could see his black satin sheets tangling around her pale golden skin, her amethyst eyes glowing up at him in invitation. Her long hair would spill out like a silken waterfall over his pillows, and her scent of sun-ripened fruit would linger in the supple fabric. His groin tightened.

But as they turned onto his street, he began to feel nervous. He was struck by the realization that he'd never brought a woman home before. Until now, he'd never wanted to.

He'd enjoyed his share of female companionship over the years, but it had always been casual sex with flirtatious young women who were just passing through, looking for a good time. And he'd always gone to their hotel rooms or the little vacation cottages they rented. They seemed more comfortable that way and he had never cared.

But it was different with Violet. Something about her resonated deep within him. He wanted her to see his things, experience how he lived…he wanted her to know him for everything he was, and accept him for it.

"This is a nice neighborhood," Violet commented, her lilting voice breaking into his thoughts.

Doyle looked around his street, trying to see it for the first time through her eyes. The lots were roomy and private; the low, sprawling houses set back from the shell-sprinkled asphalt. The yards were well-maintained and shaded by native scrub and towering palms, their lofty fronds lolling high above the rooftops and swaying gently in the breeze.

He smiled down at her. "Thanks. It's quiet here…peaceful really. It feels like home."

"That's a good feeling," she said softly. "Do you have nice neighbors?"

"I've lived here for ten years, but I don't know them all that well," he replied with an ironic twist of his lips. "There's an elderly couple to one side of me, and a single mother with a teenage daughter to the other. We tend to keep to ourselves, but everyone's been pleasant when I've spoken to them. So yeah, I'd say that's pretty much the mark of a good neighbor."

"No one spying through the blinds or reporting you to code enforcement for putting your garbage bin in the wrong spot?" Violet asked with a grin as they turned up his driveway, bordered by its tall hedge of sea grapes. It led up to Doyle's long, flat-roofed house, which was shaded by scattered coconut palms. Its white siding and green trim looked clean and freshly painted in the fading afternoon light.

"Nothing like that." Doyle chuckled. "Of course, I could always hex them if they did."

"Hex them!" Violet exclaimed in amusement.

"Sure," Doyle replied, his sea-green eyes twinkling with mischief. "I could put an inhibiting spell on their yard so nothing would grow. Or maybe an enhancing charm, so everything grows out of control and they have to mow it and clip it back constantly. Or if I wanted to be really nasty, I could always put an expelling hex on their plumbing."

"Doyle!" Violet chastised in mock horror. "This changes everything."

Doyle shot her a wary look. "How so?"

"Well," she said in a disappointed tone, "I had a fantasy about how things would go when you came over to trim the vines around my parents' villa. Now that I know you can use magic to get the yardwork done, it's ruined my dream of watching you shirtless and sweaty with the hedge-clippers." She feigned a sigh. "I was going to come outside with lemonade and everything. But if you can just toss a spell at it, I guess you won't be needing that massage I was going to give you for your sore muscles afterward."

A slow, sexy grin spread across Doyle's face. "Cold lemonade and a warm massage? That sounds worth the effort of manual labor."

"No, don't bother," Violet overrode him with a laugh. "I'm sure you'll just want to get the job done with as much expedience as possible."

"Actually," he denied huskily, "I'm thinking it will be much more satisfying if I take my time and give the task all the personal attention it deserves."

A thrill of anticipation shivered through Violet at his suggestive tone. "Are we still talking about yardwork, here?" she asked on a throaty chuckle.

No, they most definitely weren't, Doyle thought, hiding his smile as he unlocked the front door and braced himself for Bruno's weight. The excited dog was snuffling at the frame and Doyle didn't want him to accidentally knock Violet over. Doyle pushed open the door and Bruno nosed his way through, rearing up to place his giant paws on Doyle's shoulders in an enthusiastic greeting.

"Down, Bruno!" Doyle chastised, thinking that he should have made more of an effort to discourage such behavior in his over-sized pet. "He's kind of big, but he loves people," Doyle told Violet, suddenly anxious that he didn't know whether she even liked dogs.

He needn't have worried. Violet was beaming at the dog, who had just discovered she was there and was staring at her with intense curiosity. "Hi puppy, how are you?" she asked softly.

That was all Bruno needed to hear. He immediately lost interest in Doyle, pushing past him and promptly lowering himself onto his huge haunches at Violet's feet. His tail thumped a happy rhythm against the welcome mat, his long, pink tongue dangling from a panting mouth that came almost as high as Violet's shoulders.

He quivered with restrained eagerness as Violet patted his shaggy grey head and fondled his floppy ears, but remained sitting for her. "Good boy," she encouraged, sending Bruno's tail into a more frenzied beat.

"I think you've made a friend," Doyle commented, feeling a swell of tenderness toward both Violet and the dog. Violet grinned as she reached down to scratch the dog's chest.

"Go on boy, do your business." Doyle pointed Bruno toward the yard. The dog gave him a mournful look. "You can see Violet again in a minute. Go on." Violet ceased her petting and inclined her head in the direction Doyle had pointed. Bruno blew out a noise similar to a sigh and trudged out onto the sandy soil to disappear around the side of the house.

"That is by far the hugest dog I have ever seen!" Violet exclaimed as she followed Doyle into the cool interior of his house. "What kind is he?"

"Irish Wolfhound," Doyle answered with a grin.

"He looks like he could eat a wolf for breakfast," she commented. "And it's amazing how well-trained he is. Do you always just let him outside like that without a fence?"

"He knows to stay in his own yard, but he doesn't sit like that for just anyone. I think he likes you." Doyle smiled over his shoulder at her. "The breed was originally used to protect livestock from wolves, so supposedly he could fight one off if he had to. Although we haven't tested that theory, seeing as we don't have many wolves running amok, threatening our sheep and chickens here in The Keys."

Violet laughed. "I'll bet someone would think twice before breaking into your house, though."

"You should hear him bark," Doyle agreed with a chuckle. "So, would you like the tour?"

Violet smiled. "Lead on. I assume this is the living room?"

"Very perceptive," Doyle replied solicitously.

"I see you've got a masculine sort of wood and leather thing going on here." Violet clasped her hands behind her back and took an appraising look around.

Doyle bit his lip in amusement. "I'm glad you can see what I was trying to do with the space."

"Nice tile," she commented. "It really lightens up the room."

"Thanks. Manny and I just finished putting that in about a month ago."

"I do love a handy man," she teased, sending him a sultry glance as she moved on toward the kitchen. "What's in here?"

Doyle's sex stirred at the look Violet gave him. His little school teacher was playing with him, and it was enough to make him want to drag her into his arms and take her right there on the brand new tile. He reminded himself to take it slow and followed her around the corner.

"Who would have thought vintage seventies olive-green and modern stainless steel would work so well together," she said softly. "You have interesting taste, Doyle Thresher. Let's see what else I can discover about you." Her rosy lips curved up in an intimate smile and she held his gaze as she skirted around him, past the long counter of the breakfast bar, and wandered back toward the living room.

Doyle's mouth went dry at Violet's throaty tone, her light fruity scent tantalizing his senses as she brushed by him. "Would you like something to drink?" he offered, his voice taking on a roughened quality.

"No thanks," she called sweetly.

He followed her back out to the living room and watched her peak her head into his garage, which served as a tool shed since he didn't own a car. "How about some music?" he asked, moving to the stereo and glancing around distractedly for a suitable CD. There was something so enticing about seeing her explore his personal space.

"Do you have any Van Morrison?" Her eyes glowed amethyst in the soft afternoon light as she walked unhurriedly toward him.

"I have the same album we were listening to yesterday," he replied, unable to take his gaze from the gentle sway of her hips.

"Will you dance with me again?" she requested with a smile that was all heat and invitation.

"I would love nothing more than to dance with you, Violet. But wouldn't you like to see the rest of the house first?" He swallowed, her expression and her proximity seducing him as surely as her touch.

"Dance with me, Doyle. I can finish the tour later. There's only one other room I'm interested in seeing right now anyway."

Fire shot through his belly and his hand literally shook as he found the CD and placed it in the player. He rose to his feet and looked down into her lovely face as their need swirled between them like a living thing. "Just, ah, let me let Bruno in," he told her in a strangled voice.

The dog was waiting at the door. Doyle put a hand on his head and whispered, "If you go to bed and stay there, I'll buy you a steak."

Bruno's ears perked up as if he understood the bribe. He trotted into the house, pausing only briefly to lick Violet's hand before proceeding to the corner to collapse onto his mattress.

Doyle smiled and stalked purposefully toward Violet, capturing her eyes with his as the music swelled and he closed the distance between them to take her in his arms. "Now, where were we?" he asked in a low, thick brogue.

Violet's pulse quickened as Doyle pulled her body flush with his and eased them into a slow, erotic sway. He took one of her hands and threaded their fingers together, wrapping her in his arms, the fingers of his other hand tracing the indention at the small of her back. Her eyelids fluttered shut as he bent his head and trailed his lips in a warm, gliding path across her neck.

She sighed with pleasure. "Show me something magical, Doyle," she whispered.

His mouth traveled upward to her ear, and he nibbled at the soft flesh there, soothing it with the tip of his tongue. Violet shivered, her nipples tightening in arousal.

"I'm not supposed to use magic in this realm unless it's an emergency. But for you, I'll make an exception," he breathed. "Ready?"

Violet nodded and Doyle stepped back from her. She gasped as he simply disappeared, staring in shock at the empty space before her. Then, as quickly as he had gone, he reappeared holding a small bouquet of wildflowers in one hand.

"For you, *a thaisce*."

She accepted the deep purple blooms, fingering their velvet petals with a dazed smile. "Violets," she murmured with delight. "They're beautiful, Doyle. Where did you get them?"

"They grow wild in a meadow near where I was born."

"They're from the faerie realm?" she whispered in awe.

Heat sparked in Doyle's eyes as he nodded. He had been so afraid she would condemn him for not being human. The joy she seemed to find in the mere existence of his world meant more to him than she could ever know.

He grinned. "But now I seem to have created the problem of where to put them. Let me go get something." He hurried to the kitchen to retrieve a glass of water, wanting her back in his arms as quickly as possible. Violet lovingly arranged the flowers in the makeshift vase and he placed it onto the scuffed wooden coffee table.

She reached up to trace his stubble-roughened jaw with her fingertips as he pulled her back against him. "Thank you, Doyle, for everything. I really don't know what I would have done without you these past few days. And you have no idea how honored I am that you were willing to share the existence of your world with me."

She brushed her thumb across his lower lip and his muscles tightened with the strain of holding back his desire. "I only wish I hadn't reacted so badly to hearing about it," she added with a sad smile.

"You did fine, *a thaisce*," he said huskily. He nipped at the pad of her thumb and then drew it past his lips into the wet heat of his mouth, scraping at it with his teeth and then laving it with his tongue.

Violet's knees turned to water as every nerve-ending in her body responded to the gentle, insistent pressure he was creating with his mouth. Doyle embraced her tighter as he released her thumb, holding her gaze as he lowered his head to brush his lips against hers. He nibbled at them, teasing them with his tongue before entering her mouth in an erotic caress. He tasted of salt and the warmth of summer.

Swaying with the music, he deepened the kiss until she was lost in sensation, the movement of his body against hers, and the slow penetration of his tongue. She moaned, her hands gliding up his chest of their own accord. Entranced by his mouth, she shivered at the pleasure of his hands journeying up her ribcage in a leisurely slide, pushing her shirt up as they went.

His fingers caressed the rounded arcs of her breasts, stroking the sensitive outer curves as his thumbs rubbed the straining little peaks through the silky fabric of her bra. Desire curled through her, swelling in her womb, and she arched her back against his touch as her inner muscles clenched with need.

He raised his head and pulled her shirt the rest of the way off, tossing it over the side of the couch. His eyes devoured the delicate burgundy silk covering her breasts and she felt his erection jump against her waistband as he began to plunder her mouth once more. He reached behind her and deftly unhooked the scrap of lingerie, sliding it down her shoulders as he continued to kiss her, blindly tossing it in the direction of the couch.

He bent her backward, supporting her with his muscular arms, as his lips roved hungrily down her chin. He kissed the graceful curve of her neck, nibbling across her delicate collarbone, before finally fastening onto a bared nipple. She cried out at the shock of him drawing the hardened peak into the cavern of his mouth with one strong pull. He immediately gentled the suction, licking at the dusky tip with the flat of his tongue before suckling it again.

"Doyle," she gasped.

"Do you like that, *a thaisce*?" he asked in a voice that had turned to gravel.

"Yes, please…"

He sucked harder and liquid need rushed through her core, making her hips jerk against him.

Violet's uninhibited response to his touch drove Doyle wild. His rigid length strained against his shorts and he wanted desperately to be inside her. But first he wanted to draw out the heady thrill of exploring the pleasures he could give her.

He licked a path across the soft valley of skin to the opposite breast and took it into his mouth as his palm moved up to ease the vacancy he'd left at its twin. Violet's body bowed as he again pulled firmly on the stiffened tip and then soothed it with his tongue. Her hands tangled in his hair and she murmured incomprehensible sounds of encouragement that made him burn with desire.

Unable to wait any longer, he swept her into his arms and carried her to his bedroom. He crossed the lush carpet and lay her carefully down onto the cool satin of his comforter. "I want to see all of you, *a thaisce*," he rasped, as if seeking permission.

Violet held his sea-green gaze as her fingers slowly unfastened the button of her shorts and then pulled down the zipper. He nearly fell to his knees as she shimmied them over the ripe curves of her hips to reveal the wisp of burgundy lace beneath. "Dear Goddess, you are so beautiful," he murmured reverently, his words stealing Violet's breath and sending a tremor through her.

Doyle reached out to slide her shorts the rest of the way down, his fingertips traveling the lengths of her smooth legs. He dropped the shorts to the floor and stripped off her sandals, leaving only pale golden skin and a flutter of wine-colored gossamer against the black satin of his bedding.

He kissed the tips of her toes. They were polished a shiny mauve and reminded him of delectable little hard candies. Nipping and tasting, he worked his way up her creamy calves. His fingers joined the exploration as he roamed the gentle curvature of her knees, seeking higher to savor the supple flesh of her thighs.

Violet writhed in mindless pleasure beneath Doyle's onslaught. He seemed to know instinctively how to touch her, finding every erogenous zone and lingering over it with warm breath and questing hands, prolonging and building the sensations until she felt as if she would go up in flames.

Doyle growled deep in his throat as he approached the juncture between Violet's thighs, the flimsy scrap of fabric there barely obscuring her nest of tight, dark curls. Her honeyed scent enticed him, her sweet flowing nectar an invitation for him to taste her. He caressed her with his breath, then ran his finger over the dewy silk, nearly shattering her with the intensity of her response.

"Open your legs for me, *a thaisce*." His voice was low and roughened by desire, its sound seducing Violet as much as the raw command it gave. She acquiesced with a sweetness that made him groan, spreading her legs slowly and touching the tip of her tongue to her swollen lips as she watched to see what he would do.

He dipped his head to her core, holding her eyes as he traced a vertical indention in the silk with his tongue. Her eyelids fluttered and her breath came in short bursts as her head sank back onto the pillows. He swept the damp fabric with his tongue once more, pushing a little harder this time. She released a gasping shudder and her small fists clenched against his comforter.

"Is that good, *a thaisce*?" he murmured, his words vibrating against her.

"God…yes," she gasped haltingly. "Please…"

He replaced his tongue with the slow glide of his finger. "Please what?" he whispered.

"Please…deeper," she breathed.

Doyle groaned. He was tormenting them both. He was so rock hard now that he thought he might explode. But just a little more, and he would send Violet over the edge. He could feel it. He slid the scrap of silk to the side, revealing the perfection beneath, and tasted her nectar with a leisurely, stroking penetration.

Violet whimpered and her hips lifted from the bed to meet his mouth. He used his forefingers to spread her wider and sampled her honey again, eliciting a low keening sound from Violet's throat. His fingers slid over the slickness at her entrance. God, she was so ready for him. He slipped a fingertip easily inside her and she gave a soft moan of assent.

"Better, *a thaisce*?" he asked huskily, slowly withdrawing and then pushing deeper, as she'd requested.

"Yes!" she cried, her breath quickening as he added his tongue to the onslaught. He increased the friction and the tempo with masterful precision, until the waves of her climax broke over her. Tiny stars exploded behind her eyes and her mind flew out of her body on a cresting flood of bliss.

Violet floated back into awareness to find Doyle lying beside her, watching her with a smile of male satisfaction as he gently stroked her hair.

She melted into him and whispered, "That was amazing. Now it's your turn."

She heard Doyle's indrawn breath as she pulled her boneless body tight against his and began her own sensual exploration, nibbling and sampling the soft flesh of his lower lip, the slightly firmer curve of his upper one, making little darting forays beyond them with her tongue.

Her hands traveled below his shirt, her fingertips taking in the warm solidity of his chest; the vertical slope of his hard, tapered side; the firm strength of his back as it flexed beneath her touch. They sought out every contour and indentation, kneading muscle and brushing lightly over bone. She teased him with her shallow kisses all the while, stirring him into a mindless frenzy of pleasure.

Her fingers splayed over his pecs and she found his nipples with her thumbs, making him groan and grind his still clothed hips against her naked form. She trailed one hand unhurriedly down his stomach and cupped his erection through his shorts, just as her tongue flitted beyond his lips to brush against his.

The effect was instantaneous. He growled and rolled her onto her back, pressing his weight down into her as he took charge of the kiss. He rubbed his hardened length against her palm as he devoured her mouth, and she reveled in her ability to make him lose control.

But she needed him undressed. The friction of fabric against her sensitized flesh was driving her insane. She pushed his shirt up with her free hand, desperate to get closer to his skin, murmuring thickly into his mouth, "Doyle, take your clothes off, I want to feel you against me."

He nearly came when she told him to undress, the boldness of those words coming from her sweet lips enough to unhinge him completely. He rose to his knees, straddling her as he tore off his shirt. He forced himself to slow down as he maneuvered off his shorts and boxers, and then lowered himself to the bed to lie beside her.

Violet trembled with desire and anticipation as she watched Doyle strip. He had a curious red tattoo of intricate Celtic knot-work where one hip met his upper thigh. Although it was beautiful, appearing to almost glow in the dim light, she spared it only a brief glance. The rigid length of his erection drew her undivided attention as it sprang free of its restriction, and her core muscles clenched with liquid heat as she imagined taking all of him inside her.

"Come here, *a thaisce*," he ground out in a voice that sounded as if it had been rubbed with sandpaper.

She scooted across the cool satin of the comforter and into his waiting arms, her entire body rejoicing at having nothing between them. The surface of her skin felt as if an electric current sizzled over it, shivering and sparking wildly, only calming as it came into warm, solid contact with his.

He was all male heat and strength, mixed with aching tenderness, his body hard against hers as his fingers came up to gently frame her face. He kissed her with reverent care, seducing her senses with soft caresses of his lips and tongue, demanding nothing, offering everything. His hand brushed over her body, grazing her breast, stroking her side, skimming her hip, and then moving back up again.

He released her mouth, his hand still kindling a slow path of flames across her skin as he looked into her eyes. Violet met his steady gaze, the warmth and stillness there awakening a light within her that grew and expanded until she was sure he would see it shining back at him.

"Violet," he rasped in a heavy brogue, "I have no problem wearing a condom. But being sidhe, I can't pass any diseases to you. And I can also make certain I don't get you pregnant. I'll do whatever makes you comfortable, though."

She smiled at his consideration. "I want to feel you deep inside me, with nothing between us," she whispered.

His eyes flickered with heat and the muscles in his chest and arms tightened as if he was restraining himself. He muttered a low prayer in Gaelic as his hand moved down to nudge her leg over his so that her inner thigh curled across the top of his hip. "My God, *a thaisce*," he groaned as the thick head of his shaft found her moist entrance, "you have no idea what you do to me."

He eased the rounded swelling just inside her, sweating with the effort of holding himself back, and she gasped, her eyes flickering but staying locked to his. "I've never felt so connected to anyone in my life," he said as he eased in a little more, stretching her, allowing her body to get used to his.

She slid her hips forward in a small gliding motion over the tip of his shaft and they watched each others' expressions, both panting in pleasure. "I think I'm falling in love with you, *a thaisce*." He knew it was too soon to say such things to her, but he couldn't seem to stop himself. "I don't expect you to feel the same..." he faltered.

Violet silenced him with her mouth, her kiss scorching him with its passion. "I do feel the same," she whispered.

Doyle groaned and rolled her onto her back in a single unbroken movement, curling one arm around her shoulders and keeping them joined as he held himself above her with the other. "That's good, *a thaisce*," he rumbled, his throat tight with emotion, "because what we're doing right now is definitely making love. And I don't think I've ever really done it before. Not the way I am with you."

Violet's eyes filled with tears as she laughed. "God...the things you say to me are so amazing." Her smile was tremulous as she stared up at him, her eyes darkening beneath her wet lashes. "I love you, and I love your words, but right now I just want you to stop talking and make love to me." She pulled his lips down to hers, accepting his tongue into her mouth as she arched her hips and took his full length into her body.

They were both lost as he began to move inside her, burying himself until their hips met in deep, steady strokes that eased her aching need and made him want to shout in ecstasy. He slowed as he felt himself nearly spill over the edge, pulling back in shallower strokes, stretching and teasing her with his swollen tip until she was writhing beneath him, begging for release.

He plunged deeply once more, and she cried out, her muscles clamping around him as if desperate to keep him there. He drew all the way out and slid into her tightening passage again, holding nothing back. He repeated the driving action, slowly increasing the tempo as he hooked his arms beneath her knees. He tilted her hips upward and pushed deeper into her channel, burying himself to the hilt with each thrust.

Violet's head thrashed against his pillows, little keening sounds escaping her throat as her pleasure built to unbearable intensity and her body struggled to find release. And then suddenly she was calling his name as she shuddered against him, her orgasm milking him until he exploded in the rawest, most intense climax he'd ever experienced.

When he was able to think again, Doyle rolled onto his side, taking Violet with him, and remaining buried in her sweet warmth. Their lips met in languid joining as they both floated in a dreamlike haze. Doyle's tongue swept across Violet's, and to her surprise, she felt him stirring to life inside of her once more.

She gave him a questioning look. "Again?"

He rolled her on top of him and took the tip of one breast, then the other, into his mouth. The muscles tightened in his arms as he lifted her hips so that she glided up and down his thickening shaft.

"Again," he whispered with a wicked smile. "You're sleeping over tonight."

Chapter Eleven

Violet awoke to the delicious smell of bacon frying, and the more delicious soreness permeating her entire body. She'd never had a lover with Doyle's inventiveness or stamina. They'd stopped only for food and brief periods of rest. If she hadn't passed out on him around 2 a.m., she was pretty sure he would have kept going until dawn.

She felt like he'd wrung more orgasms from her body in one night than she'd had in her entire life. She smiled to herself and stretched her arms above her head, her back cracking with a satisfying pop as her fingers clutched at the decorative metal spokes of the headboard. The swirling sun design was still tangled with the mismatched silk ties that Doyle had pulled from a drawer at some point during the evening. Violet shivered with delight at the remembrance.

Feeling comfortably lazy, she plumped a pillow beneath her head and remained tucked between the sheets, reveling in the cool glide of satin on her bare skin. The late morning sun peeked through the cracks in the vertical blinds, casting stripes of shadow and light onto the thick forest green carpet.

Doyle's bedroom was again that curious blend of vintage and modern design. His low, teak chest of drawers and matching nightstands had a distinctly sixties feel, with their scalloped handles and splayed legs. While the sculptured metal headboard and the frosted glass light fixtures were obviously current additions. She decided that, being immortal, he must have had plenty of time to choose his favorite styles from all the eras he'd lived through.

With a pang of shock, she realized that she had no idea how old Doyle was. He appeared to be in his late twenties or early thirties, but for all she knew he could be hundreds of years old. The disquieting idea marred her sense of peace. Not because of the possible age difference, but because it occurred to her to wonder how a relationship between a mortal and an immortal was truly going to work. She would age and die; while Doyle would live on, probably continuing to look as young as the day they'd met.

A series of loud, echoing barks startled her out of her uncomfortable reverie. Doyle's voice rose above Bruno's baying as he ordered the dog to his bed, and Violet heard the unmistakable tone of a female voice. Doyle's response had the cadence of a greeting and then both voices grew muffled as they retreated further from the bedroom door.

Violet remained frozen for a moment, wondering what to do, before jumping up to retrieve her clothes. She let out an unladylike curse as she realized that her bra and shirt were still somewhere in the living room. She improvised by making a hesitant search through Doyle's drawers until she came across his t-shirts. She plucked one with *Ocean Magic*'s logo from the top, and took it and her shorts into the bathroom in an attempt to make herself presentable.

She rinsed off in the glass bricked shower, and then borrowed Doyle's comb, toothbrush and deodorant—all the while trying to tamp down her twinges of jealousy over his unknown female guest. By the time she ventured from the bedroom and stepped barefoot onto the cool, hard tile of the living room floor, she was a bundle of uncertainties.

The pungent aromas of coffee and breakfast lured her toward the kitchen, as did the voices coming from that direction. She turned the corner to find Doyle by the stove, cooking with his back to her. And between them, draped casually over a barstool at the long olive-green strip of countertop, was one of the most imposingly beautiful women she'd ever seen.

Silken, strawberry blonde hair was pulled back in a ponytail from her flawless face. She wore a clinging black leather vest, its v-neck revealing a hint of cleavage, tight blue-jeans, and supple black leather boots. She was nearly as tall as Doyle, her build and her wardrobe giving her an Amazonian appearance. The woman looked as if she would be at home wielding a sword in battle and then dropping by the spa for a manicure afterward.

She straddled the stool sideways, studying one short, perfectly rounded nail with an expression that dripped boredom. Suddenly her chin lifted, her eyes zeroing in on Violet with the intensity of a falcon sighting its prey. Her gaze raked Violet from head to toe in an assessing, almost disdainful manner. She neither smiled nor spoke as Violet blinked nervously back at her.

Doyle said something in Gaelic, his voice growing louder as he turned toward the woman, and his face broke out in a grin as he noticed Violet standing there. He dropped his spatula and jogged around the counter to greet Violet, who was patently relieved to have the other woman's unsettling stare broken.

"Good morning, *a thaisce*," he said softly, his eyes glowing with heat as he closed the space between them. "I like seeing you in my clothes," he whispered, pulling her into his arms for a stirring kiss. "How did you sleep?" he breathed against her mouth.

Her libido flickered to life with his touch, and she smiled up at him. "Fine, baby," she murmured, using the endearment she'd settled on some time during the night, as her fingers came up to caress his stubbly cheek.

Doyle growled as his body started to harden, swooping in for another, more urgent kiss. He loved the sexy way that intimate word fell from her lips, meant only for him. Violet melted into his chest, laughing at his ardor and then meeting it with her own. He was thinking about carrying her back to his bed when the sound of a throat being cleared resonated behind him.

He raised his head, giving Violet an apologetic look that quickly molded itself into a scowl, as he tucked her into his side and turned to face the source of the interruption. "*A thaisce,*" he began, in a gentle voice that belied his irritable expression, "meet my sister, Scarlett. Scarlett, this is Violet."

Violet's eyes widened in her flushed face, and she managed an embarrassed smile for the other woman, discerning physical similarities that she had been too flustered to notice before. Including the fact that Scarlett's eyes were the exact same shade of sea-green as Doyle's. "It's so nice to meet you," she said warmly. "I guess my parents weren't the only ones who had a thing for giving girls colorful names."

Violet's smile faltered when Scarlett's only response was to transfer her unimpressed gaze to her brother. Doyle squeezed Violet's shoulder reassuringly and made an aggravated face at his sister.

"Violet knows all about us, Letty. She knows we're sidhe." Scarlett's mouth dropped open in outrage and Doyle spoke louder to override any protest that was forthcoming. "She knows about our realm and she has a faerie guardian that she can see.

"And if you can't get over your ridiculous prejudice against humans long enough to be nice to her, then you can just blink your butt back home, because she and I are spending the day together. If you want to, that is, *a thaisce,*" he added, lowering his voice and sending Violet an affectionate grin.

Violet looked uncertainly from Doyle to Scarlett, who had snapped her mouth shut and appeared to be fuming in her continued silence. "Are you hungry?" Doyle asked Violet, proceeding to ignore his sister. "I'm making bacon and omelets again. With lots of cheese," he dangled enticingly.

Violet couldn't help grinning back at him. "I'm starved."

"Good. Come get some coffee. There's a mug and some cream and sugar on the counter there." He pointed. "Breakfast's almost ready. There's some placemats and napkins in that drawer, and silverware in the one next to it, if you wouldn't mind setting three places." He dropped a kiss on her forehead and sent a warning glare at his sister before returning to the stove.

Unnerved by the other woman's chilly demeanor, Violet retrieved the place settings and laid two of them on the breakfast bar in front of empty stools. She pushed the third one into place in front of Scarlett, attempting a friendly smile at the women, who only persisted in pretending Violet wasn't there.

Violet sighed and stepped around the counter to make herself a cup of coffee. She almost offered to refill Scarlett's, but thought better of it, not eager to be rebuffed again so soon. The steaming pot of liquid trembled in Violet's hand as the other woman's musical Irish brogue suddenly rang out behind her in a resonant Gaelic dialect.

Doyle's jaw tightened as Scarlett asked about his best friend, Pat. Her curiosity wasn't surprising—she'd held a torch for Patrick Sparrow for as long as he could remember. But her insistence on speaking their native language in front of Violet chafed at his temper.

"I haven't spoken to Pat for a couple of months, Letty," he deliberately answered her in English. "Last I heard he was still living in his apartment in Seelie City, working as a lead detective for the force. But next time I talk to him I'll make sure to tell him you said 'hi'."

He began scooping pieces of omelet onto plates, leaning over to brush his lips against Violet's cheek where she stood propped against the counter, gratefully sipping her coffee. Scarlett continued badgering him to give Pat the message that she, and his cousins from their village, missed him and wished he would come home for a visit. Again she used Gaelic, and Doyle had to bite back his anger.

"It's rude to purposely speak another language in front of someone who can't understand you," he told her quietly, refusing to acknowledge her request.

She huffed and crossed her toned arms over her leather clad breasts. "I was merely trying to have a conversation with you in our native tongue. But fine, if you want me to speak English, all you had to do was ask. I don't need my little brother chastising me to impress his girlfriend."

"No one's trying to impress anyone, Letty," he said in a weary voice as he placed a full plate and a fresh cup of coffee in front of her. "Let's just try to have a nice breakfast, shall we?"

Scarlett began eating without comment. Doyle plunked the other two plates onto their mats and steered Violet around to a barstool, placing himself between the two women. He bent down to give Violet's earlobe a playful nip and whispered, "Ignore her. It's nothing personal."

Violet smiled at him as she took her seat, deciding to take his advice and not take his sister's attitude too personally. But she thought she'd take a different tack than ignoring Scarlett, especially if they were going to be spending the day together. She figured being friendly toward the other woman could only improve the situation, seeing as nothing she said could make Scarlett like her any less.

"This looks delicious, Doyle," Violet complimented in a cheerful tone. "So, Scarlett, has Doyle always been such a good cook?"

Scarlett sent her a sulky glance, as if to protest being forced into conversation. She made a show of chewing her mouthful of food and washing it down with coffee before responding with the word, "No." Then she quickly took another large bite.

Doyle snorted. "My sister. The great communicator." He smiled at Violet. "Actually, if you'll notice, the only thing I've ever cooked for you is breakfast." Violet caught Scarlett's smirk and felt her cheeks warm, but

Doyle seemed oblivious to the innuendo. "I'm afraid my culinary talents don't go much beyond eggs and bacon. I pretty much live off of sandwiches and takeout. But I can make tacos," he said, waggling his eyebrows.

Violet chuckled. "I love tacos. Mexican food is my favorite."

"Scarlett loves them too, don'cha, sis?" He elbowed her in the side and she blocked him as if he'd gone for her ticklish spot, looking torn between ire and amusement.

Scarlett swallowed the bacon she'd been munching and narrowed her eyes at Doyle. "Don't! You're gonna make me choke," she complained.

Doyle let out a muffled chortle around his mouthful of omelet. "Gonna tell Mum and Dad on me?" he taunted.

"I'll tell Ma you were asking about Nancy Spinner," Scarlett threatened in a laughing tone.

"Who's Nancy Spinner?" Doyle asked in confusion.

Scarlett's eyes danced with mirth. "Tom Finch's niece. The one with the spots on her face who followed you around like a moon-eyed calf the last time you came for a visit. She turned eighteen a couple of months ago."

Violet bit her lip at Doyle's comical look of horror, thoroughly enjoying their sibling banter. "You wouldn't, Letty. That's really low," he pleaded.

"She's actually not so bad looking now that her spots are fading and she's toning up from her sword training," Scarlett said with a snicker.

Violet's eyes widened as she recalled what Doyle had said about the sidhe being a race of warriors. It looked like her guess that Scarlett would be at home wielding a sword hadn't been too far off the mark, if the girls from his village started weapons training at eighteen.

Doyle groaned. "Don't you dare. Mum would have the poor girl thinking I'd proposed before I even had the chance to open my mouth."

Scarlett's grin was merciless. "Come on, Doyl-ie," she goaded. "Ma just wants you to settle down with a nice, stable girl and give up your wandering ways. Maybe pop out a grandkid or two for her to dote on."

Doyle scowled. "I'm hardly a wanderer. I own my own business and I've lived in the same house for ten years. And I'm not popping out anything, that's your job. I'll never understand why you aren't the one she's trying to marry off. You're older *and* you're her only daughter."

Scarlett's face instantly shuttered. "I've made it more than clear you're her only hope as far as that goes. She knows better than to try that matchmaking crap with me."

Doyle's brow furrowed in sympathy. "I wish you'd give up that torch you're carrying for Pat, Letty. It's been almost two hundred years."

"Drop it, Doyle," she stated in a flat tone, digging back into her omelet with a stony expression.

Doyle sighed and crunched a piece of bacon, watching his sister from the corner of his eye. Since she'd been a teenager, she'd never shown the slightest bit of interest in any man other than Pat. Which made her prejudice against humans all the more unreasonable, since Pat was half human. He'd asked his best friend about it before, but Pat always insisted that he and Scarlett had never been, nor ever would be, anything more than friends. Then he inevitably clammed up as tightly as she did.

Violet frowned as the joking interplay between Doyle and Scarlett ceased at the mention of her starting a family. It was obvious that Doyle attributed it to his sister's unrequited love for his friend, Pat. But something deeper had flickered in the other woman's expression, making Violet wonder if there wasn't more to her reticence than a long-held crush.

"Just exactly how old are you guys?" Violet asked in amusement, trying to lighten the mood again.

Doyle grinned. "I'm not telling. You're liable to leave me for a younger man."

"Doyle turns one hundred eighty-nine this November," Scarlett answered with a smirk. "How old are you, human?"

"Scarlett," Doyle snapped, his grin fading.

Violet put a restraining hand on his shoulder. "It's fine, Doyle." She looked past him to meet Scarlett's defiant gaze. Rude or not, the other woman deigning to speak to her was an improvement of sorts. "I'm twenty-seven."

"And are you passing through on vacation, like all the others?" Scarlett's tone was light, but there was no mistaking her stinging intent.

A muscle twitched in Doyle's jaw and Violet's fingers tightened on his shoulder in a silent warning that she wanted to handle the question. "I live about two hours north of here. I teach fourth grade and I'm off for the summer, so I came down to stay at my parents' place for a couple of weeks."

"I see," Scarlett said airily. "Well, you'd better watch out then Doyle. You're not used to having to answer to Mummy and Daddy when you have your little flings. You might end up with another set of parents trying to marry you off."

"Violet is not a 'fling'," he ground out from between clenched teeth. "And her parents' passed away a couple of months ago."

Scarlett blinked and had the grace to look uncomfortable.

"It's okay," Violet told her softly. "You couldn't have known. I'm actually down here packing up their things."

Scarlett swallowed and her eyes darted away from Violet's. "I'm sorry." There was a pregnant pause, and then she stood and walked into the living room, with a muttered, "I'm going to take Bruno out."

Violet heard the excited jangling of the huge dog's collar, followed by the slamming of the sliding glass door leading onto the backyard.

Doyle puffed out a regretful breath. "I'm sorry about her, *a thaisce*. I completely forgot she was visiting today. I would have made other arrangements if I'd realized, but I didn't have the heart to send her home when she showed up this morning. And it's just for a few hours. She'll be gone before dinnertime. She's really not a bad person, despite the abysmal attitude you've been subjected to so far. I've never known where she got such an irrational bias against humans. It's certainly not from our parents. But she's had it as long as I can remember."

"Something happened to her," Violet said automatically. She wasn't sure where the thought came from, but she felt it for truth as soon as it left her mouth.

Doyle frowned at her. "What do you mean?"

Violet shrugged and shook her head. "It's just a feeling I have."

Doyle looked thoughtful as he began clearing the breakfast plates. Violet got up to help him and playfully bumped his arm with her shoulder. "Anyway, don't worry about it. I like getting these glimpses into your past, even if it is through a relative who doesn't particularly care for me. Maybe I can talk her into bringing naked baby pictures next time. I'll just convince her they're the last thing you'd want me to see."

Doyle dropped both their plates by the sink and spun her into his arms. "Why waste your time on pictures, when you can have the real thing?" He waggled his eyebrows at her and then captured her mouth, his hands sliding down to cup her bottom. He lifted her up onto the counter and she wrapped her legs around his hips, welcoming the press of his hardening body against the sensitive juncture of her thighs.

He rubbed her in concentrated little circles through the soft material of her shorts, matching the rhythm with slow thrusts of his tongue, until she was nearly mindless with need. But the thought of Scarlett walking in on them distracted her and she finally pulled away. "We're going to have to wait until your sister leaves, baby. I refuse to give her another reason to look down her nose at me."

Doyle moaned in protest, continuing the arousing movement of his hips as if determined to change her mind. Violet laughed as she tried to ignore the tingling pleasure he was giving her and the wildfire that was beginning to rush through her veins.

"You should go spend some time with her. You probably don't see her that often," she suggested breathlessly.

"I'm obviously not doing my job correctly if you can think so rationally right now," he growled.

"Actually, ignoring what you're doing right now could be classified as torture," Violet groaned. "But just think of how good it's going to feel later, when we can take our time and have the whole house to ourselves."

Doyle gave her a slow, seductive smile. "Does that mean you're spending the night again?"

Violet closed her eyes and shivered, unbelievably close to orgasm from his grinding thrusts alone. "Yes, if you want me to. And we can even pick up where we left off right here," she murmured.

Doyle stilled and she leaned into him, both grateful and frustrated at the reprieve. "Now there's a thought," he remarked in a heated tone. "We never did leave the bedroom last night. And I have an entire house full of rooms we can explore. Walls, countertops, chairs and couches…the bathtub," he added on a throaty rumble.

Violet whimpered into his chest as erotic images of making love with Doyle in every room and in every possible position flooded her mind. Doyle brushed her hair back from her face and lifted her chin for a quick kiss.

"You've given me new purpose for getting through the day, *a thaisce*. Maybe you should rest up for this evening while I play host to Scarlett," he recommended with a grin.

Violet chuckled. "What have I gotten myself into now?"

"It was your suggestion, *a thaisce*, and a very good one at that." He trailed his lips down her neck. "Although, come to think of it," he mumbled huskily, "I have no problem sending Scarlett home right now. I've already made her breakfast. That must count for something as far as my brotherly duties for the day."

Violet let out a bark of laughter as she pushed him away and jumped down from the counter. "Forget it, buddy. I'm not going to be the reason you cut your visit with her short. I'll do the dishes and you go hang out with her and Bruno."

She turned her back on him and flipped on the spigot, starting to scrape leftovers into the disposal. He wrapped his arms around her from behind, gently cupping her breasts and thumbing her nipples as he whispered in her ear, "I love you, *a thaisce*."

He brushed his mouth across her shoulder and released her, leaving her tight and needy for his touch. She sighed and reminded herself that letting him spend time with his sister was the right thing to do.

"What do you think about maybe meeting up with Manny and Melody for lunch at the crab shack later?" he called from the living room.

"Sounds good," she replied.

She was going to need *something* to distract her from her achy impatience for nightfall.

∞∞∞∞∞∞∞∞∞

"Come on, Scarlett, I know you for ten years. I don't care what anyone say. You just a softie beneath all that guff you throw around," Manny teased, his dark eyes twinkling beneath the slouching brim of the white golf cap he'd pulled down over his forehead.

Scarlett ignored him, transferring her scowl to the nervous waiter. She'd already laid into the poor guy for messing up the dressing on her salad and bringing fries that were too well done. His loose Hawaiian shirt flapped in the ocean breeze as he hurried away from their table. Violet felt sorry for him, suspecting that he was receiving the brunt of Scarlett's aggravation over Doyle's admonitions to be nice to his friends.

"So, how long are you in town for, Scarlett?" Melody asked. She looked cool and tranquil in a turquoise sundress, the familiar blue beret perched atop her riotous curls.

"Just for the day," Scarlett answered distractedly, the usual malice missing from her tone.

"That's nice," Melody commented with a smile. "What have you guys been doing so far?"

Scarlett shrugged a sleeveless shoulder that was cut with toned muscle. "Just hanging around the house, playing with the dog."

"Oh, you have a dog?" Melody asked, her face lighting with interest.

Scarlett described Bruno in a tone that bordered on affection, and Violet shook her head. Despite Doyle's warnings not to take his sister's attitude personally, she couldn't help feeling a little hurt at the almost amiable way in which Scarlett had taken to Melody. Although maybe it was because Melody wasn't dating her little brother, Violet reflected.

Melody's eyes widened when Doyle described Bruno's imposing size.

Violet chuckled, adding, "But he's very sweet and well-behaved."

"Yes, *mi amor*," Manny agreed, caressing the back of Melody's neck beneath her clouds of hair and giving her an adoring wink. "There is no need to fear Bruno. He may be as big as a horse, but he is a good dog."

"He loves to play fetch with the fallen palm fronds in Doyle's backyard," Scarlett told her. "They're as big as he is, and he drags them all over the place. And he loves to go to the beach."

A smile flickered over Scarlett's impassive face as she described the dog to Melody. It was the only time Violet had seen her smile all day, other than when she was joking with Doyle in private.

"He loves to go out on the boat too," Doyle said with an animated grin. "Hey, we should all go out on the boat together on Monday. We can bring Bruno."

Melody gave a frantic shake of her head and Manny resumed massaging her neck, while sending Doyle an apologetic look. "It is a nice suggestion, *hermano*, but Melody is afraid of the water. I try to persuade her to come out on the boat, but no use. She don't even like to talk about it." He shrugged and leaned in to kiss Melody's cheek, murmuring soothing words in her ear.

Doyle's sister frowned at Melody, as if she couldn't believe the other woman was really afraid of the ocean. She looked as if she wanted to comment, but Doyle glared her into silence.

"Everyone's afraid of something," Doyle said in an understanding tone.

"Yeah, it's no big deal, Melody," Violet agreed. "There are plenty of other things we could do."

Melody gave them a grateful smile and changed the subject. "How is the packing going, Violet?"

The question filled Violet with guilt. For one entire, wonderful night, she hadn't thought about her parents at all. She knew they would have wanted her to be happy. But she couldn't help feeling that being *this* happy was a betrayal of their memory. Especially in light of her recent discovery regarding the merrow and their deaths.

Doyle picked up on her mood and reached for her hand, unfolding her fingers to place a lingering kiss on her palm. She smiled, forcing herself to concentrate on answering Melody's question. "It's going alright. I took the day off, but I'll get back to it tomorrow. It's mostly going through paperwork at this point."

"You be sure to let me know when you need some help," Melody replied with an earnest expression.

"I will be glad to help also, *lindita*," Manny offered.

Violet swallowed, their generosity touching her. "Thanks, guys."

"Can I get you anything else?" the waiter asked in a timid voice, stepping up behind Melody and avoiding Scarlett's gaze.

"Just a check," Doyle replied, using the pad of his thumb to trace patterns on Violet's palm and inner wrist beneath the table. The hidden intimacy of his touch made her shiver with the anticipation of being alone with him again later.

They paid and said their goodbyes, except for Scarlett, who stood off to the side looking impatient as she waited for Doyle and Violet. Then the three of them were walking back to Doyle's house in the fading afternoon sunlight, Doyle taking a strategic position in the middle.

"I'm glad you came, Letty. It's always good to see you," Doyle said softly as they turned up his street.

Scarlett reached out to ruffle his soft honey-brown hair with her trim manicured fingers. "It's good to see you too, baby brother." Her eyes flicked grudgingly toward Violet. "I'm glad you're happy," she mumbled.

Doyle beamed and pulled her roughly into his side for a hug, walking the rest of the way home with his arm around her. She put up a weak protest, but Violet thought it was mostly for show. He only let go of her to unlock the front door with a campy call of, "Release the hound!" making both women groan.

Scarlett crouched down to say goodbye to Bruno, sticking her hands into her tight jeans pockets as she rose, as if to avoid another hug. Once inside the door, she leaned forward to peck Doyle on the cheek, muttering another goodbye that may have been meant for Violet. And then she disappeared.

Violet was left with a sense of relief, mingled with an odd sadness at her departure. There was something about the other woman that stirred Violet's compassion, despite Scarlett's animosity toward her.

Doyle puffed out a breath and shook his head. "Well, now you've met my sister. I only hope you won't judge all the sidhe by her piss-poor attitude."

Violet smiled and rose up on her toes to taste the enticing fullness of Doyle's bottom lip. "I don't know," she teased. "You may have to work at swaying my mind back to a more favorable position."

He put his hands around her waist and lifted her higher, stealing control of the kiss and robbing her of breath. "As it so happens, I am prepared to do just that," he said against her lips. "I have a little surprise for you."

"What is it?" Violet demanded, pulling back and grinning.

"You'll see." He lowered her to the tiled floor and laced his fingers with hers, tugging her with him into the kitchen. Two delicate crystal champagne flutes stood on the counter and he opened the stainless steel refrigerator door to reveal a chilled bottle of her favorite champagne and a bowl of her favorite fruit, ripe raspberries.

"How did you know?" she asked with a pleased exhalation.

He hid his smile. "A little faerie told me."

"You are sweet, Doyle Thresher," she said, a soft heat kindling in her violet eyes. "And I think you deserve a reward."

"Mmm...I like the sound of that, *a thaisce*," he purred in a roughened brogue, putting her in mind of a large tiger. "Let's take this in the other room and turn on some music."

Doyle popped the champagne open and tipped the effervescent liquid into the flutes, handing one to Violet as they settled back into the soft leather couch cushions. Violet grabbed the bowl of berries and popped one of the succulent morsels into her mouth as she took a crisp, cold sip of champagne.

She smiled in bliss. "Excellent." She chose another raspberry, plucking it from the dish with her forefinger and thumb and feeding it to Doyle. "I love a man who knows how to pick out good produce," she told him in a sultry tone. "Here, taste the fruit of your efforts."

Doyle chuckled as he caught the berry on his tongue, capturing her wrist with his hand and drawing her forefinger between his lips to lick the juice from it. "Didn't you say something about a reward?" he inquired, nibbling the tips of her other fingers in turn and sending thrilling little shockwaves up her arm.

Violet sipped her champagne, holding the bubbles on her tongue before swallowing. She felt giddy and alive, and happier than she had in a long time. Sticking a berry in her mouth, she picked out another one for Doyle and crawled onto his lap to straddle him. He hardened instantly beneath her and she gave him a seductive smile.

"So impatient," she chastised playfully. She took the second raspberry between her lips and leaned forward to place it in his mouth, her tongue pushing gently behind it.

Doyle groaned and cupped the back of her head with one hand, pulling her tighter against him as he ran his other palm over her bare silky thigh beneath her shorts. Her fragrant dark hair floated around his face as he inhaled her scent of sun-ripened fruit mingled with the sweetness of the crushed raspberry. He kissed her hard, bruising the soft berry between their tongues, its sugar combining with the sharpness of the champagne and the heady flavor of Violet's mouth. He'd never tasted anything so good.

Violet withdrew, tormenting him with a subtle rubbing of her hips against his erection, so softly that he could have almost believed she was unaware of the effect she was having on him. But her siren's smile told him differently. "I was thinking just a little reward," she breathed, sliding off his lap to kneel before him.

She stretched across him to retrieve a throw pillow and placed it on the tile beneath her knees, as if she planned to be there for a while. When she leaned in to unfasten his shorts, fire shot through Doyle's veins. By the time she got them off him, he was hard as a rock.

Violet gave him a coy look from beneath her lashes as she took him in her hand, rejoicing in the effect she had on his body. She stroked him, long and slow, brushing the moisture from the tip of his shaft with her thumb and massaging it lightly into his sensitive flesh. He leaned back into the couch, his breath coming faster as he watched her. When she licked him from base to tip and took him into her mouth, his eyes fell shut and he growled low in his throat.

She took him deeper and then retreated, swirling her tongue around his head, watching as all the muscles in his body tightened and his hands clenched at the edges of the cushions. She suckled him harder, releasing him with a little pop of her lips and then taking him between them again. When she added her palm, sliding it along the slickness beneath her mouth, and began a vibrating hum deep in her throat, his hips gave an involuntary thrust as if he'd been electrocuted.

Violet was lost in a haze of sensual power and passion. Her hips jerked with Doyle's, her body so in tune with his that it seemed to recognize the physical sensations he was experiencing. As her mouth caressed him, her palm slipped over his hip, her fingers splaying above his Celtic knot-work tattoo. It tingled, as if it was shooting little sparks of energy into her hand.

She felt the rushing buildup of his climax even before he began muttering low and fast in Gaelic, only breaking into English to moan, "Ah…Goddess…*a thaisce*," as he pulled himself from her mouth. She was shocked to realize that she'd had a mini-climax of her own.

With a smile of dazed satisfaction, she grabbed a paper napkin from the coffee table behind her and gently wiped him dry, before crawling back up onto the couch beside him to take a mouthful of champagne.

He cracked an eyelid and stared at her with a look of glazed awe that made her smile widen. "Do you feel rewarded, baby?" she asked softly.

His muscular forearm snaked out and she squeaked as he yanked her against him and then twisted to push her into the cushions beneath him. The glazed look in his eyes faded, to be replaced by a stark hunger that made her desire flare as his mouth descended to take purposeful possession of hers.

"I feel like rewarding you, *a thaisce*," he growled.

Violet's breaths came in short gasps as he trailed one hand down her body and slowly undid her shorts, all the while teasing her tongue with his.

"Open your thighs for me." His command came on a soft breath as he kissed her and she groaned as a hot, needy ache spread through her. She slowly widened her knees and his clever fingers slid beneath the waistband of her panties to draw firm, unhurried circles over her clitoris. The ache grew into a restless need and she squirmed beneath him, pressing her hips upward into his hand.

"Do you want more, *a thaisce*?" he inquired silkily.

"Please, Doyle," she begged.

The sweetness of her request nearly undid him. He slid one finger down between the plump lips of her vagina, feeling how swollen and ready she was for him. He teased her, slowly tracing the opening to her body and drawing his finger back up through her soft, sensitive flesh, over and over, until she was trembling with the pleasure of it.

"Please, baby," she whispered again.

"Like this?" he murmured as he finally pushed one long digit deep inside her.

She cried her assent as her hips rose to meet him, sending a shockwave of desire straight to his groin. "You're so wet for me," he groaned, withdrawing his finger to circle her clit before returning to plunge two digits inside her.

Violet felt wild and wanton as she lifted her hips to meet his thrusting fingers. He was so gentle, yet he was also stretching her, testing her limits. And still she needed more. She thrashed beneath him, mutely requesting that he fill her, that he let go and lose control as she was.

Doyle sipped at her lips, staring intently into her dazed eyes as he pleasured her with his fingers. "What do you need, *a thaisce*?" he purred, as if sensing her conflict. "Tell me."

"You, Doyle," she gasped finally. "I need you inside me. Now."

His hand stilled, a surge of desire, potent and wild, rushing through him at her demand. He'd meant to bring her to completion first with his hands and his mouth, but instead he found himself pushing her shorts and panties down in a single jerking motion. He slid the full length of his cock into her slick passage in one fluid glide, as he claimed her mouth with his tongue.

Violet's entire body shook with savage pleasure as he took her. And she knew that she was taking him as well, enveloping him within her, coaxing him to lose himself in their raw, carnal union.

Doyle groaned, spearing into her with a feral rhythm, helpless to resist her cries of bliss as she met his every thrust. He felt her tighten around him, signaling the approach of her climax, and he knew he'd never felt anything so good or right in his entire life. Unable to control his own pleasure, he released himself inside her with a shout, her cries of fulfillment echoing his own as they both exploded into orgasm.

After long moments of incoherence, Doyle came to his senses and rolled to his side, pulling her with him. "No fair," he murmured, as they both lay in a boneless, sleepy afterglow.

"Wha'do'you mean?" Violet slurred.

"You seduced me before I had a chance to give you your full reward."

Violet giggled. "I'm not sure I could have survived my full reward."

Doyle smiled and pulled her closer against him. "I'd better give you a few minutes to recover before we christen the chair, then."

He nodded toward the overstuffed leather recliner beside the couch and Violet stifled a groaning laugh.

Chapter Twelve

"Hey Violet."

Violet looked up from the receipts she'd been reviewing and smiled at the miniature winged woman hovering in the air before her. "Didn't even startle me this time," she said smugly.

Eleanor heaved a dramatic sigh. "Gone are the days when I could amaze and astound you with my very presence."

Violet snickered. "So whatcha been doing?"

Eleanor zoomed over to sit on the computer desk, her bare feet dangling from the edge. "Mostly planning for Obie's birthday party next week—inviting the neighborhood kids, making decorations, planning games."

Violet leaned back, propping her hands on the carpet behind her with a grin. "What sorts of games do faerie children play at parties?"

"Oh, just the regular stuff," Eleanor shrugged, "'pin the tail on the hobgoblin', 'musical toadstools', that kind of thing."

Violet's grin widened and Eleanor narrowed her tilted eyes at her as if she knew she was being laughed at. "Anyway, that's what I've been doing. I'm not even going to ask what *you've* been doing for the past couple of days. I should have warned you how virile the sidhe are. They take satisfying their women very seriously. If they don't do a good job, their bonded mates can take them to Aeval the sorceress' midnight court and have them judged unworthy." Eleanor smirked. "I'm surprised you can still walk straight."

A blush crept up Violet's cheeks and Eleanor gave a tinkling chuckle. "So, have you found anything merrow-related in all these papers?" she asked.

Violet rolled a kink out of her shoulder blades and sighed. "Nope. That $3500 cash withdrawal was the last thing that looked remotely out of place. There's been nothing since, paper or otherwise. Doyle said he was going to call his friend from the Seelie Police Department to see if someone can help us track down the merrow." She scowled. "If I ever get my hands on the murdering bastard, I plan to make merrow fin soup."

Eleanor winced at Violet's ferocious tone. "I want to catch him too, Violet, and I promise you we will. But you have to promise *me* you'll stay away from him. Let the immortals handle it. Speaking of which, Doyle sent me to tell you that he got through to his detective friend, and someone's coming to meet with us later today."

Violet's mutinous expression vanished with a rush of excitement at having the help of the Seelie Police. *Finally they were taking some action!* "Where and when?" she asked.

"5:30 down by the docks," Eleanor replied. "Doyle said something about having to stay later than usual for cleanup today."

"Oh, yeah. He owes Manny for cutting out on him two afternoons in a row." Violet broke into a guilty grin, remembering that she'd been the reason he'd neglected his duties both times. "So do you know who's meeting us?"

"No idea." Eleanor lifted her pastel-clad shoulders in a graceful shrug. "But I'm sure they'll be good. The Seelie Police only hire the best." She fluttered her shimmering wings and rose to her feet, tapping the computer's keyboard with her toes. "Anyway, I just wanted to drop by to tell you that. I've got to get back to Obie. Oh, and can you bring that recording your parents made?"

"Yeah. I think there's a walkman around here somewhere." Violet frowned, trying to remember where she'd seen the CD sized square of plastic, and hoping it hadn't already been stuffed into a box.

Eleanor gave her a quizzical look.

"Portable thing to play the recoding on," Violet supplied with a smile. "I'll figure it out. Anyway, you go on. And give Obie a kiss from his Auntie Violet."

"Will do," Eleanor agreed with a cheerful wink as she blinked out.

∞∞∞∞∞∞∞∞∞

Violet walked up the dock toward the *Ocean Magic* with a spring in her step, happy at the prospect of seeing Doyle again, and thrilled to be doing something proactive in the search for her parents' killer. She spied her immortal warrior on his boat, sexy and shirtless, his skin bronzed by the late afternoon light as he leaned back against one of the benches lining the deck. His face was relaxed and peaceful, with his eyes closed and a breeze teasing his soft hair. She wished she had a camera to capture the alluring image.

She carefully ascended the gangplank and walked past the captain's wheel toward the stern, coming to a stop before Doyle. "Hi baby," she said softly, not wanting to startle him.

His eyes remained closed, but his delectable lips spread in a slow smile. "*A thaisce*, I was just thinking of you. This was where you were sitting the first time I saw you. I was thoroughly entranced by your loveliness."

Violet chuckled in disbelief. "You were not."

Doyle cracked an eyelid and raised a brow. "I assure you I was. And I still am." He stretched a hand out toward her. "Come here," he commanded silkily, "and I'll show you just how entrancing I find you."

Violet took his hand, laughing as he pulled her onto his lap.

"Ahhh…that's better," he sighed, banding his arms around her back and running his fingers through her long hair.

"Did you have a nice day?" she murmured, smoothing her thumb over his lower lip and smiling into his eyes.

"It was bearable. But it just got much better." He was on the verge of kissing her senseless, when a small voice piped up nearby, halting his momentum.

"Titania's wand! Can't you two go half a day without crawling all over each other?" Eleanor floated just out of reach, her tiny hands planted on her hips.

Doyle glanced at his watch and then smugly back up at the sprite. "It's been half a day."

Violet's entire body tingled as she remembered him waking her at 5:30 that morning and lazily making love to her until it was time for him to get up for work. "He's right, Eleanor. It's been twelve hours." She grinned and kissed him soundly, then slid off his lap onto the bench beside him. "But I suppose we have work to do."

"At least one of you can control her hormones," Eleanor grumbled with a dry look at Doyle. "It's a wonder the poor girl isn't falling asleep on her feet."

"Who is your Seelie friend sending?" Violet asked, placing her hand on Doyle's arm to divert his attention from the glare he was directing at Eleanor.

He grabbed his shirt from the back of the bench and pulled it over his head, his voice momentarily muffled as he answered, "Pat said he was going to try to get Daisy from the Marid djinn tribe, which would be great, because she's an expert on underwater lore and probably knows more about the merrows than anyone else in the faerie realm."

"Marid djinn tribe?" Violet repeated.

"The djinns are a race of magical beings that can take on spirit form," Doyle explained. "There are four tribes, each with an affinity for one of the elements in nature. The Marids are the water djinns, but there are earth, air and fire djinns too. All of them are generally lovely people, except for the fire djinns, who are also known as 'death djinns' because of their dealings in the soul trade."

Violet blinked at his revelation about this newest legend come to life. "Djinn…as in genie? As in rub the lamp and get three wishes?"

"It's those damned death djinns that have my sister's charge in such a bind," Eleanor fumed, oblivious to Violet's glazed stare of disbelief. "They've got her tied up in one of their soul contracts, and if she makes one more wish they'll be able to claim her for eternity."

Doyle looked thoughtful. "Pat's involved in a major investigation of the death djinns right now. He's been in charge of several raids that have uncovered large numbers of illegal unaligned souls found in numerous death djinn containment safes."

"Good," Eleanor replied fiercely. "I hope the Seelie Court nails those bastards to the wall. It's about time they did something about those disgraceful soul contracts."

"Sorry I'm late," chimed a feminine voice, interrupting Eleanor's rant. A breathtakingly beautiful woman appeared out of thin air to stand on the deck before them. She glided forward, her wavy red hair seeming to billow in an unseen wind, and extended a graceful hand to Violet. Her smile was radiant beneath her watery turquoise eyes. "You must be Violet. I'm Daisy."

"Nice to meet you," Violet replied, trying not to gape.

Daisy squeezed her hand gently before releasing it and turning to the sprite hovering by Violet's shoulder. "Good day, little sister," she said. She tucked her chin respectfully down toward her loose flowing blouse, which was the same brilliant shade of turquoise as her eyes.

"I'm Eleanor, Violet's guardian. Thank you for taking the time to meet us, Daisy."

"My pleasure." She turned to Doyle with a familiar grin. "Pat made me promise to keep you out of trouble, Doyle Thresher."

Doyle stepped up to give the woman a quick kiss on the cheek and she pulled him into a hug. "You may have bitten off more than you can chew on that count, Daisy. But I'm glad you're the one he sent."

Jealousy surged in Violet's heart and she pushed it down with surprise, unused to experiencing the uncomfortable emotion.

"I hear you're having some problems with a merrow." Daisy lowered herself onto the bench next to Doyle and crossed her long legs, the hems of her thin, white linen pants fluttering in the breeze above her leather thong sandals. With a twinge, Violet noted that even her feet were extraordinarily shapely and lovely.

Air flickered softly by Violet's ear as Eleanor alighted on her shoulder, and Doyle took one of her hands between his warm palms. Affection washed through her as she realized they were lending her their silent support for the coming discussion about her parents. Eleanor cleared her throat with a small sound and began to speak.

"A few days ago, I saw a merrow try to drown Violet. She was out on Doyle's boat with a group of humans, and she's a very good swimmer, so I didn't think anything of her being in the water. I didn't even sense the danger until he was dragging her down." The faerie frowned. "I figure my signal must have gotten fouled up by his magical field."

Daisy's delicate brow wrinkled in a troubled expression. "The merrows aren't known to be violent toward humans. On the contrary, they tend to avoid humans at all costs."

"We know," Eleanor agreed with a vigorous nod. Her wings sped up, sifting purple dust onto Violet's shoulder. "But this merrow came after her a second time. I felt his approach because I was looking for it, and I tried to warn her out of the water, but she wouldn't listen. Luckily, Doyle got to her before the merrow did. That was when we decided we had to reveal ourselves. It was the only way I could think of to keep Violet safe."

Daisy directed an intimate grin at Violet. "It sounds like you've had quite a week."

Violet smiled back, not immune to the other woman's warmth, despite her familiarity with Doyle. "It's certainly been interesting."

"But you've had no contact with the merrows prior to these two recent episodes?" Daisy asked, her expression sharp and calculating.

Violet shook her head. "I had no idea they even existed. But Eleanor pointed out that it was an odd coincidence that my parents were killed taking their boat out around here a couple of months ago. And then we found this." She pulled the walkman containing her parents' CD from her shorts pocket, untangling the earphones and holding it out for Daisy.

Daisy took the plastic contraption, her eyes glowing with sorrow as they met Violet's. "I'm very sorry for your loss," she said quietly.

"Thank you," Violet replied, trying to ignore the discomfort that always came with telling someone that her parents had passed away. She showed Daisy how to use the walkman and the four of them sat in silence as the djinn listened to the contents of the CD.

Daisy removed the earphones slowly after several minutes, concern marring her perfect features. "This is disturbing news. The merrows have always been a solitary race, but it is truly terrible to think that one of them would resort to murder to keep themselves hidden. Especially when retrieving the chart your father mentions would have preserved their secret just as effectively. Do you have any idea how your parents gained possession of such a chart in the first place?"

Violet shook her head sadly. "I've been going through their things, and all I've found are this CD and a couple of unusual expenditures on their credit card and bank statements. They spent quite a bit on gas toward the end, but that can be explained by the frequent use of their boat. The weirdest thing was a $3500 cash withdrawal that I can't seem to match up with any purchases." She frowned. "Do you think they could have used the money to buy the chart?"

Daisy nibbled her lip as she thought aloud. "Only if your parents bought it from another human. A merrow wouldn't have any use for human coin. Which begs the question, why *would* a merrow reveal their city to a human? Your mother says in the recording that they planned to return the chart to its owner.

"I wonder if its owner was the merrow your parents saw. And if that's the same merrow who is now after you, and who we are assuming was responsible for their deaths. Or could there be more than one of them involved?"

Violet sucked in a breath as she envisioned not just one, but a horde of murderous mer-creatures, lying in wait for her beneath the waves. Doyle sensed her unease and reached up to run a soothing hand through her hair.

"I'm fairly certain it was the same merrow after Violet both times. He had an unpleasantly sticky aura about him." Eleanor wrinkled her tiny nose in distaste. "But you're right. We have no idea if he was the same one Violet's parents saw."

"Either way, he's definitely our starting point," Daisy mused. "And since he zeroed in on you twice," she gave Violet a meaningful look, "we have to assume that he has a tracing spell on you. It's likely he got hold of something that belongs to you. Something you wore against your skin would work best, like an article of clothing or jewelry…"

"My anklet," Violet exhaled on a shocked breath, "I lost it in the water the first time he came after me."

Daisy nodded. "That would be perfect for a tracing spell."

"But how did he find her before he had it?" Doyle asked shrewdly.

Daisy thinned her lips as she thought. "Something he got from your parents?" she suggested to Violet in a questioning tone.

"Something they had on their boat when it went down?" Violet replied in a distant voice. "A picture, maybe?"

Daisy let out a humorless little sniff. "That would work, though not as well as your anklet undoubtedly does. I hate to say this, but I'm afraid if you really want to find this merrow, we're going to have to use you as bait. From what you've told me, we don't have anything else to go on."

"Absolutely not!" Eleanor exclaimed. "It's far too dangerous. Violet almost died once at his hands already. Do you even realize how easily he could finish the job? She's not immortal like you! There has to be something else we can lure him with."

Daisy raised her hands in placation. "I mean no offense little sister," she responded calmly. "And I don't wish to endanger your charge. I will do everything in my power to keep her safe. But if you don't want to chance it, I understand. Are you sure there is nothing else of significance in your parents' belongings?" She turned her sharp gaze on Violet.

Violet shook her head. "No," she admitted. "I've looked and looked."

Daisy's eyes flickered apologetically to Eleanor. "Then, going by the information you've given me, this is the only way I can see to draw out the merrow that's after her. Violet can try to stay out of the ocean for the rest of her life. But if you want to neutralize this danger and discover what truly happened to her parents, she is the only tool we have at our disposal that's sure to bring him to us."

Doyle's heart sank at Daisy's calm logic and Violet's growing expression of determination. "How would you keep her safe?" he demanded.

Eleanor gaped at him, as if she couldn't believe he'd even entertain the idea.

His jaw tightened at her silent accusation. "I think you know your charge well enough to recognize the look she has in her eyes right now. Would you rather she lures the merrow with or without Daisy there to help protect her?"

Eleanor flitted forward to hover in front of Violet, purple dust filtering in a heavy stream from her agitated wings. Violet greeted her with an obstinate stare and Eleanor transferred her pleading gaze back to Doyle. "This is madness. You tell her. She'll listen to you!"

Doyle's lips twitched in a grim smile. "I've known her for less than a week, and I already know better than that."

Violet's shoulders relaxed and she leaned into Doyle's side, grateful for his understanding. "How *do* you intend to keep the bastard from drowning me?" she asked Daisy with a humorless smirk.

"Well, it would be helpful if Eleanor was there to keep us apprised of the merrow's approach," Daisy replied with a rueful glance toward the sprite. "Doyle and I would remain nearby, using a cloaking spell to help conceal our presence. Then, the moment the merrow reached Violet, we would blink to her and attempt to subdue him. I have a special binding net that's resistant to magic. It should hold him."

"And what if you don't get there in time and he pulls her under and takes off with her?" Eleanor demanded.

"I don't intend to let that happen, little sister," Daisy answered gently. "But I will provide Violet with a spell allowing her to breathe underwater for a short period of time. Long enough for us to give chase and retrieve her if the plan backfires."

"I want to do it." Violet focused her uncompromising stare on her faerie guardian. "That bastard isn't going to get away with what he did to my parents. I trust Doyle and Daisy to keep me safe. I trust you too, Eleanor," she added softly. "And I need your help."

Eleanor winced. "That's emotional blackmail."

"No it's not. It's the truth. *Please* help me do this."

Eleanor squeezed her eyes shut. "Fine," she agreed unhappily. "But I really hate this idea."

∞∞∞∞∞∞∞∞∞

Violet walked barefoot across the heated stretch of sand toward the gently foaming surf. She reflected on the surreal perfection of the scene, trying not to betray her nerves to Eleanor, who hovered at her shoulder trailing fretful clouds of faerie dust behind them.

The sun was sinking toward the horizon in a blaze of rose and carnelian. It was the perfect time for a stroll or a refreshing dip before dinner, but she had the beach to herself due to Daisy's warding spell. The water beckoned, a sleek, translucent sheet of ripples offering to envelop her body with its warmth and healing minerals.

Too bad going in meant offering herself up to a murderous fish creature intent upon drowning her. At least he didn't intend to take a bite out of her like *Jaws*, although that was a small comfort at this point. Dead was dead. She could hear the creepy two-toned theme music now.

She knew Doyle and Daisy were waiting somewhere behind her, hidden by both a cloaking spell and the undulating landscape of waving beach grasses and dunes. She glanced over her shoulder, those dunes seeming awfully far away as her toes met the first soft spill of the incoming tide. She stuck her hand in her pocket, fingering the odd, hard little capsule that Daisy had given her.

It was a perfectly round pebble of opaque sky-blue, the size of a large pea, and slick to the touch. If she was pulled under, she was to hold her breath until she could get the thing into her mouth and swallow it. Daisy said it would begin working immediately, allowing her to acclimate to any depth and breathe underwater for approximately one hour.

Violet had scoffed at Eleanor's misgivings over the logistics of getting it from her pocket to her mouth while being manhandled by a merrow. But the truth was, she thought her faerie guardian had a valid point. One she sincerely hoped wouldn't be put to the test.

It still seemed a better plan than holding it in her mouth where she might accidentally swallow it, and then being ocean bound with her parents' killer until it wore off.

Violet waded forward to where the water reached her knees, taking more exaggerated steps as it came up past her thighs, to her hips. The hum of faerie wings was an anxious counterpoint to the tranquil lap of waves against the shore. Violet's shorts and half of her shirt were soaked as she used one hand to propel herself deeper, keeping the other in her pocket to grasp the magical bead that might save her life if things went badly.

"That's far enough," Eleanor chirped in a tight, pleading voice.

Violet halted where she stood, the water buoying her up so that her bare feet were drifting above the sandy bottom. "Take it easy, Eleanor," she soothed. "Everything's going to be fine."

"How can you say that?" the faerie snapped. "This is a rash, un-thought-out plan, and I don't see why it couldn't wait until tomorrow."

"Because Daisy has a job that she needs to get back to and because the plan wasn't going to change between now and then anyway," Violet explained for the tenth time, trying to keep the aggravation from her voice. "Can you feel the merrow nearby?"

Eleanor shut her eyes. Whether it was in exasperation or to help her focus, Violet wasn't sure. "No," she replied in a clipped tone. "I don't sense any danger." She drifted forward several feet, her face pointed out toward the open ocean as she hovered there in silence.

Seconds stretched to minutes as Violet watched the placid swell of the water's surface, the fading, angled sunlight giving it a quicksilver luster that left her blind to what might be moving beneath. She felt suspended, by the water and the waiting, her tension growing into an unbearable internal vibration that felt as if it would explode out of her at any moment.

Violet felt something sharp brush her toes and let out a terrified squeak. Eleanor darted back toward her in alarm, ready to call for help. And Violet gasped, "Fish!" She gulped a relieved breath. "Just a fish nibbling my toes. It's alright. It must have gotten used to me standing here and come to investigate."

Eleanor fussed over her, her wings leaking purple dust like a sieve. "You scared the life out of me!"

Violet gave a wild little laugh, tinged with the mindless fear that had just clawed through her. "Hard to do, seeing as you're immortal," she managed.

Eleanor glared at her, obviously not amused. "I can't sense anything, Violet," she said in agitation. "And the last time you got in the water, I felt him coming for you almost immediately. Maybe he's decided to leave you alone."

"After trying to kill me twice?" Violet countered doubtfully. "Maybe he's just coming from further away this time."

"Or maybe he knows it's a trap," Eleanor suggested, her tone rife with impatience.

"But the cloaking spell," Violet argued, although her confidence in their plan was rapidly deflating. "You don't feel anything?"

"I…" Eleanor narrowed her eyes, focusing on some invisible point in her mind. "There's something, I can't quite…not the merrow, but…"

Violet let out a yelp as she was suddenly dragged beneath the water. It felt as if thin, slimy bands of iron had wrapped themselves around her ankles. She tried to kick them off, but her feet were bound together and all she could manage was a panicked thrust of her knees that did nothing to free her.

She struggled with her arms, trying desperately to drag herself back up to the surface, but it was a useless, flailing waste of energy. At once she realized two things: that she was being dragged along the bottom out into deeper water, and that her lungs were beginning to burn and she needed to get Daisy's capsule into her mouth.

She reached toward her pocket with difficulty, water rushing over her body with increasing momentum, her awkward limbs creating resistance and making it nearly impossible for her to force her hand down toward her target. She maneuvered her arm so that it was tucked tightly against her body and slid her fingers lower, along her belly, past the waistband of her shorts. They brushed the edge of her pocket and she almost sobbed with triumph, her brain's directive to breathe so imperative she knew that she wouldn't be able to override it much longer.

There was a disturbance in the flow of water just above her, and something wrapped around her wrist, trapping it in a ruthlessly tight grip. It felt like long bony fingers, encased in thin, oozing gloves. Her eyes flew open and a face floated toward hers out of the blurry, deepening gloom. A brittle, weedy mane spread out around it in a drab parody of hair. Round eyes peered at her, black as sin and rimmed in poisonous green. Slit-like nostrils flared above grotesque, rubbery lips that spread in a sneer to reveal jagged, algae-coated teeth.

Violet screamed out her remaining air, helpless to prevent the inhalation of seawater that followed.

∞∞∞∞∞∞∞∞∞

Frantic, Eleanor blinked to the location where Doyle and Daisy had agreed to wait for her signal. Praying they were nearby, but unable to see or sense them beyond Daisy's cloaking spell, she began shouting herself hoarse, her wings emitting a piercing shriek of their own. Daisy dropped the spell, and Eleanor glimpsed them both for a split second before they blinked out into the water. Daisy's face was calm, her lithe form wired and alert. Doyle's sea-green eyes were stricken with a terrible mix of fear and rage.

"Nixes!" Daisy spat the word like a curse, just as Doyle and Eleanor appeared beside her. "The merrow has hired help. Stay here, sidhe, and let me handle this. You don't want to tangle with the water pixies on their turf." She faded into a smoky outline and disappeared.

"The hell I will," Doyle ground out in fury. "Eleanor, where is she?"

"Follow me!" Eleanor gasped. She blinked toward her charge's urgent distress signal, utterly terrified as she felt it begin to weaken. She reappeared where Violet was being dragged beneath the water, helpless to do anything but dart forward above her, acting as a homing signal for her rescuers.

Doyle popped into the water several yards away, whipped his head around until he saw Eleanor, and then dived beneath the surface. Daisy beat him there, and he saw that she had transformed to suit the element she was most at home in. Her long, flippered feet propelled her forward, her webbed hands tight to the sides of her streamlined body, her hair a reddish blur flying out behind her.

He followed, unable to see much past her in the murky, darkening water, a fear like he'd never known gripping his heart. Suddenly a streak of liquid green flame came shooting out of the gloom. Daisy rolled to the side to avoid it, her swift progress barely hindered. Doyle, however, was forced to stop and push hard off the seafloor, shooting upward just as it rushed past his legs in a scalding flash of agony.

He ignored the burn and catapulted himself forward again, cursing the delay and the distance it had put between him and Violet. He could see

Daisy's outline moving through the water ahead, fainter than before, then abruptly growing brighter in a broad flash of white and silver as she flung something away from her body.

He put on a determined burst of speed when he saw that he was gaining on her, but then realized that it was only because she had stopped. She drifted cautiously downward, following the progress of an eerily glowing net. The thing bulged and strained as it sank to the bottom, as if something was trapped beneath it and struggling to get free.

Flares of green flickered against its silvery glow, sparking at its edges and weakening the net's integrity until a fiery shock of viridian blasted through it. Doyle watched in horror as the molten flames shot straight at Daisy. She calmly threw her hands up and the flames broke apart just before striking her, guttering into weak green sputters and petering out as if they'd been doused by an invisible shield. She continued her careful progress toward the damaged net.

More green fire surged through the hole, deflected again by a steadily approaching Daisy. But the gash was widening too rapidly, spreading across the net's silvery webbing like a virulent canker until it fell apart in shreds. Two nixes burst free from the wreckage of their prison, their bodies thin and scaly beneath their leering visages. They came up shooting acid flames from their webbed hands, moving to flank Daisy from either side.

Daisy dropped like a stone and whipped both her arms up to hurl two more silver-white nets at them. But they were already retreating, the nets falling short of their flipper-like feet and melting away to nothing behind them as they disappeared into the dim depths. Furious, she launched herself after her quarry. She felt more than heard Doyle's anguished cry, still yards behind her, and paused to look down.

Violet's deathly still form was tangled beneath the quickly fading remains of the torn net. With a heartfelt expletive she shot to the bottom to retrieve the human. Holding the girl in her arms, she blinked back to shore, trusting Doyle would realize what she'd done and follow.

Daisy began CPR immediately, the sprite hovering above them, making a high-pitched noise of fright as her wings dusted heavily onto Daisy's shoulder. Violet's pulse was thready, but Daisy sensed the girl's spark of awareness, and it was enough to assure her that Violet would be alright as soon as she got the water out of her lungs. Daisy muttered an incantation, adding magic to the physical action of pumping Violet's chest and breathing into her mouth.

Beneath the tang of the ocean, Violet had a light scent of sun-ripened fruit, and her lips were petal soft as Daisy placed her mouth against them. *Doyle was a lucky man*, she thought as she continued to administer a mix of human and faerie first aid. Violet's head lurched violently as she finally came to and expelled the water she had inhaled. She turned her face to the side and began coughing in rough gasping spurts.

Daisy was easing her up from her prone position, just as Doyle blinked in beside them and pulled the human woman gently into his arms. He leaned her over his shoulder, patting her back and murmuring soothing words of love in his native tongue of Gaelic. Daisy was surprised at the little shock of jealousy that zinged through her when he took over the job of providing Violet comfort.

"Are you alright?" she asked softly.

Violet nodded, her eyes wide and wet. "What the hell was that thing?" she managed on a croak.

Daisy smirked. "Ugly, wasn't he? There were two of them, and they're what we call nixes, or water pixies. Your merrow must have hired them to come after you."

Violet blinked. "Water pixies? I thought pixies were supposed to be cute, like faeries." She broke out in another coughing fit and missed the indignant look that Eleanor gave her.

Daisy gave Violet's shoulder a comforting squeeze. "Sorry we didn't get to you sooner. And I hate to cut and run like this, but the longer I wait to go after those vermin, the less chance I have of finding them."

"Did you recognize them?" Doyle asked grimly, holding Violet within the protective circle of his arms as if he never intended to let her go again.

"As a matter of fact, I did," Daisy replied with a sour smile. "They're brothers, Ligan and Lagan, a pair of particularly slippery mercenaries for hire. We've been trying to pin something on them for ages. Kidnapping, theft and political sabotage are just a few of the skills on their resume. Murder's a bit out of their league, though."

She stood and dusted off some of the sand that clung to her. "I'll check back with you by tomorrow afternoon. Right now I have nixes to hunt. And they won't slip out of my nets so easily next time." Her expression was fierce as she turned to smoke and disappeared.

Doyle felt a cooling tingle spread across his leg and looked down in surprise to find Eleanor sprinkling silver healing dust over the burns he'd received from the nix fire. "Thanks for that," he told her quietly, still rubbing Violet's back, though her coughing was subsiding.

Eleanor didn't respond, merely continuing to sprinkle dust over the burns until the angry red skin calmed and faded back to its usual shade of golden tan. Doyle grimaced, his tone wary as he asked, "Just how mad are you, little sister?"

Finished with the healing, she flitted up so that she was level with his face, her eyes bright and hard as crystals. "How mad am I that you allowed my charge to be used for bait and almost got her killed?"

Doyle winced. "You're right. Things went badly." He held Violet tighter to him. "Almost catastrophically," he murmured in a pained voice. "But I love her, Eleanor. I would do anything to keep her safe. And you know she would have gone after her parents' killer with or without our help. Without would have been much worse."

Eleanor looked away. "Things wouldn't have gone nearly as badly if I didn't have such a problem sensing magical threats," she muttered guiltily. "I would have been able to warn you and Daisy about those nixes before they grabbed Violet, and you might have caught them. If the merrow has hired mercenaries after her, she'll never be safe until we stop him."

"Would you guys stop talking about me like I'm not here?" Violet interjected, her speech rough with saltwater and irritation. She turned and pulled away from Doyle, who let her go with reluctance. "It was my decision, and I'd do it again. At least Daisy has something to go on now. If she finds those creatures...nixes," she expelled the word as if it had a bitter taste, "then she'll find out who hired them and we'll have my parents' killer.

"It's nobody's fault that things went the way they did today. So can we just stop talking about it? I want to get out of these wet clothes."

"Are you sure you're alright?" Eleanor asked worriedly.

"As alright as I can be while wet and pissed off," she mumbled. "Can we go now?"

Doyle and Eleanor shared a helpless look. "Well, the warding spell is still in effect. How about if I break the rules this once and blink us home, *a thaisce*? Then you can take a hot shower while I go see to Bruno and come back with some takeout. I don't know about you, but I think a nice quiet evening at home might go a long way toward calming everyone's nerves."

Violet's face split into a crooked grin. "That's the best plan I've heard all day." She turned to Eleanor. "Will you join us? We could get you that fruit salad again."

Her small chest heaved in a resigned sigh. "No, I'm sure you two would like some time alone, and I need to get back to my family. But if anything else happens, just call my name, or concentrate on it in your mind, and I'll hear you, okay?"

Violet gaped at her. "And I'm just now finding this out?"

Eleanor rolled her eyes.

Violet grinned. "Will do. And Eleanor," she added just before the faerie blinked out, "it wasn't your fault."

Eleanor sent her a grateful, if troubled, smile as she disappeared.

"Hold on tight, *a thaisce*," Doyle murmured as he pulled Violet back into his arms. "Traveling this way can be a bit uncomfortable if you're not used to it." He chuckled at her apprehensive look. "But don't worry. I have a way to distract you."

"What's that?" she asked warily.

"This," he whispered, brushing her lips with his. Her eyelids fluttered shut and she held him tighter as she felt a thrilling roller coaster drop in the pit of her stomach. When she opened her eyes, they were standing in the living room of her parents' villa.

She couldn't tell if the feeling in her stomach had been from his kiss or the magical travel. So she kissed him again, just to be sure.

∞∞∞∞∞∞∞∞∞∞

"I thought I told you not to come back here without the girl," Hagar said in a dangerous tone.

He regarded the nixes imperiously from his throne-like chair in the chamber he used for spell casting. Fashioned from stone shot through with veins of gold, the chair's tall, carved seat gave him the advantage of height over his guests. Intimidating sets of shackles were bolted into the rock walls lining the chamber, and the stone altar at the opposite end of the room was stocked with the more subtle threat of his magical implements.

"I'm afraid our deal requires renegotiation," hissed Ligan as he nursed the burns on his webbed hands that he'd received while trying to burst his way through the Marid's net.

Lagan shot him a quelling glance and drifted forward over the pebble-scattered cavern floor to address the furious merrow. "What my brother means is that there are certain critical details about this job which were not disclosed to us. Details which make the completion of the task considerably more difficult."

Hagar narrowed his eyes in agitation and pulled at his bristly orange beard. *A beard which hid the weak chin of a bully*, Lagan thought, not for the first time since meeting the merrow.

"If you slimy nixes think you can wheedle a higher price out of me than what we originally negotiated, I'll take my business elsewhere."

"Fine with me," Ligan grumbled under his gills, earning another cutting look from his brother. He bared his algae-coated teeth in a sneer, but kept his mouth shut. He would have liked nothing better than to leave this Triton-forsaken ocean and forget about the scurvy merrow and his hassle-ridden job. But Lagan was convinced that if they played their cards right, they'd end up coming out on the rich side of the deal.

Lagan's rubbery lips bent up in a parody of a polite smile. "We both know that you won't find anyone to do the job for less than the paltry price you've offered us. And even if you did, you'd never find anyone capable of grabbing the girl out from under the nose of a Seelie Police officer for that price."

Hagar's eyes widened in shock, flickering greenish-blue in the dim luminescence from the conch shell lanterns lining the walls of the cavern. "What the devil are you talking about?"

So he didn't know about the Seelie's involvement, Lagan thought with satisfaction. "I'm talking about the fact that you had us swimming right into a trap, Hagar. We tracked the girl into the water today, pleased that there was no sign of the sidhe warrior who foiled our attempt at the docks. We sent out feelers to see if he was nearby before approaching her, and found no trace of anyone but her and a harmless sprite.

"Imagine our surprise when, as soon as we grabbed her, we had a Marid djinn hot on our flippers. We barely escaped from her nets, and had to leave the girl behind. I recognized that Marid, Hagar, and she's with the Seelie Police. You told us that neither the girl nor the sidhe had any idea you were after her. You certainly never warned us that the Seelie Police might be involved, lying in wait behind a cloaking spell.

"I'm sure you can see how this changes the rules of the game, makes things more difficult, even calls for a bit more hazard pay." Lagan held out his palms, which had been burned worse than his brother's, displaying the ugly flaking black of the webbed skin and the raw oozing green beneath. "Have you ever had to blast your way out of a Marid net before, Hagar?" he asked quietly, flexing his hands for effect and watching the merrow wince and look away.

"This job is not turning out to be as simple as you promised. Don't get me wrong, we'll still get you the girl. But we want triple the fee."

"Triple!" roared Hagar, propelling himself upward to tower menacingly above the scaly little swindler.

The infuriating creature merely raised its scraggly grey head and stared up at him with its soulless green-rimmed eyes. "Triple."

Hagar gnashed his teeth and lowered himself back onto his throne, brushing his fingers over the cowrie shell at his throat in an effort to calm himself. It wasn't working. "I want that girl brought to me so I can make sure she's finished. I'll pay you your...*triple*," he thrust the word from his tongue as if it disgusted him, "but you just make sure you aren't caught. If the Seelies come sniffing around my grotto, so help me Triton, I'll have both your miserable hides."

"Agreed," Lagan spouted crisply, offering his wounded hand to seal the bargain.

Hagar grimaced at the oozing appendage in disgust, ignoring the other nix's surly reply of, "You could try, but we'd have your miserable tail for fin-covers first."

Hagar didn't see the point in antagonizing the creature while he still had a use for it. He had no intention of tripling the fee. Now that the Seelies were involved, he couldn't chance leaving the nixes with the knowledge of what he'd done. It had been a mistake to hire them. Thefts and kidnappings were one thing; murder was quite another, even if it was only a human.

And they definitely seemed the types who wouldn't be above blackmailing him over it.

<u>Chapter Thirteen</u>

As she drifted on the edge of sleep in Doyle's arms, Violet mused that the day hadn't ended up so badly after all. Sure, she'd almost drowned for the second time that week, but it had been worth it to get another step closer to catching her parents' killer. And she was grateful to have Daisy on their side. The other woman had been amazing. She'd blinked in, assessed the situation, made a plan and executed it.

She was tough and in charge. But there was also a graceful beauty to the casual ease with which she did her job. And her magic was amazing. The pale blue oxygen pebble that Violet had never gotten the chance to swallow had appeared out of thin air in Daisy's hand with only a few words. And it had been eerie to watch her and Doyle disappear behind the cloaking spell, knowing they were right there, but no longer being able to see or hear them.

Earlier that evening, as they sat at the mosaic table in the kitchen nook eating takeout from Styrofoam boxes, Violet had asked Doyle how he knew Daisy. He told her about a prank that his best friend, Pat, had pulled years ago. When he first made detective on the Seelie Police Force, he persuaded Daisy to arrest Doyle on a bogus charge. And she'd played the part well, convincing Doyle for a full hour that he was accused of smuggling danger-ous magical artifacts into the human realm.

When Violet made an innuendo about Daisy having him in handcuffs, Doyle assuaged the last remnants of her jealousy with his pronouncement that Daisy would have likely much rather had *her* in them, since Daisy wasn't into men.

But that did nothing to quiet the other nagging doubt that had begun to plague Violet's mind. Doyle was immortal and she wasn't. How were things ever going to work out between them? She didn't want to ruin their time together by fretting over an uncertain future. But she was getting herself in deeper with him every day. Every time he made her laugh; every time he smiled into her eyes and brushed his lips over hers; every time he sank inside her body and whispered soft words of love.

School started in a few weeks, and she would have to return to her apart-ment and her own life. They would be separated by a two hour drive, and a magic that he wasn't supposed to use, even though it could bring them closer. She wasn't sure if it was fair to either of them to pursue a relation-ship together, but the thought of letting him go was a dull ache pressing against her heart.

Violet sighed and snuggled closer to him, taking comfort from his warmth and trying to shut out her fears. She was floating into the realm of dreams when something tugged her back to consciousness. Her sleepy eyes blinked open and she looked around her parents' bedroom. The streetlight across the way faintly limned the closed blinds with its glow, the room dim and silent but for the slow whirl of the fan and Doyle's breath gently stirring her hair.

Her eyelids drooped shut once more, but a strange rustling sound made her frown and open them again. It had likely come from some night-owl neighbor, or an animal prowling around the garden. But Violet couldn't quell the thought that it had sounded more like it was coming from somewhere inside the villa. She held her breath and listened.

There it was again. This time accompanied by a louder sort of shuffling clink, followed by a complete hush, as if someone had gone deliberately still after making an unintentional noise. Wide awake now, Violet's muscles stiffened with growing apprehension. The next sound, like something heavy being lowered to the ground with a muffled thump, left her frozen with a terrible certainty that there was someone other than Doyle and she inside her parents' home.

She gave Doyle an urgent shake, wishing they had Bruno with them. The huge wolfhound probably would have scared the intruder off by now. Doyle tightened his arm around her and nuzzled her with his chin. "Ready again, *a thaisce*?" he mumbled drowsily.

"There's someone in the house," she whispered, her voice thin with fright.

Doyle tensed, coming instantly awake and reaching with all of his senses into the straining silence. There was a quiet scraping sound, and he knew without a doubt that someone was in Violet's garage. "Wait here. Lock the door behind me." He leapt noiselessly from the bed and pulled on a pair of shorts before stalking from the room.

"Screw that," Violet hissed indignantly, "I'm not staying here alone."

He sent an irritated glance over his shoulder as she appeared mutely behind him in her hurriedly donned robe, a heavy pewter candle holder from her parents' dresser gripped tightly in her fist. She stood her ground and waved him forward, forcing him to resign himself to her refusal to stay behind.

They crept barefoot across the cool wooden floor, the soft scuffing noises growing louder with each step they took toward the garage. When they reached the door, Violet stood rigid and ready at Doyle's back, waiting for him to yank it open so they could surprise the intruder. But to her shock, he simply disappeared.

Cursing silently, nerves stretched to the breaking point, she lifted her hand to the knob. She heard a clatter and a stifled scream, and rushed through the door with her makeshift weapon held high, ready to defend Doyle. Two figures struggled in the darkness on the far side of the woody wagon. Faint shadows writhed against the wall, illuminated by an indistinct light shining from below, as if from a dropped flashlight.

Violet flicked on the overhead light, squinting against the sudden brightness, and charged toward them to find that Doyle had already subdued the other, much slighter, figure. The prowler wore jeans, a t-shirt and a knit cap, all in black, but the cap had fallen askew during the tussle to reveal a tangled spill of red-golden curls. When Violet moved closer to look into the intruder's face, she gasped as Melody's panic-stricken eyes stared back at her. Those eyes quickly filled with tears as the other woman sagged, defeated, in Doyle's grasp.

"I'm so sorry, Violet," she cried. "It's all my fault."

Violet exchanged a bewildered look with Doyle and stepped forward to hesitantly place her hand on Melody's shoulder. "What's all your fault, Melody? And why on earth are you sneaking around my garage at four in the morning?"

"I gave it to them so I could get away from him," she sobbed. "You must believe I had no idea he would do this. I have to go back to him now. It's the only way he'll stop." Melody wept as if her heart was breaking, her speech becoming incoherent and her slim body shuddering against Doyle's firm grip.

"Let her go," Violet told him quietly.

He reluctantly released Melody into Violet's arms, keeping a wary eye on the other woman as Violet led her inside to sit on the couch.

"Could you get her some water?" Violet requested in a soft tone, her arms wrapped around Melody's trembling form. Her cap had fallen off and Violet reached up to smooth the tangles from her hair, murmuring soothing words of comfort as she waited for Melody's hysteria to subside.

Doyle returned with three bottles of cold water, setting two of them on the tiled coffee table in front of Violet without comment. She opened one and grabbed some Kleenex from the side table by the lamp, offering both to Melody, who gave a soggy sniff and accepted them with shaking hands.

"You wouldn't be so nice to me if you knew what I'd done," she whimpered.

"Nonsense," Violet replied. "I'm sure there's a perfectly good explanation for you breaking into my parents' garage in the middle of the night, as well as for any other crimes you may have seen fit to commit lately."

Melody raised her tear-filled eyes to Violet's and said in a stricken voice, "It's my fault your parents were killed."

Violet jerked as if she'd been struck. "What?" she asked tonelessly.

Melody took a shuddering breath. "Your parents, they were such kind people. I never meant for them to be harmed. But they helped me, and it got them killed." She squared her shoulders and made a determined effort to stifle another sob. "Before Manny," she began with a glance at Doyle, "I was involved with another man." She faltered as if unsure how to continue.

"The stalker," Violet replied, remembering their conversation the day Melody came over for coffee.

Melody nodded, her expression turning hollow, as if she was distancing herself from the memory. "We were together for two years. He seemed so strong and charming at first, so determined for us to be together. I thought he loved me; that he'd take care of me. And things went well between us for a while. But then the petty jealousies started cropping up, the mean little comments and accusations. It got to the point where he didn't want me to spend time with anyone but him.

"I suppose I should have seen it coming, but the first time he hit me it came as such a shock that I believed him when he said he'd never do it again." She squeezed her eyes shut, her voice going hoarse as she continued. "After the third time, and a trip to the healer to mend a broken arm, I knew I had to get away from him."

"Oh, Melody," Violet breathed in sympathy.

"Does Manny know about this?" Doyle asked, his speech strained.

Violet looked up to find his jaw clenched in barely controlled anger. She could relate. She'd like to have a half hour alone in a room with a pewter candlestick and the coward who had beaten up Melody herself. During her tenure as a teacher, she'd seen wives terrified of their husbands, and children terrified of their parents, and it always burned her up with helpless fury.

Melody's eyes flew wide and she shook her head frantically at Doyle. "No. Manny cannot know. You must promise me you won't tell him. He would try to protect me and it would only get him killed." She released another shuddering sob and turned back to Violet in anguish. "Your parents helped me get away from Hagar the first time, and they ended up dead. He has threatened to come after both you and Manny if I don't return to him."

Violet looked hard at the anxious redhead. "I have a pretty good idea how my parents were killed, Melody. What I don't understand is how it could possibly have had anything to do with you. You said before, in the garage, that you gave them something so you could get away from him. What exactly did you mean by that?"

Melody looked down at her lap and didn't answer.

"Were you the one who gave my parents that nautical chart?" Violet asked, watching the other woman for a reaction.

Melody's head snapped back up in shock. "How did you…?"

"We found a recording my parents made before they died," Violet replied quietly. "My father spoke of discovering a race of underwater creatures called merrows. He spoke of a map that would reveal one of their underwater cities. We suspect that one of the merrows killed them for what they knew." She paused and frowned.

"Did you sell them that chart? They made a large cash withdrawal not long before they died and I've been wondering what it was for. But they were killed at sea. What does this have to do with your stalker ex-boy-friend?"

Melody dropped her face into her hands. "I didn't sell them the chart. I let them borrow it in gratitude for their kindness. I knew I shouldn't have given it to them, but they were so excited about seeing one of our cities, and I thought it would be alright just once, if they were careful." Her voice broke. "They made me take the money because I didn't have anywhere to go, and no way to feed or clothe myself."

Her eyes rose pleadingly to Violet's. "Your parents saw me out on the reef one day. They believed, and they saw me. And I was so desperate to get away from Hagar, that I gave them my favorite red cap. I gave it to them so I could leave the sea, so he wouldn't ever find me again."

Violet transferred her confused gaze to Doyle, who was staring at Melody in sudden comprehension. "The legend's true," he murmured in astonishment. "You were trying to take it back so you could resume your form and return to the sea."

"What legend?" Violet asked.

"There's an old sailors' legend," Doyle explained, his brogue husky with disbelief. "It says that if a human takes a favored personal item from a mermaid, she will take human form until the item is returned to her. And if the item is destroyed, she will remain human forever." He looked sharply at Melody. "It's still here, packed away in one of the boxes in the garage, isn't it?"

Melody nodded miserably. "I couldn't bring myself to ask Violet's parents to destroy it. They promised to keep it safe for me." She swiped at a fresh tear. "But then they had their accident. I assumed the chart was lost to the sea, but I knew my cap must still be hidden somewhere in their house. I wasn't sure what to do, so I just watched and waited for someone to come.

"And then I met Manny," she said with a hitch of emotion, "and I knew that if I could stay with him, I would be happy remaining human. I thought of destroying the cap, but still I waited.

"When Violet showed up and spoke of her mother's hat collection, I was sure that was where it would be. Hidden in plain sight among all of Vicki's other caps. But Violet had already packed them up by then. She promised to let me look through them before giving them away, so I decided to be patient just a little while longer.

"But tonight I was walking by the docks, on my way to meet Manny for dinner, and Hagar called out to me from the water. I wanted to ignore him, but he was in a rage, and began shouting about what he'd done to Violet's parents. He said he knew I was being unfaithful to him. He threatened to kill both Manny and Violet if I didn't come back to him."

Her eyes were haunted as she looked from Violet to Doyle. "He's been spying on me. He must have taken some of the things I left behind and used them to cast a shadowing spell. I tried to tell him the cap had already been destroyed, but he knew better. He said he knew I was looking for it. He suspected I thought Violet had it. He's given me until sunset tomorrow to reclaim it and return to him.

"And I must do it. I won't bring death to anyone else who's been kind to me," she gazed at Violet with regret etched deeply into her features. "Or anyone I've come to love," she added softly. There was such pain in her voice that Violet knew she grieved not only for Vicki and George Hendrickson, but at the thought of losing the love she'd found with Manny.

Violet wrapped her in a fierce hug. "Melody, you listen to me. I'll destroy every hat in this house before I even think about letting you go back to that monster."

Melody stiffened. "You don't understand the kind of man he is, Violet. He'll stop at nothing until he gets what he wants."

Violet drew back, still grasping Melody's thin shoulders in her hands. "You don't think I understand? He killed my parents. I don't blame you," she added at Melody's wince, giving her a gentle shake. "But we do know what we're up against with this asshole. He's tried to kill me at least twice. Did you know he hired mercenaries, a couple of nixes, to finish me off?"

Melody's mouth went slack in horror. "I should have known. That day you told me you had almost drowned," she said hollowly. "My foolishness has cost the lives of your parents, and now it has nearly cost you yours."

"No, Melody," Violet ground out. "Hagar's viciousness has been the cause of all of this. And he needs to be stopped. So before you throw your life away by going back to him, just take a moment and think about whether you really trust him to call his assassins off once he has you back.

"You must know, deep down, that one of these days he'll end up killing you too. That's why you left in the first place. And with his possessive streak, do you honestly believe he won't go after Manny in a fit of jealous rage? I'm surprised he hasn't already."

"Manny isn't a big beachgoer," Doyle commented. "The only time he's probably ever in the water is on our tours, and he sticks pretty close to the customers."

"And it's obviously served him well so far, but how long do you think he'll last if Hagar is really determined? Apparently I've been his top priority because of what my parents knew and how they died, not to mention Melody's cap being right under my nose the whole time. Once he has me out of the way, though, do you truly think he'll leave Manny alone?"

"Stop, please," Melody cried softly.

Violet turned back to Melody, her expression compassionate but firm. "I'm sorry, sweetie. I can't imagine how hard this must be for you. But you have to realize that going back to that bastard isn't going to accomplish anything except for getting you killed.

"Doyle has a friend with the Seelie Police Department, and we already have one of their water djinns going after the nixes Hagar hired. When she checks back with us tomorrow, we can tell her who's behind this. If she hasn't found out by then on her own," Violet added.

Melody gave Doyle a surprised look. "*You* have a friend with the Seelie Police?"

"I'm sidhe," he explained. "And I didn't sense that you weren't human either," he said with a frown, "although now that I'm looking for it, there is a faint aura about you."

"The only thing holding me back from being fully human is the existence of my cap," she replied in a quiet tone. "My merrow senses are almost completely dampened, and it's not surprising that your senses would be fooled. Although now that I think about it, your sister may have guessed when we met."

Violet's eyes widened. "Melody *was* the only 'human' that Scarlett seemed not to have a problem with the other day," she mused aloud to Doyle. She couldn't help feeling redeemed by the thought that Scarlett might have only liked Melody because she wasn't human.

"But speaking of people knowing your secrets," Violet gave Melody a searching look, "you do realize you're going to have to tell Manny about all this, right?"

Melody's expression was an agonizing mix of guilt, fear and sadness. "I had thought to destroy the cap and become fully human without him ever being the wiser. What if I tell him and he no longer wants to be with me? What if what I am disgusts him? Surely he'll be angry that I have lied to him these past weeks..." she trailed off wretchedly.

Before Violet could form an answer, Doyle rose and moved to sit on Melody's other side. He took her hand in his and said, "I know you're afraid of losing him, but he deserves to know the truth. And Manny loves you, Melody. He may find this all a bit strange, but have some faith in what he feels for you. You can't leave this secret looming between you. You have to allow him to accept you for everything you are." His gaze rested on Violet, his heart in his eyes as he spoke.

Violet smiled at him as she added, "He may even think it's one of the coolest things that's ever happened to him, and decide he loves you more because of it. Once he gets over the shock."

"I hope you're right." The look Melody gave them both was still painfully uncertain. "But I must make sure that Hagar is out of our lives first. What am I to do? He expects me back by sunset with the cap. And I don't like to think of what will happen if I'm not."

"I think we should take a page out of Daisy's book—she's the water djinn from the Seelie Police," Violet told Melody. "We should be proactive and make a plan to trap him while we know where he's going to be."

"Daisy should be here for this discussion," Doyle interrupted, worried by the determined gleam in Violet's eyes.

"You're right," Violet agreed, to his momentary relief, "but it doesn't hurt to have an idea of what we should do ahead of time. After all, we don't know what time she'll get back to us tomorrow. Or today, rather," she corrected with a grimace at the clock. "Don't you think we should start coming up with a plan sooner rather than later?"

Doyle's stomach knotted at the thought of Violet being involved in another dangerous scheme, but he knew she'd be thinking about it whether they discussed it or not. "Alright," he sighed. "Theoretically only, let's hash it out. Where are you supposed to meet Hagar, Melody?"

"He told me to meet him back at the docks at sunset with my cap," she answered nervously.

"And did he tell you to bring anything else? Was he going to give you any sort of guarantee that he'd leave Violet and Manny alone after you went with him?" Doyle asked.

Melody looked embarrassed. "No," she admitted. "I'm just supposed to show up with the cap."

Violet patted her arm consolingly.

"I suppose the next step would be to make sure we actually have the cap," Doyle said. "What does it look like?"

"It's a red beret made out of a shiny kind of plastic," Melody replied. She straightened, as if the thought of having it again sent a zip of excitement up her spine.

Violet let out a startled breath. "I saw two of those, almost exactly alike, when I was packing up my mom's collection."

"Vicki told me she had one just like it," Melody said sadly.

Violet stared at her, the realization that Melody had probably been one of the last people to see her mom alive washing over her. She cleared her throat and jumped up to diffuse the awkward pall. "Well, let's go find it, then." She headed toward the garage, relieved when Melody and Doyle followed without further comment.

Melody had nearly completed the job of uncovering the hat boxes herself during her stint as a cat burglar, and Doyle made quick work of pulling them the rest of the way out. She zeroed in on the correct box immediately, as if the cap's presence drew her. When Doyle unsealed it, a flash of shiny red was visible just beneath a stack of baseball caps and a black pillbox hat with a lacy veil.

Melody pulled the beret out with slow reverence, running her tapered fingers over it gently, like it was an old friend. Her eyes glowed as she placed it on her head, the shiny red a smart contrast to her black outfit.

"So how does the magic work, exactly?" Doyle asked in interest.

"Now that the cap has been returned to me, as soon as I step foot in the ocean, I will return to merrow form."

"And will it work both ways, now that you've been human?" he prodded. "Would you be able to return to human form by leaving the ocean?"

Melody smiled sadly. "No. Once back in merrow form, another human would have to possess the cap for me to become human again."

Doyle gave a thoughtful nod and glanced down at Violet, still rummaging through the hat box. She pulled out a second red vinyl beret that looked remarkably like the one Melody wore.

"I wonder if we might be able to use this one as a decoy." That crafty little smile was back on her face, pulling Doyle's stomach into a tighter knot. "You know, keep Melody away from the water, but use this to lure him close enough to capture him. Does Hagar wear a cap? Maybe we can snatch it from his head and force him onto our turf this time."

"There was a shell he always wore around his neck," Melody began.

"Whoa," interrupted Doyle. "I completely agree that Melody should stay away from the water, and so should you, Violet. I'm sure that Daisy is perfectly capable of apprehending Hagar on her own. And if not, she can call for Seelie backup. We just need to tell her what we know and let her do her job."

Violet reached up to plant a kiss of reassurance on his mouth. "I know, baby. We're just being theoretical. Of course we'll let Daisy handle it. But it's good to know your enemy's weaknesses," she added with an impudent grin.

Doyle pulled her against him, the thought of losing her like a branding iron searing his soul. He looked beyond the silken top of her head to the panes of glass set high across the garage door. A faint grey light heralded the dawn, and he cursed silently, wishing he and Manny didn't have tours already planned for the day.

He had a sudden, very strong desire to spend the next twelve hours in bed with Violet, making her forget her plots for revenge and remember only him.

Chapter Fourteen

None of them bothered going back to sleep. Doyle drove home to take care of Bruno, grabbed some cooking supplies, and returned to make them all breakfast before leaving for work.

Violet tried calling Eleanor just by thinking about her and saying her name, and was surprised to find that it actually worked. After rehashing the night's events, the two of them finally persuaded Melody to go home and get some rest. They made her swear not to go near the water alone, and promised in return that Eleanor would blink over and tell her as soon as they heard from Daisy.

But neither they nor Doyle heard anything from the djinn all day.

Sunset was approaching fast, and Violet paced her parents' living room, growing more and more agitated with each step. "I don't know how you can just sit there so calmly," she burst out.

Eleanor looked up from her perch on the edge of the coffee table and tucked away the miniscule book she'd been reading so that it disappeared inside her color-shifting dress. "There's no sense in working yourself up like this. Daisy will arrest Hagar one way or another. It doesn't have to be tonight."

Violet blinked at her in frustrated disbelief. "We have no idea where Daisy is! She was supposed to get back to us this afternoon. What if something happened to her?"

"It's still afternoon," Eleanor pointed out, but she looked uncomfortable as she said it.

"The sun goes down in an hour! And with Daisy going after his nixes, it can't be long before Hagar knows the Seelie Police are on to him. He's not going to just stick around, waiting to be arrested. Our best chance of catching the bastard is now. I guarantee he won't give up the possibility of getting Melody back. He's obsessed with her!"

Violet jumped as Doyle appeared in the middle of her living room. "What the...?" she began in confusion.

"Sorry," he said quickly, "but I don't have much time. I'm supposed to be in the head and it won't be long before someone realizes I'm gone. I came to tell you that we're running late because the *Ocean Magic*'s engine died on us. The marine towing service is on the way, but Manny and I have a boat full of tourists to keep calm and I have to get back."

He gave Violet a quick peck on the lips and she clutched his shoulders, her mind whirling with panic. "But what about Daisy, and Melody's meeting with Hagar at sunset?"

He gave her an apologetic look. "I still haven't heard from Daisy, so I'm afraid we're going to have to postpone tonight's plan."

Violet's eyes widened. "But we have no idea what Hagar will do if Melody doesn't show up!"

"It will be okay, *a thaisce*," Doyle promised softly. "If Hagar waited this long to get Melody back, I'm sure he'll wait a little longer. We'll bring him to justice. We just have to be patient." He nodded at Eleanor. "Please let Melody know what's going on. I have to get back." He brushed his lips against Violet's forehead and was gone.

Violet stood there for a moment, blinking in disbelief, and then her gaze flew to Eleanor. "This is bad. Hagar is going to flip out when Melody blows him off. And Doyle, Manny, and all those people are stuck out there in the middle of the ocean!"

"Doyle can take care of himself," Eleanor soothed. "And he said the towing service was on the way."

"Doyle may be able to take care of himself, but he's alone on that boat with a bunch of humans who can't," Violet argued. "And for all we know, Hagar or his nixes sabotaged their engine and he's just waiting to make good on his threat to kill Manny if Melody doesn't show."

Eleanor's wings buzzed in alarm, but she took a deep breath and forced them to a stop. "I know it's hard, but try not to let your imagination run away with you. Don't human engines break down all the time?"

"But today, of all days? Doesn't that seem a little too convenient to you?" Violet barely resisted the urge to stomp her foot in frustration.

"He had no problem sinking my parents' boat," she added. "What do you think will happen to all of those people if he decides to go after Manny?"

Eleanor flitted over to hover directly in front of her charge, her expression sympathetic. "You're human too, Violet. And you're in just as much danger as they are. Doyle can handle a merrow, if it comes to that."

"Do you think he can handle a merrow *and* two nixes?" she asked, swiping angrily at a tear.

Eleanor sighed. "I have to let Melody know what's going on before it gets any later. Stay here. I'll be right back."

"I can't stand this waiting, Eleanor," Violet replied with a mutinous expression. "I need some fresh air."

Eleanor zipped into Violet's path as she stalked toward the door, her tilted eyes narrowing in suspicion. "Violet Marie Hendrickson," she warned, "don't you lie to me. You're planning on going down to those docks to meet Hagar. And just what do you expect to do, pull him from the water and take him down yourself? If you get anywhere near him, he'll pull you in and drown you in a heartbeat."

Violet stared at her faerie guardian, hovering there with purple dust streaming from wings vibrating rapidly enough to emit a high-pitched whine. And she knew Eleanor was right. But she couldn't let her parents' killer get away without facing him at least once.

"I'm just going to stall him long enough for Doyle and Manny to get the boat back to the docks. I'll stay out of his reach."

She stepped around Eleanor and pulled the extra beret from where she had folded it into her shorts pocket, her fingers brushing the slickness of the small, hard pebble beneath it. Smoothing out the vinyl cap, she placed it on her head and opened the door.

"I'll tell Melody what you're doing," Eleanor threatened desperately.

Violet gave her a somber half smile and proceeded down the cobblestone path toward the picketed fence. "No you won't. Because you know she'll just offer herself to Hagar in my place."

"Blast it, Violet! *You're* my charge, not Melody!" Eleanor yelled.

"It wouldn't do any good. I'd just follow her, and then he'd have us both."

Eleanor goggled at her, realizing with a sinking heart that, short of having Doyle there to physically restrain her, Violet wasn't going to be dissuaded.

"Stubborn human!" the faerie swore bitterly as she blinked out.

∞∞∞∞∞∞∞∞∞

Doyle watched Manny joking with the passengers and tipping more rum into their cups of soda. It was a good thing they always kept a few emergency bottles stashed on board. He transferred his troubled gaze back toward shore, scanning for the Sea Tow boat as a cooling breeze picked up and ruffled his hair.

He'd intended to keep the schedule tight on this last tour so he could get back to Violet. But a pod of dolphins swam by just as he was calling the snorkelers in, and they'd lingered in the water ooh-ing and ah-ing. When he'd finally gotten everyone on board, the damn boat had refused to start. It was the devil's own fickle timing, and he had to wonder if there wasn't something else at work against him.

At least the passengers weren't complaining. The dolphin sighting, along with Manny's charm and generosity with their secret stash of rum, had the lot of them grinning ear to ear despite being stranded. He wished he could join in their ease. But something wasn't right.

Daisy had contacted neither him nor Pat since yesterday. Pat insisted the djinn could take care of herself and didn't sound worried that she hadn't checked in. And though he agreed it would be a shame if she wasn't back to arrest Hagar at sunset, he couldn't spare any of his other agents from his current death djinn investigation to help.

But the dread that had been slowly seeping into Doyle's veins over the past few hours wasn't only due to Daisy's continuing absence. There was a storm coming. Doyle could feel it in his bones, though the skies were clear. And he wanted more than anything to get back to Violet before it broke.

Eleanor materialized at the railing several yards away and motioned for him to come closer. Up until he'd blinked in to tell them about the engine, she'd been appearing all afternoon with increasingly frustrated messages from Violet. Now the sun was sinking toward the horizon in a blazing ball of tangerine, and no doubt the sprite was here one last time to ask if he'd heard anything from Daisy.

Doyle sighed and glanced at the jubilant group of passengers gathered at the stern of the ship before slipping around toward the bow to deal with Eleanor.

"Violet's going to meet with Hagar." She spoke as soon as he was near enough to hear, her expression stony with suppressed anger and fear.

"What?" he hissed. "Why didn't you stop her?"

"With what?" she asked in a biting tone. "My superior size and strength? I warned her. That's all I can do. I can't interfere in free will, even if it is to stop my troll-brained charge from getting herself killed. Keeping her out of the water was supposed to be your job!"

He cursed in two languages. "I can't just disappear from here, Eleanor. There are eleven people on the other side of this boat who know there's nowhere for me to go!"

"Well, you'd better think of something fast, then, hadn't you?" she said grimly, and disappeared.

He muttered a few more choice words as he stood staring after her, and then he went to get Manny.

Doyle tried to smile as he interrupted the passengers' raucous laughter over a particularly bawdy joke. "I wonder if I might borrow my first mate from you ladies and gentlemen for a moment."

"I believe you've made a mistake, sir, my husband's no gentleman!" interjected a giddy, sun-burnt young woman with brown hair and sparkling eyes. The comment brought a renewed bout of hilarity from the others, and Doyle worked hard to expel a weak chuckle as he pulled Manny away from them.

"What up, *hermano*, you looking a little green around the gills. You been hitting that last bottle of rum alone?" Manny frowned worriedly as Doyle continued to pull him toward the bow until they were out of the passengers' sight.

Doyle's eyes flickered anxiously to the darkening sky and back to his friend. "Manny, we've been friends and partners for ten years. I'd trust you with my life, brother, but there's something about me that I've never told you."

Manny crossed his sun-browned arms over his chest and gave Doyle a cautious look as he waited for him to continue.

Doyle released an apprehensive breath. "This is going to sound completely crazy. But just do me a favor and hear me out. Violet's in trouble and I have to get to her. I'm going to go into the head, lock the door, make it sound like I'm getting sick, and then I'm going to disappear. I want you to tell the passengers that I ate some bad oysters for lunch and I just need to be left alone. I'll explain everything later. Will you do it for me?" He stared pleadingly at Manny, willing him to understand.

The Costa Rican lifted his dark brows, a grin teasing his rounded cheeks. "You messing with me, *hermano*?"

Doyle's tormented gaze took in the swift progress of the setting sun. "I'm sorry brother. I don't have time to explain things now. Don't freak out on me. Just watch." He locked eyes with Manny, blinked out for a few seconds, and then reappeared where he'd stood.

Manny was gripping the railing and his tan had gone a few shades lighter, like coffee that had been diluted with cream.

"It's me, man," Doyle implored. "You know me. And if I don't go now, Violet might die. I love her, Manny. I wouldn't have chosen to spring the disappearing act on you like this, but I have no choice. I have to go, *now*, and I need your help."

Confusion swirled in Manny's eyes, but he nodded.

Doyle sent him one last desperate look and sprinted for the head with a thickly muttered, "I think I'm going to be sick."

Manny stared after him in disbelief. "*Dios mio*. I always knew there was something different about that crazy Irishman," he mumbled to himself.

∞∞∞∞∞∞∞∞∞∞

The sun's rounded edges wavered with heat as they burned through the clouds, its lower rim nearly touching the sea. Violet glanced around cautiously as she approached the docks. A streetlamp flickered to life with a sulfuric buzz nearby, in preparation for the coming darkness. She could hear the sound of laughter from the deck of the crab shack across the adjacent parking lot. But the wharf was deserted.

She tried not to look at *Ocean Magic*'s empty slip as she stepped onto the ramp of timbers that leveled out into the wide stretch of dock. The boat's absence was a hole inside her chest, a breeding ground for fear. And the red beret perched atop her head was beginning to feel like some sort of malevolent beacon.

She stood as close to the center of the planks as she could, her eyes darting between the spans of inky water to either side, feeling terrifyingly exposed. She wondered if this was what agoraphobics felt like when they stepped outside. This almost paralyzing urge to flatten herself against the solidity of the ground beneath her and crawl back to a place where she felt more sheltered.

She stiffened her spine and forced herself to walk out further over the water, nearly stumbling when a voice rang out behind her.

"Melody? I didn't feel your approach."

Violet turned slowly and looked down to her left to find a shaggy-haired man with a bristly, orange beard treading water alongside the dock. His eyes were a Caribbean blue, just like Melody's, but held a harshness that would have appeared alien on the other woman's face. His expression went blank with shock for a moment, and then rapidly molded into a sneer.

"You. What are you doing here, *human*?" he spat. "Where is my Melody and why do you wear her cap?"

Violet felt the first stirrings of anger begin to override her fear. "Melody doesn't belong to you, and she never will, *Hagar*." She suffused his name with as much disdain as he had the word *human*. "As a matter of fact, she can't wait to sever her last tie with you. So I just came to let you know that I'll be destroying this cap personally. Do you think you'll still be able to spy on her like a lowlife stalker once she's fully human?"

Hagar bared his teeth in outrage and the water stirred into a livid boil around him, buoying him up higher to reveal a bare chest, lightly furred with golden-orange hair. "You dare speak to me this way? I'll watch you struggle for the final breath you will never take, your weak human eyes exploding from the pressure of the depths as I feed your still warm flesh to the eels!"

"Empty threats and ugly words from an ugly excuse for a man," Violet taunted recklessly. For nestled at his throat she had spied a small cowrie shell threaded onto a piece of twine. And she thought that if she could only draw him close enough to snatch it away, she would have him. "You're a coward who beats up women because you can't hold your own with real men."

The black water churned violently, throwing angry flecks of foam onto the surface of the dock, as if spitting venom. It ripped the barnacles away from their tenacious grip on the pilings and seawall, and uprooted oyster shells from their shallow burial in the mud below. The seething whirlpool flung the sharp debris wildly into the air. Violet threw her hands up to protect her face and felt the stinging bite of the shrapnel as it sliced at her palms and forearms.

The water spun in a vortex around Hagar, pushing him higher still, so that his shoulders came even with the edge of the wooden timbers and Violet could see his flat, muscular belly where it 've'd into the thick tail that made up the lower half of his body. His round, silvery-green scales glittered like paillettes made flesh in the yellow dock lights that shone down into the murk.

"I'll savor the panic in your eyes as you die, human. Almost as much as I enjoyed watching your meddling father's clumsy attempts to reach your mother as I held her down until the ocean filled her lungs. I didn't have to wave a tailfin to take him. He came right to me, and so claimed his death as well."

Blind rage consumed Violet, an obsidian cloud obscuring all thought, driving her to act from mindless hatred. She lunged at him, only faintly hearing the shouts that rang out behind her as she went for his throat, reveling in the fact that her nails tore at his flesh as she grasped for the shell that lay against it. A dark triumph filled her as she hooked two fingers around the twine and yanked. She felt the snap as the tension in the braided rope gave way; felt the small shell slide across her palm.

And then she hit the dock with cruel force, the impact driving all the air from her lungs, bruising her ribs and knocking her momentarily senseless. Her muscles went slack, and in the brief seconds it took to come out of her stupor, the shell fell through her fingers and disappeared into the frothing maelstrom below. Violet's mind cried out in silent denial at its loss, some distant corner of her still clinging to the tenuous hope that ripping the thing from his neck had been enough.

But it hadn't.

Thick arms banded around her and dragged her roughly forward. Behind her, panicked shouting and a high-pitched scream joined the sound of feet pounding against the planks. And then Violet was rushing headfirst toward the churning water, the rancid odor of decaying fish the last thing that assailed her senses as she held her breath and was pulled under. She choked back the urge to waste air on crying out as the beret was brutally yanked from her head, along with what felt like a sizable chunk of her hair.

She felt more than heard the resounding splash of another body breaking the surface nearby, but Hagar was already rushing through the water at impossible speed, crushing her bruised ribs with his ruthless grip. She could see nothing in the pitch blackness of the night ocean; feel nothing but the pain in her abused body, and the overwhelming terror that seized and began to devour her.

This time, however, she had come prepared.

She maneuvered the slick pea-sized pebble from beneath her tongue and manipulated it back into the dry tightness of her throat, swallowing convulsively until it slid deeper, trying not to gag as it jammed in an uncomfortable lump halfway down. Ignoring her straining lungs, she methodically worked saliva into her mouth, and then swallowed harder, trying to relax her throat.

The bead hit her stomach like she'd swallowed a cube of ice, the sudden flood of oxygen through her system so sweet it brought tears of relief to her eyes. For a full minute she could only concentrate on the miracle of breathing, the smooth, cool flow of the water past her nose and mouth like air made liquid. Gradually she realized that her eyes were becoming acclimated to the gloom as well.

Dazed, she saw that they were already approaching the coral reefs, flying through the depths with the grace of a hawk soaring across the skies. The underwater scene took on an eerie beauty, Violet's magically enhanced vision discerning contrasts of color and texture that her human eyes could have never distinguished. A field of glowing white points spread out end-lessly before them, like molten fingertips of heat reaching up from branch-ing stalks of sage. With wonder, she recognized it as a meadow of fire coral, its true vibrancy something she had never before seen.

Fish swam all around them, unafraid, a bright shifting jungle of infinite colors and patterns. Their movements were a kaleidoscopic dance, the angels and butterflies flowing past in their lithe ballet, the clowns frolick-ing in a whimsical freestyle, the parrots bobbing and weaving with rhyth-mic agility. Violet stared in wonder, trying to take it all in. This was the ocean's unfiltered beauty, experienced in a way that not even her parents had been able to appreciate.

And with that thought, the reality of her situation crashed over her once more. She struggled against Hagar's grip, catching him in the gut with a sharp jab from her elbow. He snarled a harsh curse of surprise as he tight-ened his arms around her, squeezing her aching ribs with such ferocity that she could only gasp and hope they didn't crack.

"Why aren't you dead, human?" he growled.

"Surprise, asshole. If anyone's dying tonight, it'll be you," Violet blus-tered, taking satisfaction in the fact that her voice didn't waver with pain or fear. It was surprising that the words came out at all, considering she was underwater, but they flowed from her lips as easily as air.

Hagar scoffed mockingly, but sent a nervous glance over his shoulder and picked up speed. Violet thought of trying to mentally call Eleanor, but what good would it do? Maybe just letting her know she was okay was enough. Violet pictured the faerie in her mind and tried to send her a mes-sage.

Her helpless amazement overshadowed her panic once more as she and Hagar approached what was unmistakably a sprawling, underwater city. It looked as if it had been constructed from glittering, quartz-flecked sand, in varying shades of rose and cream. The architecture alone was dazzling, all rounded swirls, like huge fanciful shells—some wide and low with scal-loped edges, others whirling upward in towering spires like giant upright whelks.

Some structures captured the curling edges of crashing waves, frozen in unbroken permanence far below the reach of the actual whitecaps they depicted. Others portrayed massive, sphinx-like creatures, with the heads of people or lions or birds of prey. But their lower halves all took the form of either fish-tails or coiled masses of tentacles.

Hagar veered away from the city, racing along its outskirts as he barreled toward an immense natural cave. Violet saw that the seafloor surrounding it was laid out like a well-tended garden, with ordered beds of anemones in alternating colors. Long strips of seaweed hung like a beaded curtain at the arched entrance of the cave, brushing softly against Violet's face as Hagar swept through and carried her into his lair.

The rough-hewn interior was illuminated by glowing conch shell lamps, mounted at intervals high along the walls. Jewel bright pebbles carpeted the floors in a decorative touch that would have never passed the test of human feet. Hagar muscled her into a rectangular room dominated on one end by a raised throne, carved from smooth gold-veined stone. He had her against the wall before she realized he intended to shackle her there.

Violet wrestled wildly against his efforts to trap her arms above her head, kicking out at him and kneeing him viciously in what would have been his groin had he been human. The resistance of the water dampened her movements and her blows merely glanced off the slickness of his scales. She almost caught the flesh of his arm with her teeth, but he hauled the appendage out of reach just as the manacles snapped over her wrists and her jaws snapped shut on empty water.

He backed away, studying her as if she was a particularly interesting science experiment. "What have you done that allows you to survive at this depth, and with no air?" he wondered aloud. When Violet remained stubbornly silent he curled his lip in a nasty smile. "What's the matter, human? Not feeling brave enough to run your filthy mouth any longer? No matter. I'd bet a considerable amount that it's some spell whose effects will wear off eventually. I have but to wait."

He surged forward and slammed her legs roughly into the wall with his shoulders, catching her by surprise and shackling her ankles as well. Not straightening immediately, his hands lingered at her feet, sliding slowly, probingly up her legs. She clenched her teeth and tried not to give him the satisfaction of cringing when he paused, his face level with her hips. An intent glow lit his aqua eyes as he gazed at the clasp of her shorts.

"You skin is so terribly pale, yet so enticingly smooth," he muttered, as if mesmerized. His eyes lifted to hers and she saw that they burned with an unnatural fervor. "I have always wondered what lies at the juncture between these oddly separated growths you humans call legs. How different you are from our own females. Maybe before your air runs out, you will show me."

He trailed a finger along the line of her zipper and she swallowed the bile that rose in her throat, allowing the full force of her hatred and disgust to show on her face. Her revulsion only heightened his greedy excitement. As he straightened, she saw that there was a slit in the upper front area of his tail, where a human man's sex would be. It was only noticeable now because something swelled behind it, bulging forward to separate the scaly skin, beginning to push through the opening.

She turned her head away, unable to stop herself, and he barked a cruel laugh.

"Before we take this any further, I have a small bit of magic to perform in honor of our lovely Melody. You have no objection to waiting a bit for our play to begin, do you, my dear? I've found that a mix of anticipation and fear always increases the pleasure." He sent her a nasty grin over his shoulder as he bent to retrieve the vinyl beret from where he'd dropped it in order to shackle her.

He drifted toward the end of the room opposite the stone throne, where a low table rested against the wall, littered with multi-hued jars. "Let's see," he mused aloud, "it should be simple enough to reverse this spell and return our Melody to her rightful merrow form. Not my fault if the bitch happens to be land bound. Fitting, actually, for her to have to slither back to me on her belly."

He separated two of the jars from the clutter, one containing a sickly grey-brown substance, the other, a thick mucous as red as freshly spilled blood. "I think a little jellied eye of lamprey and some hagfish slime will do the trick." He opened the jars, foul odors and tastes immediately permeating the water of the room and making Violet gag.

"Oops," Hagar said maliciously, "should have warned you about that."

His broad back blocked Violet's view, but from what she could tell, he was smearing the hat with the unpleasant contents of the jars and whispering some sort of incantation. A flourish of his hands seemed to signal the end of the spell, but she could sense his confusion as he continued to stare down at the beret. He lifted it slowly, studying it more carefully, his heavy shoulders beginning to heave in agitation.

Suddenly he flung it away and turned on Violet, his eyes glinting with murderous wrath. "You thought to trick me." He advanced on her, muscles coiled to attack. "I won't be bested by a human," he grated, "and especially not a female," he spat, crowding her with the weight of his body.

He hauled his arm back and slapped her so hard her teeth rattled. She supposed it would have been worse if they hadn't been underwater, but she couldn't imagine how. Her vision was streaked with light and her cheek felt as if it had been reduced to a pulpy mass of soreness. He used his other arm to give the same treatment to the opposite cheek, and she mused hazily that it hadn't hurt quite as bad that time. Either it was his weak arm, or she was becoming numb to the pain.

"I hear you've been fucking that sidhe warrior," he whispered hotly against one still-ringing ear. "Do you enjoy mating outside your own species?" he enquired as he lifted the weight of her breast in his palm.

"Filthy whore," he growled, giving her nipple a hard pinch. "Let's see how much you like it with me." He grabbed at her shorts and began to yank them down over her hips, not bothering with the zipper.

Violet cried out and thrashed uselessly against her chains. The thick metal of the shackles tore the flesh at her wrists and ankles, but she felt nothing in her blind panic. Curses broke out in front of her as Hagar's groping hands were ripped from her body. She nearly howled with relief. Doyle had found her. And he had Hagar in a choke hold from behind, the merrow struggling fiercely against his grip.

A sword suddenly appeared in Doyle's hand as if he had called it into being. It was a claymore, long and heavy, its double edges honed to razor sharpness along a blade inscribed in runes that flashed with blue fire. One of its deadly edges pressed against Hagar's throat, a thin line of blood welling and dispersing into the water. "You will *never* raise your vile hand to her again, do you hear me, you worthless piece of shite?"

Doyle's anger was a palpable thing, like the sword he had conjured— hard, bright and deadly. Violet took a deep gulping breath, her tears mixing with the saltwater around her as Eleanor darted into the chamber behind him. She was floating inside an iridescent bubble, safe and dry, but winded with fright and exertion. She squeaked as she saw Hagar and the sword, flitting forward to hover anxiously in front of Violet.

Violet gave the sprite a humorless smile through teeth gritted in pain, realizing that the parts of her that didn't hurt had gone numb. "Nice bubble," she mumbled.

"Something I cooked up. Just in case I needed to follow you underwater." Eleanor drifted forward with a look of agonized sympathy, her hand against the inside of the filmy sphere as it gently brushed Violet's cheek. "I heard you calling to me before. Oh, Violet!" she sobbed. "What has he done to your face?"

Hagar grunted as Doyle's muscles tightened in barely restrained fury, deepening the sword's bite. The bastard was lucky Doyle hadn't already cleaved him in half.

Violet attempted a smirk. "Here I am, shackled to the wall, and you're worried about how pretty I look. Can you get me out of these things?" she asked hoarsely, giving her chains a weak rattle.

Eleanor spun to face Hagar, black dust dripping from her wings to pile at the bottom of her bubble like shimmering cinders of onyx. "Where is the key, you miserable waste of life?"

Her voice was so cold it sent a shiver of ice up Violet's spine. For the first time, she thought to wonder what the faerie would be capable of if she ever decided to abandon her vow to harm none.

"On my altar," Hagar managed tightly. He appeared to be trying to avoid swallowing.

"March," Doyle demanded, letting up on the sword and giving the merrow a shove forward. "Slowly. Get the key and release her. One false move and I'll gut you like the cold-blooded fish you are. And don't think for one second that I wouldn't be more than happy for the excuse to rid the world of you."

Hagar drifted stiffly across the room toward the altar, the point of Doyle's sword pricking into his bare back. He fumbled among the myriad jars until his fingers found a ring of oddly shaped keys that appeared to be made out of the same dull metal as the shackles themselves. His progress was equally rigid as he made his way toward Violet, his muscles tensing at Doyle's warning growl when he lowered himself to free her ankles.

She flexed her feet in relief as the heavy weight of the chains dropped off, and then forced her face into blank passivity as Hagar straightened and looked into her eyes while reaching up to free her wrists. He scrabbled with the lock, mumbling to himself as if he was having trouble opening it. Then, faster than her vision could track, he twisted and hurled something green and viscous at Doyle.

Doyle heard Violet's scream just as something splattered against his face and began to burn his eyes like acid. He struck out with a vicious sweep of his sword, but his forward movement was restricted for fear of hurting Violet. He felt the weapon graze flesh and heard the merrow grunt. He knew it was only a shallow cut, but he took a grim pleasure in it all the same.

"Now you fools!" shouted Hagar as he whipped his tail around in a low, powerful circle to unbalance Doyle.

Suddenly two identical thin, scaly creatures appeared several feet away, their brittle grey hair floating around their heads, their expressions wary and confused. "Did you think to just hover there silently and do nothing?" Hagar screamed. "You can't use a cloaking spell against me in my own spell casting chamber! Get the sword!"

Ligan and Lagan both shot toward Doyle. Violet tried to yell a warning, but only a croak made it past the increasing rawness in her throat. And it was three creatures that were accustomed to moving in water, against one blinded immortal warrior who wasn't.

One of the nixes blasted the sword from Doyle's hand. The bulky weapon spun across the room, landing on the floor and cutting a wide swathe through the carpet of pebbles before coming to rest against the wall near Violet. Doyle fought with fists and kicks, unwilling to summon his sword again for fear of striking Violet or Eleanor. He tried to blink out, only then realizing that the room had been bound against such escape techniques.

He gave as good as he got, leaving his assailants bruised and bleeding despite his inability to see them, but they eventually strong armed him to the wall across from Violet and managed to get him into shackles. Eleanor bobbed helplessly overhead swearing heartily at them all, until Hagar snatched her in one fist. He tried to squeeze the bubble, fully intent upon crushing the sprite inside of it, but Eleanor's magic was too strong.

He sneered and conjured a cage, trapping both the bubble and the faerie inside it.

Breathing heavily, he picked up the abandoned key ring and dropped it on the altar as he twisted open a jar of blue ointment. Bringing a palm-full back to Doyle, he carelessly flung it at the sidhe's eyes. Doyle hissed as if it burned, blinking rapidly against the sting, but his vision began to return almost immediately.

"Wouldn't want you to miss anything," Hagar jeered. "And if I'm not mistaken, the show's about to start." He gestured toward Violet with a mocking sweep of his hand.

Doyle's bloodshot eyes darted to where she was still chained by her wrists to the wall, directly across the narrow room from him. She looked as if every breath was causing her agony, her chest heaving in silent wheezes as she fought for air. "I'd say her underwater breathing spell is wearing off, wouldn't you?" Hagar asked with malicious glee.

Doyle thrashed against his bonds, bellowing his grief and helplessness.

"I had planned to provide you with a more...*intimate* demonstration," Hagar continued in a cruel tone, "but I'm afraid I've never been one for necrophilia. Perhaps I could find a way to prolong her life, if you'd be interested in seeing a more entertaining display?"

Doyle's eyes locked onto Violet's. The pain and pleading in her gaze made him want to double over in anguish. She shook her head, maybe only to clear her increasingly oxygen starved brain, but he knew she would prefer to die sooner rather than later under Hagar's terms. "I'm so sorry, *a thaisce*," he whispered, his voice breaking on the endearment.

"Now isn't that touching?" Hagar asked malignantly. "And I suppose that's a *no* on my offer. The shorter version of the show it is, then." He drifted forward in order to observe the human's contorted expressions for himself, careful not to obstruct the sidhe's view of her death. Excitement began to build within him as he watched her struggle for air, watched how the panic escalated in her eyes, so potent he could almost taste it.

This was better than the unexpected thrill he'd received when he'd dragged her parents down from the surface. It was over far too quickly that way. Here, in the privacy of his grotto with his shackles and spells, he could prolong that delicious fear.

Maybe after all of this was over, he would choose another human to bring here at his leisure. Perhaps he could push her to the edge of death, and then pull her back in order to watch the scene play out more than once. The very thought stimulated him. Maybe he shouldn't be so hasty to force Melody back into merrow form after all.

"You're a sick bastard, Hagar." A steely feminine voice made him start guiltily from his dark fantasies. He whipped around to face the newcomer, just as an opaque blue pebble shot through the water past him. He heard the human girl gasping and sobbing behind him, and her sidhe lover muttering heartfelt prayers of thanks. Hagar knew with an instant flash of rage what had happened.

"Ligan, Lagan—behind me!" he shouted. "Her magic can't touch me in my own spell chamber!" The nixes rushed to crowd behind his back and he sneered at the female djinn.

She only blinked at him calmly. "You're under arrest, Hagar."

"I don't think so, Seelie whore. It's three against one, and your magic is useless against me here."

Her lips curved in a hard, mirthless smile. "And I think your arithmetic is off. You really ought to learn to pay your mercenaries better."

It was then that he felt the point of the sword at his back.

"Thanks, boys," Daisy drawled, her grin turning wolfish. "Good thing the Seelie Police have their own generous fund set aside for such expenses.

"Now, let me see," she continued in a thoughtful voice, "two counts of murder, one count of attempted murder, resisting arrest…I have a feeling you're going to be locked away in a Seelie prison for quite some time, Hagar. I happen to be somewhat familiar with the underwater division. Do you know you'll be the only merrow in residence? I'm sure the other inmates will find you a fascinating addition."

The implication in her tone was far from friendly.

"Ligan. Lagan," she barked. "Whichever one of you isn't holding that sword, get the keys and unchain these good folks." Daisy glided forward with a dangerous smile, summoning a pair of thorny black throwing stars into her webbed hands. "You're just full of oversights, aren't you, Hagar? You should have gone the extra fathom and expanded that magic binding spell of yours to prevent the summoning of physical weapons. I'm a pretty good shot with these. Don't give me an excuse to slit your worthless throat."

Hagar glared at her with impotent rage. And then, without warning, he simply vanished.

Daisy let out a stream of words that would have burned the ears of a hardened sailor, and dashed from the room. She darted up the hall toward the cave's entrance, hoping that he only had the power to cast a localized escape spell and blink just outside his grotto. She'd willingly hunt the asshole to the ends of the oceans for what he'd done, but it would be so much simpler if she didn't have to.

Luck was with her as she spotted his fleeing form several hundred yards away.

She started to give chase, but as she gained on him, she noticed that something odd was happening. Instead of swimming forward to put as much distance between them as possible, he was swimming upward toward the surface. And his movements were becoming awkward and flailing, instead of the smooth, flowing mobility he should have had.

Hagar started to sink toward the bottom, his limbs jerking and twitching before going completely motionless. Daisy slowed, fearing trickery, her hand ready to cast a net as soon as she was close enough. Over a hundred yards of open water remained between them, and she proceeded at a wary crawl, erecting her shield just in case he threw something nasty at her.

She approached him cautiously as she came within casting range, but he remained slumped and unmoving on the seafloor. She continued forward and stopped a few yards away. Instead of netting him, she sent a thin jet of boiling water at his back, just enough to force him to stir if he was playing dead. But Hagar didn't move a muscle.

She studied him more closely, and it was only then that she realized what was wrong. In place of his streamlined tail, a pair of useless human legs was folded beneath his crumpled body.

She rushed over to him in shock, bending down to turn him on his back. She focused on conjuring another oxygen pebble, but by the time she managed to push it between his blue, lifeless lips, it was too late.

Hagar had drowned.

Daisy lifted his sagging form in her arms and blinked his body to the Seelie morgue. She woke the surly attendant and gave him a hurried explanation before rushing back to check on Violet, Eleanor and Doyle.

Though things hadn't gone quite the way she'd planned, at least she'd gotten there in time to save Violet. *Too bad she wasn't the hero who was going to end up with the girl today,* she thought with a smirk.

<u>Chapter Fifteen</u>

Violet sat with her sandaled feet swinging over the edge of the dock, the picnic basket she'd packed by her side, as she watched a boat that she hoped was *Ocean Magic* heading shoreward.

"Hi Violet," said a soft voice behind her.

She turned to find Melody standing there looking cool and bright in a yellow sundress. Her long, red hair curled down over her pale shoulders, topped with a new yellow beret. The last time Violet had seen the woman she had been in merrow form. She'd shown up at Hagar's cave in a panic after all the excitement was over.

"Hey Melody," she greeted.

"I am happy to see you looking well again, after Hagar's mistreatment." Melody's eyes were filled with apology.

Violet's fists clenched as she remembered the helplessness of being chained while the horrible merrow put his hands on her. But she took a deep breath and shook it off. The miserable creature was gone, her parents had been avenged, and she had escaped with her life.

"Thank you," she replied after a beat. "I had some bruises, but Eleanor healed me."

Melody cleared her throat into a silence that was thick with her regret. "Are you waiting for Doyle?"

"Yep. We have a date." Violet grinned down at her picnic basket. "What about you? Are you meeting Manny?"

"Yes," Melody replied with a shy smile as she dropped to a seat beside Violet.

"I guess he took the news about you being a merrow okay, then." She leaned over and gave Melody a friendly nudge. "Eleanor told me that you found Hagar's necklace, and that you asked Manny to destroy it."

Melody's expression clouded over. "I was so scared," she whispered. "Turning Hagar human was the only thing I could think of to save you. Eleanor said she saw you rip the necklace off him and drop it in the water. But it took me so long to find it, I was sure I was too late. If you had died…" her words tapered off, her eyes wide and haunted.

"It wouldn't have been your fault, Melody," Violet said quietly. "It would have been Hagar's. He was sick and twisted, and he was the only one responsible for his actions.

"If you hadn't found that necklace and destroyed it, he might have gotten away. You gave me and my parents justice. That monster deserved to feel what it was like to drown."

Violet took a breath and forced the vehemence from her tone. "But I don't want to talk about him anymore."

Melody nodded in understanding.

"I want to hear how Manny reacted to finding out you were a merrow. It obviously went better than when Doyle told me he was sidhe," Violet said with a grimace.

Melody cocked her head. "I don't think Manny really understood what I was telling him until he saw me transform," she replied slowly. "Lucky for me, Doyle had blinked out in front of him on their boat earlier. I guess that somewhat prepared him for the shock."

Violet laughed. "So he handled it as well as could be expected."

Melody's smile was giddy. "When I returned to the docks last night, he was wating for me. I offered to give him my cap so that I could return to human form. He not only took it, he destroyed it for me. I can hardly believe it. I am fully human now!"

Violet pulled her into a tight hug. "I'm so glad things worked out for you."

A blush crept up Melody's cheekbones to stain her peaches and cream skin. "He said he wanted to make sure he never lost me again."

"That's one sweet man you have there," Violet said with a grin. She nodded at the incoming boat. "Speaking of which, I think our boys are back. What are you two doing tonight?"

"Manny said he has a special surprise planned." Melody beamed.

"Ooh, that sounds promising." Violet waggled her eyebrows and Melody giggled. "I thought I'd surprise Doyle with a picnic on the beach." She nodded to the basket beside her.

"That sounds romantic," Melody replied softly.

"I hope Doyle thinks so. I'm afraid that after the last week with me, he might be sick of anything to do with the beach. But I love it too much to give it up, so this is my sneaky plan to give him some fonder memories."

"I am sure you will succeed." Melody smiled.

They sat and watched as the boat pulled in and the passengers filed off, keeping each other company as Doyle and Manny went about their cleaning. When it looked as if the men were wrapping things up, Violet and Melody stood and made their way toward the gangplank.

"Hurry it up, boys," Violet called. "Melody and I have plans for you this evening."

Manny straightened from padlocking the last equipment locker and crossed his arms over his chest. "Hey *hermano*, come here for a minute."

Doyle appeared from the other side of the boat, his handsome face breaking into a grin as he saw Violet. Manny motioned him over and draped a friendly arm across his shoulders. "What a beautiful sight, eh?" he asked. "We must be the two luckiest *hombres* alive."

"Without a doubt," Doyle replied, his eyes full of heat as they gazed into Violet's. He leapt down the gangplank and strode over to take her in his arms. She sighed with pleasure as he found her lips and coaxed them apart, dipping his tongue between them, tasting of ocean air and the warmth of the sun.

When he broke away she smiled and said, "So, nothing unusual happened today, I hope?"

Doyle tucked a strand of hair behind her ear and dropped a kiss on her forehead. "Nope. Everything appears to be back to normal."

He glanced over at Manny, who was whispering softly to Melody. "The mechanic told Manny that it looked like some wires had been cut in the engine yesterday." Manny looked up at his name. "We figure it was Hagar, trying to keep us from getting back in time to stop his meeting with Melody."

"I *told* Eleanor your engine was sabotaged," Violet said smugly.

Manny's dark brows drew together at the mention of the merrow's name, and he began to mutter angrily in Spanish. Melody placed a gentle hand against his cheek and he closed his eyes, turning his face into her palm to kiss it. When he opened his eyes again, they held only love, and the faintest hint of regret.

He pulled Melody tight against his side and turned to Violet with a grin. "So, *lindita*, you have anything you want to tell me?"

Violet gave him a questioning look.

"Well, with these other two legends come to life," he nodded to Melody and Doyle, "I think maybe you can tell the future," he suggested. "Or sprout wings and fly like a bird?"

Melody gave him a shove for his teasing. He grabbed her hand and pressed his lips to her knuckles before reclaiming her with his arm.

Violet laughed. "No, I was just as surprised as you to find out about all this magical stuff. I'm afraid I'm just a plain, ordinary human." She tried to keep her voice blithe as she said it. But it weighed on her that a human was all she would ever be, while the man she loved was a powerful immortal. At least Melody and Manny had a chance at a normal life together now.

"There is nothing plain or ordinary about you, *a thaisce*," Doyle replied quietly.

"You see that charm, *lindita*?" Manny murmured to Violet. "He learn it all from me."

Doyle let out a good-natured snort.

Manny's cheeks bunched in a grin. "Melody and I have to get going, *mis amigos*. Dinner reservations," he said with a twinkle in his eye.

"Where are we going, Manny?" Melody asked as he retrieved his t-shirt and began leading her down the dock.

"It's a surprise, *mi amor*, you'll see."

Their voices drifted away, leaving Violet and Doyle standing alone. "Get your shirt, baby. We have dinner reservations too." Violet urged him toward the boat with a mischievous smile.

"We do?" he asked in surprise, pulling his t-shirt over his head and retracting the gangplank.

"Mmhm." She waited for him to jump back onto the dock and handed him the picnic basket. "There's a beach blanket in there with our names written all over it."

∞∞∞∞∞∞∞∞∞

Violet leaned back on one elbow as she nibbled a piece of cheese with a bite of apple wedge, savoring a sip of red wine and allowing the flavors to blend on her tongue. The waves broke against the shore in a soothing, endless rhythm, and a gentle breeze stirred against her bare arms and legs.

The first stars were beginning to appear in a cloudless sky, each one a tiny jewel of mysterious beauty, burning bright in the growing darkness. As much as Violet loved the sun-drenched warmth of the day, there was something mystical about the beach at night. It seemed to bring a dormant magic to life deep within her soul.

Doyle ran his fingers through the loose length of her hair and she smiled up at him. "Daisy stopped by today," she told him idly. "She wanted to get my version of what happened last night."

Doyle grinned. "She stopped by to see me too, when I went home to take Bruno out between tours."

"I still can't believe the Seelie Police put those nixes on the payroll instead of arresting them," Violet commented with a distasteful twist of her lips.

"I know it seems like a questionable decision, *a thaisce*, but I wouldn't worry too much. I talked to my buddy Pat, and he said Daisy's keeping them on a tight leash. Apparently she put the same kind of shadowing spell on them that Hagar had on Melody.

"And they'll be much more useful as informants than they would be locked up. They have a reputation among the criminal element in my realm. Daisy thinks she can use them to bust some of the major players that the Seelies have been after for ages."

Violet's face broke into an expression of grim pleasure. "It *was* pretty great when Daisy showed up and they turned your sword on Hagar. I only wish they'd done it sooner."

Doyle shrugged uncomfortably. "She instructed them not to reveal themselves until she gave the word. But let's not think about that right now." The memory of Violet struggling for breath as Hagar taunted them was far too fresh in his mind.

He forced the thought away. "It's a beautiful evening, and you've packed this lovely meal for us. Although I must admit I'm surprised that Eleanor let you out of her sight again so soon, after the way she hovered over you all last night."

Violet chuckled. "She must be exhausted after the healing she did for us. Not to mention it's her son's birthday tomorrow, and she's been planning a big party for him all week."

She smiled softly at the thought of Obie. He was such a sweet baby. And he was lucky to have Eleanor for a mother; lucky to have two parents who loved each other so much that they'd committed their immortal lives to one another.

"What's the matter, *a thaisce*?" Doyle asked gently.

Violet realized that her smile had turned sad. She leaned back onto the blanket and looked up into his sea-green eyes, searching for an answer to the questions that plagued her. She loved him so much, and she knew he loved her. But was it fair to ask him for a commitment, when her life was so finite compared to his, and her youth even more fleeting?

"I love you, Doyle," she said softly.

"I love you too, Violet." His voice was warm and sure, as were his hands when they came up to cup her shoulders, and his lips when he leaned down to kiss her with slow, stirring heat.

A tear leaked from her eye and he brushed it away with his thumb, feathering kisses over her cheek. "Why so sad, *a thaisce*?"

She took a shuddering breath and tried not to cry. "What's going to happen to us, Doyle? You're immortal, and I'm not. What kind of life can we have together? Eventually I'll start to get old and wrinkly and you'll stay young and handsome. And I've always wanted kids…and someone to raise them with, and to share the kind of love my parents had…"

She broke off as he lowered himself onto his back beside her, wondering if she'd said too much. They had only known each other a week. He probably didn't want to hear about kids and forevers right now. But she couldn't stop thinking about it, and it was tearing her up inside.

He threaded his fingers through hers as they stared up at the night sky together. "I want those things too, Violet," he spoke softly into the silence, making her tears well up again.

A shooting star streaked across the heavens above them, bright and intense, leaving a trail of green flame in its wake as it burned through its celestial journey. Violet gasped in appreciation and Doyle squeezed her hand. "Close your eyes and make a wish, *a thaisce*," he whispered.

Her eyelids fluttered shut. She felt the warmth of his fingers joined with hers, the perfect feel of his body pressed against hers, and she wished with all the love in her heart that they could somehow remain happy together. The night seemed to take a waiting breath, the wind brushing over them to tease her hair against her cheek. Doyle shifted and her body tingled as his hip grazed hers.

And then the moment passed. She opened her eyes with an inward sigh, chastising herself for darkening their time together with melancholy thoughts. She jumped up and gave him an impish grin. "I'm going for a swim. Catch me if you can."

She raced toward the water, pulling her shirt over her head and tossing it carelessly behind her, shooting an inviting glance over her shoulder as she undid the clasp of her shorts and let them fall to the sand. She dashed into the surf, launching herself into a dive as soon as she was deep enough. She came up laughing as Doyle caught her and turned her into his arms.

As he bent his head to hers she wrapped herself around him, arms clasped behind his neck, legs enfolding his hips, clinging to him in sudden desperate abandon as she fiercely returned his kiss. She felt him harden against her and moaned her need as she pressed tighter to him. A swift, reckless passion consumed her, her body aching to be filled with his rigid heat.

Doyle felt as if he was drowning beneath her sensual onslaught, the urge to pull aside the thin fabric between them and thrust himself inside her almost more than he could contain. He groaned as Violet reached down and freed him from his shorts, caressing him once before she brought him to her and pulled aside the fabric of her bathing suit herself.

"Come inside me now, Doyle. I need to feel you." Her voice was husky with both a command and a plea, and it forced all thought from his mind as he took her hips in his hands and drove himself deep inside her.

They both cried out with the sudden shock of sensation. He moved with mindless carnal demand, lifting her hips to increase the momentum, finding her wet and ready for his plunging thrusts. She urged him on, harder and faster, craving the wild, frenzied heat of their union, until they were both breathless and lost in desire.

Violet screamed his name as her body shuddered in a violent climax, her muscles milking him in relentless fists, until he followed her into his own explosion of ecstasy. Dazed and spent, he looked down to find her clinging to him limply, her eyes closed. Cursing himself for being too rough with her, he brushed his mouth against her damp forehead in apology.

"Are you alright, *a thaisce*?" His voice was like gravel.

Her eyelids fluttered open in surprise. "Better than alright," she mumbled with a sated smile.

His lips spread in a slow, satisfied grin. "I'm glad. But next time I promise to be gentler."

"I like it both ways," she insisted with a languid sigh. Her eyes opened wider and she raised a brow as she felt him pulse inside her. "Is it next time already?"

He chuckled and gave her a swift kiss. "Well, maybe I can wait until we get home. If we hurry."

He lowered her to her feet and they straightened their clothing before wading hand in hand to the shore. Violet bent to retrieve her discarded shorts from the sand, and paused as she noticed something dark on her hip. She brushed her hand against it, thinking it was dirt or tar, but the mark didn't smear. She peered at it more closely, gasping in surprise as she realized what it was.

"Uh, Doyle?" she asked in a quavering voice.

"Yes, *a thaisce?*"

"Why do we have matching tattoos?"

He froze and stared down at the symbol on her hip with the strangest look on his face. Then he swallowed and pulled her into a tight hug, murmuring a prayer in Gaelic.

"I take it this is a good thing?" she asked, her words muffled by his shoulder.

He held her away from him, his eyes bright with awe as he looked at her. "It is a legend among my people. I have seen it in bonded sidhe couples…" he faltered. "I always half believed that they had their matching tattoos inked on in secret."

She smiled at him, feeling an odd welling of joy and excitement. "I haven't had time to get a big Celtic tattoo on my hip in the last twenty-four hours. Besides, look—it's completely healed." She took his hand and brushed his fingertips over it so that he could feel her smooth, unblemished skin.

He shook his head in disbelief. "It's called an Aegishjalmur," he mumbled. "All sidhe get them the year before we come of age. They are supposed to give us magical protection and irresistibility in battle. But there is another legend," he gazed into her eyes, "a legend that says we will know when we have found our soul mate, because the matching mark will appear on their body."

"*This means we're soul mates?*" Violet breathed in wonder.

Doyle gave a solemn nod. "And it means more than that, *a thaisce,*" he whispered, watching her intently. "According to the legend, as soul mates, our life-forces are bound together for as long as we live. Which means, you will share my immortality."

Tears pricked Violet's widened eyes and fell silently down her cheeks.

Doyle stared at her, breathless with hope and fear. "Are those happy tears, *a thaisce*? Does the thought of spending eternity with me please you, or frighten you?"

She choked out a laugh and threw herself into his arms. "Of course they're happy tears! I can't imagine being with anyone else. Ever. I didn't need some magical tattoo to tell me that."

Doyle held her tight, burying his face in her fragrant hair as he allowed the silken strands to absorb his own tears of joy.

"I mean, don't get me wrong." she continued with a sniffle. "The idea of immortality is going to take some getting used to. I guess we'll have to move around so people don't get suspicious when we don't age. And poor Eleanor," she added on a hysterical giggle, "she probably didn't know she was signing on for eternity when she decided to be my faerie guardian."

Doyle let out a chuckle. "You'd probably be shocked to find out what kinds of secret knowledge the sprites have hidden away. I wouldn't be surprised if she's known all along. But at least now I won't have to worry so much the next time you decide to go and do something crazy, like getting yourself dragged beneath the ocean by a demented merrow."

She drew back from him and made an unsuccessful attempt at a scowl. "Totally not my fault. But speaking of getting dragged beneath the ocean," she said, brightening, "this means I can go diving without a tank! Do you have any idea how much treasure has to be buried down there? Spanish Galleons and pirate ships…"

Doyle silenced her with a laughing kiss that melted her with its tenderness, and rekindled her passion into a slow burn. He framed her face with his hands and said, "You asked me what *a thaisce* meant before. That is what it means—*my treasure*. You are my treasure, Violet. I knew it from the first moment I saw you. You are worth more to me than anything in this realm or beyond. I have spent my life looking for you, whether I realized it or not. And I will be honored to spend the rest of eternity by your side."

Violet gave him a tremulous smile. "You say the sweetest things, baby," she whispered. "I love you, and I love your words. But right now all I want to do is spend eternity in your bed. Or at least the next thirty hours or so."

Doyle grinned and unceremoniously dumped everything back into the picnic basket before grabbing Violet's hand and blinking them directly to his bedroom.

Epilogue

One Month Later...

Violet's bare feet flexed against the soft carpet of cool grass as she smoothed her hands nervously over the exquisite dress Doyle's mother had given her to wear for their bonding ceremony. It was made of a filmy, opalescent white fabric that felt light as a breeze against her skin and flowed down her body in a simple, straight line to float around her ankles. The small sleeves were gathered just off her shoulders, and despite the gown's no-frills design, it managed to hug her most pleasing curves and hide her imperfections.

A meadow of wild violets swelled out in a huge arcing circle around the area they had chosen for their ceremony. Eleanor fussed with a delicate wreath of the purple flowers that she and her sister Lorien had woven for Violet's hair. It was the very same meadow that Doyle had brought her flowers from when she'd asked him to show her something magical.

The passage of time was a funny thing, even stranger now that so much of it stretched before her.

She and Doyle planned on having a human wedding as well, for all of her friends to attend. Doyle had already asked Manny to be his best man. But this bonding ceremony in his realm, before all of his family and childhood friends, was equally important to her. It was symbolic of their union and the bridge it created between their worlds.

The new school year had begun back home. At first she'd been unsure about the logistics of Doyle living and working in Key Largo, while she carried on with her life a two hour drive north. But he had officially petitioned the Seelie Court for the right to use simple magics in the human realm. And with his ability to blink them between places, the distance became less of an issue. Though poor Bruno was still having trouble getting used to being magically transported.

A soft hand squeezed hers, thin but strong, and Violet turned to find Doyle's mother standing beside her, a tall, willowy woman with kind eyes and a ready smile. Doyle had her eyes and her amber hair, but he had his father's bulky build and handsome features. "You're a vision in that dress, dear," she whispered fondly.

"I feel like a faerie princess," Violet admitted with a grin.

Marjorie Thresher's eyes sparkled. "And today, you are. I should have known there was a reason my son was always so drawn to the human realm. You are it, Violet," she said, pulling her into a hug.

"Thank you, Mrs. Thresher. And I'm really glad I'm not wearing makeup right now," Violet said with a watery sniff.

"I've told you to call me Marjorie," the woman scolded. "And stop fussing, Eleanor," she added as she pulled away, her gaze drawn to where the faerie was still plumping the petals in Violet's headdress. "Her hair is perfect. You and your sister outdid yourselves."

Eleanor poked at one last petal and darted backward to assess her handiwork. Her tilted eyes shone happily against her silvery skin. "She does look lovely, doesn't she?"

Violet blushed beneath their admiring stares, but she lost her train of thought as Doyle approached. He was resplendent in fitted robes of white trimmed in gold, his sword strapped to his side with its runes of blue fire burning along the blade. His feet were bare like hers, in observance of his people's tradition. It signified that they went into their bonding grounded, and in perfect harmony, with the earth supporting them.

"It's time," Marjorie announced with a slight wobble in her voice.

A deep music seemed to spring forth from the land itself, a thrumming resonance that rose and swelled, vibrating up through Violet's feet and filling her body, opening her consciousness and her heart until she felt as if she was brimming with a joyful light. The smile she directed at Doyle was the embodiment of sheer happiness as they fell into step, side by side.

Doyle's mouth went dry when he saw Violet there waiting for him. Her radiance dazzled him, and the love in her eyes was so strong that it made his heart squeeze painfully inside his chest. He had no idea what he'd done to deserve that kind of love from her, but he intended to spend the rest of his life showing her that he was worthy of it.

They began their slow walk down the center aisle, surrounded in two half-circles by Doyle's sidhe kin, gathered to stand in witness to their bonding. Suddenly a tiny, dark-haired faerie child separated from the crowd, riding on the harnessed back of a miniscule golden-brown frog. He hopped forward across the grassy aisle at the feet of the couple, giggling merrily and jiggling the frog's thread-like reins in his fists.

"Obie!" cried a scandalized voice. Eleanor's sister Lorien darted after the boy, shepherding him back into the onlookers, her color-shifting dress flashing blue, purple and green in the sunlight. The crowd chuckled, and Lorien's human charge, Sydney, gave Violet a wink as they continued the procession.

Violet had liked Sydney immediately upon meeting her. She possessed a dry, quiet wit and piercing, dark eyes that seemed to see through to the heart of things. She was dating Doyle's best friend, Pat, and they made an attractive couple. Her pale loveliness was a striking contrast to the bold, sexy image Pat portrayed, with his trim goatee and multiple tattoos.

Violet smiled at her as they passed and approached the end of the aisle to stand before Aeval, the powerful sidhe sorceress who performed the bonding ceremonies.

Pat stood witness to Doyle's right, and Scarlett to Violet's left. Eleanor hovered at Violet's shoulder, shedding green dust. Both Pat and Scarlett wore swords at their hips, as did all the adult sidhe in the crowd. They were a race of proud warriors, and looked every inch of it. They were also some of the kindest, most down-to-earth people Violet had ever met.

Violet was a little nervous about having Scarlett stand for her, though. Doyle's sister hadn't said two words to her, but had insisted to Doyle that she wanted to be a part of the ceremony. Violet hadn't been able to find it within herself to refuse.

Aeval stood tall before them, beginning the rite in Gaelic. She carried herself with a stern beauty, in her stately robes, her flowing black hair falling like a curtain around her. Violet had been given the translations beforehand, so she understood what was being said. And she had practiced pronouncing the few words she was to repeat during the bonding.

The ceremony was brief, and before Violet knew it, Doyle was gently turning her around to face their audience.

A rousing cheer went up, echoing through the meadow, and the metallic ring of swords being drawn filled the air. The sidhe raised the sharpened points high in salute, the silver and gold of blades, and fiery runes in every color of the rainbow, flashing brilliantly in the sun. The strains of children's laughter joined the music as the youngest members of the village were released to dance and twirl among the field of flowers.

Violet felt an uncertain hand against her shoulder and turned to find Scarlett looking at her with an odd expression on her flawless face. Doyle's sibling hesitated for a moment, and then quickly pulled Violet into a hug, as if forcing herself to do it before she changed her mind. "Welcome, sister," she whispered.

Tears sprang to Violet's already damp eyes as she squeezed the other woman's lean, muscular frame. "Thank you, Scarlett," she replied in a choked voice.

Doyle was beaming at them both as they parted. Scarlett blushed and looked away. Aeval's officious tone brought their attention back to her as she spoke a brief, final sentence in Gaelic. The woman's imperious expression broke into a hale smile as she added in heavily accented English, "That means ye may kiss yer bride, Doyle Thresher. And ye'd best be doin' a good job of it or ye may find yerself in me midnight court of an evening."

Violet sputtered a laugh as Aevel gave her a hearty wink, and Doyle swept her into his arms. He kissed her with such sweet passion that she forgot the crowd of people around them, forgot everything but his lips caressing hers and the stirring invasion of his tongue as it whispered to her of wilder rhythms to come.

Finally he released her, leaving her breathless and with color high in her cheeks as they smiled out over the applauding crowd. Doyle bent to her ear and whispered, "Look up, *a thaisce*."

Violet raised her eyes and caught her breath as her pounding heart skipped a beat. Four pegasuses soared high above them, twisting and dipping in a graceful dance, their immense wings spread wide from bodies that gleamed chestnut, grey, black and palomino in the sun.

"Eleanor said you'd asked about them. And her sister Lorien is on good terms with one of their leaders," Doyle told her quietly.

Violet looked at Eleanor with incredulous, tear-blurred eyes. "They're magnificent," she breathed.

Eleanor beamed.

Violet lifted her face to the sky once more to watch them in silent awe as Doyle pulled her into the steady warmth of his side. In a single month, her life had become more incredible than she could have ever dreamed. She knew her parents wouldn't have been so surprised, though. They had always known that such deep wonders lay just beneath the surface of the everyday, only waiting to be discovered.

All it took to find them was a little belief, and a dash of passionate magic.

The End

Dear Readers,

If you enjoy my books, I'd truly appreciate it if you would take a quick moment to add positive reviews online at Amazon.com, B&N.com, and/or your Goodreads.com shelf. Your recommendation is the best advertising!

An excerpt follows from my novel *Grey's Magic*. It features Doyle's sister Scarlett, and has lots of cameo appearances by Sydney and Sparrow. It contains an exciting blend of fantasy and romance, though it is a bit darker than *Passionate Magic*. I hope you enjoy it!

- Dawn Addonizio

Scarlett Thresher doesn't like humans. She's an immortal warrior. She's lethal with a sword. And she can hold her whiskey better than most men. But visiting the human realm gives her panic attacks.

Too bad her baby brother is getting married there and skipping the wedding isn't an option.

But when Scarlett stumbles across FBI Agent Greyson Derrington at a murder scene, she realizes that his killer is quite literally inhuman. And he's going to need cooperation from the faerie realm to have any hope of stopping the monster.

As they close in on an insidious evil that's stalking human women through their dreams, Grey begins to awaken parts of Scarlett that she long believed were shattered beyond repair.

Can he help her to release her fear and let go of the past, before time runs out for the next victim?

Chapter 1 of Grey's Magic

Scarlett yanked irritably at the dark purple hem of her bridesmaid's dress as she lowered herself onto a wooden barstool. She supposed she should be grateful that her new sister-in-law hadn't chosen one of the more frilly contraptions she'd seen at the bridal shop.

Whoever had designed some of those dresses bore an unhealthy obsession with making women look like giant cupcakes.

At least this frock had a simple cut and was short enough to give her a full range of movement. Though Scarlett still preferred the loose robes that her people, the *sidhe*, wore for such ceremonies. Or even better, her jeans and leather vest. Not that the pointy heels her mother had insisted she wear didn't have some intriguing possibilities…too bad they all involved using them as weaponry instead of shoes.

She ordered a shot of whiskey from a Hawaiian-shirt clad bartender and tilted her head back as she tipped it past her lips. Her eyes closed as it burned a fiery path down her throat. She sighed in appreciation, thankful that her father had insisted on paying for a full bar.

Tapping the empty glass with two fingers, she signaled the bartender to make the next one a double, and tried not to fidget as she waited for him to finish with another order.

Scarlett's face ached from the strain of forcing a smile for the pictures. And it was going to take a week of sparring with her cousins to work out the knots in her shoulders and neck from sitting through getting her hair and nails done.

Being surrounded by all of these humans made her tense as hell.

She downed the second shot, the warmth in her belly beginning to take root, and reached up to massage the base of her neck. A man in a rumpled suit grinned at her from down the bar and she turned a glare on him.

It wasn't the deterrent she'd hoped.

His smile widened and he slid over until he was seated on the stool next to hers. The crinkles around his eyes glowed white against his too-tanned face. Combined with his shaggy, sun-streaked hair, it was a sure bet that he was one of her brother's beach bum friends.

"You're Doyle's sister, right?" he slurred, confirming her observation. "He never told me how pretty you are. Let me buy your drink, I insist."

He laughed at his own joke and Scarlett cringed. This piss artist had obviously been drunk long before the bar opened.

"No," she growled, adding a grudging, "thank you," as she remembered her mother's dire warnings to be nice to Doyle and Violet's guests.

"I'm Joe," he continued, unfazed by her refusal. The human leaned forward and brushed against her shoulder, the alcohol fumes on his breath wafting into her face as he called out to get the bartender's attention.

Scarlett jerked away, sweat trickling in an uncomfortable path between her breasts. He was oblivious to her anxiety as he pointed for her glass to be refilled, then accepted a fresh drink and clinked it against hers with a hearty, "To Doyle and Violet!"

Nearby guests cheered and raised their glasses in salute. It seemed she was expected to do the same, and she tried to steady her shaking hand enough to lift her own drink.

People crowded closer to tap her glass, a suffocating mass of bodies hemming her in. Their voices crashed against her senses, loud and unintelligible through the blood pounding in her ears.

Scarlett looked up toward the rustic wooden planks of the ceiling and tried to suck more air into her lungs. Her vision wavered as she blinked at the roof timbers decorated with white paper garlands and strings of tiny lights. The myriad twinkling points grew brighter and slowly coalesced into a dazzling supernova. Scarlett swayed on her stool.

Suddenly there was a hand at her elbow, pulling her to her unsteady feet and leading her away from the cluster of humans.

Pat's familiar scent of woodland spice enveloped her and she almost sobbed with the relief of it. He was her brother's best friend, and one of the few men outside her family that she trusted.

"*Easy there, Letty,*" he murmured in Gaelic as he steered her outside the restaurant and toward a quiet bench near the docks. Tiki torches lent a velvety glow to the walkway. They flickered in the breeze, their fiery reflections shimmering on the rippled surface of the water.

Pat urged her to sit.

Scarlett's panic faded to annoyed embarrassment. "*I'm fine,*" she snapped in their home tongue.

He sighed and gave her a look so filled with pity it made her want to scream. "*Letty, you haven't been fine for almost two hundred years.*"

She scowled at him. "Well, I would be if I didn't have to visit the blasted human realm every time I want to see my own brother. Now that he's taking one of them as his soul mate, he'll probably never come home," she predicted with disgust.

Pat arched a brow at her. "Violet is perfectly lovely, and she makes him happier than I've ever seen him. Besides, you know we don't choose our soul mates. If we're lucky, fate allows us to find them."

Scarlett knew he was right. She had even developed a grudging affection for her brother's human, Violet. But the look in Pat's eyes when he spoke of soul mates left her no doubt that he was thinking of his own date.

"I suppose you think you've found your soul mate as well," she scoffed. "Though, in that sleeveless dress of hers, it's hard not to notice that your Aegishjalmur tattoo hasn't imprinted on her yet. At least Doyle's human can claim that much."

Excerpt from *Grey's Magic* by Dawn Addonizio

The warmth in Pat's eyes fled. "You and I have been friends for a long time, Letty, but I'm warning you to tread lightly on the subject of Sydney. She **is** my soul mate. My tattoo reacts to her touch. The fact that it didn't imprint on her skin must be because my human blood has always interfered with my sidhe magic."

"Sparrow?" called a concerned female voice. "Is she okay?"

Scarlett smiled sourly at the human in question. Sydney appeared ethereal in her ankle length, strapless gown. Her long, golden-brown hair floated in a cloud around her pale shoulders, and she looked softer and more feminine than Scarlett would ever be.

"Yes, love, just give us another minute if you don't mind," Pat replied.

"No problem." Sydney smiled at him, her eyes sympathetic as they travelled to Scarlett before she turned and went back inside.

Humiliation stained Scarlett's cheeks as she wondered what Pat had told his human about her. *"Sparrow?"* she mocked. *"Do you think you and your 'soul mate' will graduate to a first name basis any time soon?"*

Pat's jaw clenched. "You need to stop pretending you're jealous of her," he snapped in English. "You've used me as an excuse not to live your life for far too long."

He got up and followed Sydney back to the reception, leaving Scarlett feeling as if he'd slapped her. She squeezed her eyes shut, refusing to allow the tears to escape them.

She needed to get out of here. But she'd never hear the end of it if she left her brother's reception this early to return to the faerie realm.

She rose from the bench, wondering if her mother had already noticed her absence. Maybe she had time to slip away for a calming walk on the beach before she was missed. The heel of her shoe snagged on a wooden deck plank and she expelled a vivid curse, barely catching herself from toppling over.

She'd give both pinky toes to be able to conjure her favorite pair of leather boots right now. But unlike Pat, she didn't have Seelie clearance to use gratuitous magic in the human realm.

Muttering to herself, Scarlett yanked off the ridiculous shoes and set out barefoot down the ramp and away from the party.

∞∞∞∞∞∞∞∞∞

Greyson stood in the shadows outside the quaint beachside cottage. Ceramic garden gnomes peaked out from the colorful hibiscus and bougainvillea blooming along the fence-line, and a welcome mat embroidered with butterflies beckoned visitors onto the front porch.

The cheerfulness felt grotesque, considering the profanities that had been committed inside the cottage less than forty-eight hours ago. The profile fit the unsub he'd been chasing for three months now. He'd been to three other crime scenes, just like this one, spread across the country from

New Hampshire, to Colorado, to Texas, and now Florida.

He couldn't figure out how the bastard was choosing his victims. Much less how he found the time to travel across North America stalking them.

He sighed and shook his head, trying to push his frustration aside and get into the mind of the killer.

Key Largo was a beach community. It thrived on tourism. None of the residents would think twice about a stranger hanging around this neighborhood.

The perimeter of the yard was a thick mass of foliage. Normally it would provide an ideal place for a predator to lie in wait. But the thorns on these bushes would scratch the hell out of anyone who tried to use them for cover.

There was no sign of forced entry. Nor was there any sign of a struggle near the front or back doors. And all the windows were locked tight from the inside.

It had been the same at each of the other crime scenes. Perhaps this victim had felt safe enough to leave her doors unlocked. But not all of the women had lived in such casual neighborhoods.

Which meant that they had to be inviting him in. Or he had keys.

Greyson gritted his teeth at the all-too-familiar theory. He wished his brain would pick up something new. His technical analyst, Liza, hadn't found any evidence of the victims having contact with professionals that had access to their customers' keys.

And when a tech as good as Liza found nothing, there was usually nothing to find. The chance was unlikely that an unsub who had killed in four states in as many months had such professional ties anyway.

Maybe Greyson would get lucky and something about this poor woman's recent history would finally give him a bead on the bastard.

A faint sound interrupted Greyson's musings, and his eyes narrowed as they scanned the surrounding darkness for its source. A lone figure approached along the sidewalk. The moon slid from behind a cloud, and he froze as its light gilded strawberry blonde hair and revealed the most incredible woman he'd ever seen.

Tall and lithe, she moved with the grace of a panther. Her sheath dress clung to her curves, flaring to a stop at mid-thigh length and showcasing toned legs with a sexy bronzed glow. Her eyes flashed with awareness as she slowed her walk, her full lips gleaming beneath the caress of her tongue, as if she was tasting the air for danger.

Greyson's heart jumped inside his chest and he inhaled sharply. Her eyes flew toward the pool of shadows in the yard, zeroing in on him. Though he knew she couldn't possibly see him from her vantage point.

He stood immobile, staring at her in fascination and feeling an odd pang of regret as she moved forward, seeming to dismiss his presence.

Excerpt from *Grey's Magic* by Dawn Addonizio

∞∞∞∞∞∞∞∞∞∞

The solitude and the salt air helped to calm Scarlett's frazzled nerves as she meandered along the deserted sidewalk. If this place wasn't infested with humans, she might actually enjoy spending time here.

She turned down a residential street that bordered the beach, Pat's parting words replaying in her mind. He'd accused her of using him as an excuse not to live her life. And if she was honest with herself, she knew it for truth.

When she was younger, she hadn't had eyes for anyone but him. Though she hadn't been just another village girl swooning after his mouthwatering looks. She'd been a terrified teenager who idolized the young man that had saved her.

She closed her eyes and slammed her mental shutters down against the memory. Shaking her head, she shuffled to a stop and peered across the unfenced yard of the house to her left.

It looked like cutting through the property would bring her straight to the ocean. There were lights on behind the windows of the house, but the curtains were closed. She was debating the wisdom of trespassing, when she sensed that she was being watched.

Her pulse sped up as she scanned her surroundings. She felt, more than saw, a lone man standing motionless in the next yard. Adrenaline spiked in her blood, fueled by anger.

This was the first moment of peace she'd had all day. She'd be damned if she'd let another human ruin it. She moved closer, pretending as if she didn't see him. Then she stopped and pivoted on her heel, her stance defensive as she faced him.

"Do you make a habit of hiding in the bushes and spying on women?" she demanded.

Chocolate brows rose in surprise above dark eyes brimming with intelligence. He recovered quickly and flashed her a chagrinned smile, revealing an intriguing dimple in an otherwise smooth cheek. As her vision adjusted to the gloom, she saw that he had a trim, muscular physique and skin the color of creamy coffee.

"Do you make a habit of walking the streets alone at night?" he countered. "This isn't the safest place to be," he added, his expression turning grim.

Scarlett narrowed her eyes at his change in tone. He had a familiar scent about him. Her nose tingled with recognition as she realized it was a pungent combination of herbs that her people used to make a very specific potion…a potent sleeping draught.

Her body tensed. "Is that a threat?"

He gave her an odd look. "No, I'm…"

Excerpt from *Grey's Magic* by Dawn Addonizio

He reached into his pocket as he spoke, and she leapt at him before he could complete the sentence. She wasn't about to give him the chance to hit her with a sleeping potion.

Greyson grunted in shock as the woman came at him full force, sweeping his leg and sending him crashing to the ground. She landed atop him with one arm braced against his neck. Her other hand rose in a powerful arc behind her head, and he had a split second to realize that it was clenched around a stiletto heeled shoe.

With the pointy end aimed at his face.

Years of martial arts training kicked in, and he sent an uppercut flying into her ribs. He took advantage of her surprised gasp and deflected her chokehold, flipping her onto her back.

Then she began to fight in earnest.

They rolled across the lawn in a wild tussle of limbs, each landing punches heavy enough to bruise bone and steal breath. She refused to be subdued, and he realized with shock that she might be able to best him in a fight.

"FBI," he panted, groaning as she landed a brutal blow to his kidney. "I wasn't threatening you. I was trying to show you my badge. I'm FBI."

He rolled off of her and held up his hands, hoping she would accept the truce. But he kept his elbows tucked into a defensive position just in case she wasn't in mood for diplomacy.

She leapt to her feet, nimble as a cat, and took a step backward. Her wary eyes never left his face as she towered over him.

"Do you want to see my badge?" he asked, pointing to his pocket. When she didn't respond, he slowly reached for it, keeping one hand up in supplication.

She took another step back, almost stumbling on one of the garden gnomes. Her face was smudged with dirt and her fancy dress was probably ruined. But her sharp, sea-green gaze tracked his every move.

"I'm Special Agent Greyson Derrington," he explained. "I'm investigating a murder that occurred here two days ago. That's why I said it wasn't safe for you to walk alone at night."

He watched her face as her mind processed his words. She glanced at his badge, but seemed to be more interested in discerning the truth from his eyes. The tension she held in her muscles relaxed and he felt his own tension begin to drain away.

"Who are you?" he asked, still incredulous that she'd almost beat him at hand to hand combat. She was both a skilled fighter, and quite possibly the sexiest woman he'd ever seen. It was a dangerous combination.

"My name is Scarlett Thresher," she answered softly.

Desire shot through his groin at the musical cadence of her Irish brogue, and the intense way she held his stare.

Excerpt from *Grey's Magic* by Dawn Addonizio

She retreated another step and shook her head, silky strands of hair caressing her cheek where they'd escaped from their array of pins. "I'm sorry. I have to go," she murmured, looking as bewildered as he felt.

She turned and fled back up the sidewalk, disappearing into the darkness before he could formulate a protest.

Greyson sat back on his haunches in the grass, stunned. A shimmer of light caught his eye, and he reached down to find an earring with a large teardrop diamond glistening in a gold setting.

He stuck it in his pocket, wincing at the twinge in his ribs. She'd kicked his ass and then bolted without so much as an explanation. He wasn't sure whether to feel impressed, offended, or turned on.

∞∞∞∞∞∞∞∞∞∞

Scarlett ran, her legs pumping faster and faster, her mind a haze of confusion. She faltered to a stop when she found herself back at the docks by the wedding reception.

Agent Greyson Derrington of the FBI, her brain whispered as she made her way over the wooden planks and past the row of tiki torches. He'd said he was investigating a murder, so he must be part of the human police force.

She puffed at the loose hair on her cheek as she pushed open the door to the building. A cool blast of air hit her, drying the sweat on her forehead. Scarlett grimaced as she realized what a mess she must look with her dirty face, torn dress and bare feet.

She sprinted for the washroom, avoiding the gazes of the other guests, and hurried through the door with the crepe-paper bride taped to it. She locked herself in the large stall with the sink and steadied her hands on the basin as she tried to calm down.

She couldn't believe what had just happened. She never should have engaged him. She should have turned and walked away. But she'd been upset and itching for a fight.

And what a fighter he was. She was almost disappointed that he'd surrendered before she found out if she could beat him. How insane was that?

He'd defended himself against her attacks, yet he lacked the arrogance of many fighters who could claim his skill. He'd attempted to subdue her, but none of his moves had been designed to truly hurt her. And there was something in his eyes that made her want to trust him, despite the fact that he was human.

That was the most insane thing of all.

And it wasn't the only disturbing thing about their encounter. There were also the herbs she'd smelled on him. If Agent Greyson Derrington had picked up the scent of her people's most potent sleeping potion from his crime scene, in all probability, his criminal wasn't human.

She couldn't allow herself to keep that knowledge a secret. Not if it could help catch a murderer.

She cursed and gave the tap a hard twist, yanking some paper towels from the dispenser so she could wipe the dirt from her face. The careful design that the human hairdresser had taken so much time creating was wrecked.

She began pulling out the remaining hairpins, and groaned as the mirror revealed her bare earlobe. *Damn it.* She'd lost one of the special dwarven-made diamond earrings that her father had given her for her birthday.

"Scarlett?" her mother's voice called from outside the stall.

She groaned again. "Yes, Ma," she replied, trying to sound composed.

"Are you alright? Paddy said you weren't feeling well." Marjorie Thresher's tone was concerned, but there was a strain of exasperation in it. It wasn't much of a leap for her mother to assume that Scarlett was hiding in the washroom to avoid mingling with the human guests.

Scarlett hesitated. One look at her dress told her that she had to avoid opening the stall door at all costs. Nothing but faerie dust was going to fix the torn and stained cloth, and she didn't have any with her.

"Not really, Ma. I think I had a bad oyster from the raw bar," she improvised. "I've been in here wondering if I'm going to be sick."

Marjorie paused and Scarlett felt her disbelief thick in the air.

"Paddy said you were going for a walk."

Scarlett dropped her head back and exhaled. "I thought the fresh air might make me feel better," she answered truthfully.

There was another moment of silence, as if Marjorie was torn between wanting to comfort her daughter, and not truly believing she was ill.

"Do you want me to come in there?" she asked finally. "I may have a soothing potion in my purse…"

"No," Scarlett replied quickly, and then added, "Thanks, Ma. I'd really just like to blink home and go to bed, if you and Da don't mind."

Marjorie sighed. "It's not your Da and me you should be asking. It's your brother's wedding you'll be leaving early."

Scarlett swallowed a lump of guilt. But Doyle probably hadn't expected her to stay as long as she had. He was well aware of how she felt about humans.

"Please tell Doyle and Violet that I'm sorry," she said softly.

Her mother hesitated, as if she wanted to say more, but then she sighed again and left Scarlett alone in the bathroom.

Scarlett released a breath and thanked the goddess that she hadn't had to explain to her mother how she'd ruined her bridesmaid's dress. She loved Ma, but no matter how old Scarlett was, Ma could still make her feel like a disobedient child.

Excerpt from *Grey's Magic* by Dawn Addonizio

She thought about retracing her steps to look for her earring, but decided against it. She didn't want anyone to see her. And she'd had more than enough of the human realm for one day.

Not to mention she'd probably lost it during the fight, and Agent Derrington might still be hanging around his crime scene. The thought of seeing him again made her belly do a weird little flip.

She told herself that her stomach was reacting to her lie about eating bad oysters, and put him from her mind as she gratefully blinked home to the faerie realm.

But a hard bodied fighter with smooth, brown skin and a dimpled smile still watched her from the shadows in her dreams.

Grey's Magic **is available now in print & for e-readers!**

Dear Readers,

My novel *A Risky Proposition* - Book 1 of The Third Wish Duology features Doyle's best friend, Pat Sparrow, and Eleanor's sister, Lorien. It is Book 1 of a two-part series that leans more toward urban fantasy than *Passionate Magic,* but it still contains a good dose of romance. I hope you enjoy it!

- Dawn Addonizio

What would you do if a sexy djinn offered you three wishes? Before you get too excited, you'd better read the fine print—because the price for pleasure could be your eternal soul.

When Sydney Corrigan tries to forget her problems with a night out in exclusive Palm Beach, the sinfully handsome Balthus is only too happy to help. Unfortunately Balthus is no ordinary man. He's a death djinn intent on claiming her soul.

Luckily Sydney has her faerie guardian on her side.

Not to mention Pat Sparrow, an exceedingly hot Irish detective who would love nothing more than to discredit the death djinns and show Sydney what real pleasure is all about...

<u>About the Author</u>

Dawn Addonizio lives in South Florida with her wonderful husband, who is a science teacher, and their beloved menagerie of pets.

When she's not working her day job, or staring into space, she spends her time writing fantasy and making jewelry, wine accessories, and all manner of other sparkly things.

You can visit her store at DawnsBoutique.Net, "like" her on Facebook/D.Addonizio, and read some of her musings at DAddonizio.blogspot.com. You can also follow her on Twitter @DawnAddonizio